The girl jumped back, alarmed, her dark eyes wide in sudden terror. She had the presence of mind, however, not to cry out. Instead, she dropped the clothing she was carrying and clapped both hands over her mouth.

So that left her standing in the moonlight, stark naked, a pile of clothing at her feet.

Longarm swiftly lowered the Colt and smiled up at the girl. "You're going to get a chill standing there like that."

"I know," she said. "As a matter of fact, Longarm, I'm already pretty chilly. But I hadn't planned on standing here like this, you see. I was hoping to find a much warmer welcome."

"Get over here," Longarm said, flipping back the fold of the bedroll.

"No more guns?"

"Not the kind that hurt, Denny. . . ."

She ran lightly toward him. In a moment she dropped beside him in the bedroll. "Now," she murmured, "warm me up, Longarm!"

TABOR EVANS

LONGARM

AND THE DRAGON HUNTERS

A JOVE BOOK

First Jove edition published November 1980

10 9 8 7 6 5 4 3 2 1

Printed in the United States of America

Jove books are published by Jove Publications, Inc., 200 Madison Avenue, New York, NY 10016

Chapter 1

Longarm stuck a fresh cheroot into his mouth, thumbed a sulfur match to life, and lit up. Then he tipped his head back to get a better look at the enormous skeleton. Through the clouds of pungent smoke that billowed about his head, he peered with narrowed eyes at the tiny skull, after which he followed the great swooping neck to the high, rounded backbone, until his gaze reached at last the powerful, incredibly long tail.

He had heard about these dinosaurs, and had read accounts of this exhibition in the Denver newspaper, but seeing them up close like this was something else again. He didn't know which was more flabbergasting—the height of the critter or its length. One thing was for sure, however: when this oversized dragon was up and about, all dressed proper in muscles and skin, it would have taken a damn sight more than his .44 to stop it.

Longarm's rapt observation was rudely interrupted. Someone grabbed his arm from behind and pulled him around. Longarm found himself looking at a very unhappy little man.

"Sir!" the fellow cried. "Must you smoke that noxious weed in here?"

"I didn't see any 'no smoking' signs, mister."

"Whether you did or not is not the point! This is a closed hall. We must keep it so to preserve the specimens and allow the plaster to harden properly.

5

There is no way to vent that foul-smelling smoke issuing from your person!"

Longarm removed the cheroot from his mouth, mildly amused; the little whippersnapper had quite a bark. "I'm plumb sorry, mister. Didn't mean to foul up your air like that. As a matter of fact, I've been trying to break the habit lately."

"Well then," the man snapped, "come back when you succeed."

"And just who might you be?" Longarm drawled, unable to keep the amused smile off his face.

The fellow pulled himself up to his full five feet five. "I am Charles Ogden Stewart. And just who are you? Visitors were not to be allowed in here until further notice."

This was the one Longarm had come to see, all right. Charles Ogden Stewart was a man in his late forties, Longarm judged, a bone-hard, wiry man with fierce, intense eyes that were as dark as obsidian. As the agitated little fellow rocked back and forth on his heels before Longarm, the tall lawman thought he could hear the man buzzing—as if, under his dark, unruly shock of hair, a swarm of bees were at work.

"I am Deputy U.S. Marshal Custis Long," Longarm replied. "And I suspicion you'd be the gent I've been sent over here to see."

"By whom, might I ask?"

"By Marshal Billy Vail—and the U.S. State Department."

"The State Department? What is this all about? Speak sense, Deputy!"

Longarm took a puff on his cheroot, his eyes gleaming merrily. "Heard tell you was about ready to start another war with the British."

"Another *war*?"

"Yup."

Suddenly, Stewart's eyes narrowed in comprehension. "Oh, yes," he said. "I see what you mean, Deputy. You are referring to Sir Thomas Dorset and the British expedition he is heading."

"Reckon that's the fellow, all right."

"That man is about to plunder Dragon Bluff—to loot it of its precious lode of fossils and take them back to England! American fossils! They belong to this country. Of course I will do all in my power to stop them!"

"Then you admit you're the one responsible for the attacks on his expedition?"

Stewart smiled craftily. "I am afraid I cannot take the credit for them, Deputy. That wouldn't be fair."

"Maybe you'd better explain that, Stewart."

"Yellow Horn and his Arapahos are in the vicinity of the dig, I believe. And also a truly belligerent Reverend Wilson. And there are others."

"Others?"

Stewart sobered, his eyes suddenly hard. "I have a rival, Deputy—a most meddlesome and unprincipled rival. His name is William Edward Pope. He is of the Quaker persuasion, though of late one could hardly believe it. He, too, would be most anxious to stop Sir Thomas from plundering my dig."

"Your dig?"

"I was there first, Deputy. It was my men who unearthed the first fossils. Yes! I consider that my dig."

Longarm shrugged. "And you suspicion that any one of these parties might be causing the British expedition trouble. Is that it?"

"Yes."

"But not members of your expedition, not men working for you?"

"Why, sir, how would I know that for certain? They are zealous men, indefatigable diggers, and I

7

pay them well. Already you see before you the fruits of their labor."

With a proud gesture, Charles Ogden Stewart indicated the skeleton that towered over them both. Longarm glanced up at the bony structure, then glanced back at the little man. That this fellow and his assistants had hauled this pile of bones from a quarry north of Denver and then propped the whole damn thing up inside this exhibition hall filled Longarm with a sense of wonder—and also a sense of incredulity at the foolish errands some men will expend their energies to complete. He shook his head in amazement at the thought.

Stewart read the meaning of Longarm's gesture. "I gather you think this is all foolishness, Deputy."

"More than that, Stewart. Why not just leave the bones where you found them? Why dig up half the West so you can prop up this dragon inside this drafty old hall?"

"I would not expect you to understand. You are a simple lawman, after all." He shook his head in pity at Longarm's lack of perception. "What do you know of science, or of the scientist's imperative need to brush aside the darkness of this age and peer into the past?"

"Is that what you call this?"

"Precisely. This animal—or dragon, as you call it—is a glimpse into past ages when such mighty creations were the lords of this planet."

Longarm glanced nervously up at the creature towering over him. "But not for long, I gather."

"Not for long, you say, Deputy? Not for long? Do you realize that these dinosaurs covered this planet and were the dominant creatures on it for close on to *one hundred million* years?"

Longarm's eyebrows shot up a notch. "That so?"

"While *man*, Deputy, has existed for a paltry one percent of that time."

"Well, then," responded Longarm, peering down at the paleontologist. "Looks like we're just getting started, don't it?"

Stewart shook his head and took a deep breath. "To answer your question," he said wearily, "I am presenting this specimen to Denver in thanks to the many public-spirited citizens who have seen fit to aid me in my endeavors over the years. It is my hope that this specimen will form the nucleus of a great natural history museum."

"That's right generous of you."

"Of course, many of these bones—the majority, in fact—are simply plaster copies of the originals. I have long since crated and sent back to Brown University the original fossils. There is much work yet to be done with each, you see. Classification, photographic plates to be made, and so on."

"That's all very interesting, Stewart. But you better do what you can to keep the members of your digging crew off the backs of them British scientists. If you don't, I'll just have to see how many bones your men can dig up in a jail cell."

Stewart's face reddened. "Are you threatening me, Deputy?"

"Call it a warning—to you and to your men."

"Do you realize who I am? I have over three hundred publications! At present I am the chief paleontologist for the Providence Naturalist Society, a world-famous association, boasting among its members some of the greatest minds of this age. Furthermore, I number Charles Darwin and Thomas Huxley among my collaborators!"

Longarm smiled gently down at the little man. "Now don't go and get your bowels in an uproar, Stewart. I heard tell of some of those men. And your reputation is mighty impressive, I sure do admit. But out here, Marshal Billy Vail is the law—and I am his agent. There's been men killed out there on

9

those digs, and Billy Vail wants it stopped. And the State Department wants them British scientists left alone. And it don't matter how eager them diggers of yours are. Billy Vail is holding you responsible for the actions of your men. Is that clear, Stewart?"

The man's face had darkened dangerously during Longarm's statement. "Perfectly," he snapped. "You are threatening me."

"Have it your own way, Stewart."

Longarm turned to go.

"Deputy!"

Longarm stopped and looked back at the paleontologist, who said, "Am I to understand that Marshal Vail expects the same discipline from William Pope and the members of his expedition? Can you assure me that Marshal Vail will not countenance any misconduct on the part of any of his crew, either?"

"That's right."

Stewart drew himself up to his full height. "Well, then, sir, I suggest you or this Marshal Vail will have his hands full. But I expect him to live up to that promise!"

"Stewart," Longarm said softly, his gunmetal-blue eyes snapping angrily, "Marshal Vail and I might just be simple lawmen to you, but we don't need anyone like you to tell us our job. Is *that* clear?"

Stewart hesitated a moment, swallowed stiffly, then nodded.

At that moment a tall, rakishly attired individual stepped out from the shadow of a large packing crate at the far end of the hall.

"Pope!" Stewart cried, outraged. "What are *you* doing here?"

Ignoring the paleontologist, the newcomer addressed Longarm warmly. "Bravo, Deputy!" he cried, as he advanced on Longarm. "That's the way to handle this mountebank!"

"And just who the hell are you?" Longarm asked, nonplussed.

"You heard Stewart," the man replied, sticking out his hand. "I am William Edward Pope, the man Stewart thinks is so dangerous."

Pope clasped Longarm's hand and shook it warmly, then turned to face Stewart. "It is about time, Stewart. I've been waiting for someone to cut you down to size, and it was a real pleasure to hear this deputy do it. You are a fraud and a liar! And I propose to reveal this fact to the world."

Stewart smiled thinly. "Do you, now?"

"Tell me, Stewart. You say you collaborated with Huxley and Darwin. Do *they* know that?"

Seething, Stewart asked, "Just what are you implying, Pope?"

Pope smiled easily, obviously pleased at the reaction his accusation was getting. "You mean you don't know the difference between collaboration and theft?"

"Theft?" Stewart cried, outraged.

"Perhaps plagiarism *is* a better word, at that."

Something snapped in Stewart. With a barely articulate snarl of fury, the smaller scientist flung himself at Pope. Before Longarm could intervene, Stewart had struck Pope with such force that he sent the taller one reeling back. Pope lost his footing and fell to the wooden floor beneath the wildly flailing Stewart. Pope did his best to fight back, and the two grown men rolled over and over on the floor, pummeling each other like schoolboys—and with just about as much effectiveness.

Longarm watched it for a moment, somewhat amused at the ineffectuality of the two men. They were like two irate women trying to beat each other to death with powder puffs. A last, impatient to be on his way, Longarm reached down and pulled the two apart. Then he hauled Stewart to his feet, hold-

11

ing him by his coat collar. The fellow was still trying vainly to punch at Pope.

Pope, little the worse for wear, got to his feet, picked up his wide-brimmed hat and began to brush off his buckskin jacket. "Thank you, Deputy. Now I *know* the little pipsqueak's bark is worse than his bite."

"Get out of here!" screamed Stewart. "Both of you! At once! Get out!"

"I guess," said Pope, "we are no longer welcome. Isn't that a shame, Deputy? I suggest we retire from battle. Join me in a cup of coffee?"

Longarm nodded curtly to the infuriated Stewart, then turned and started across the floor to the entrance, Pope at his side. Glancing at the fellow, Longarm said, "After a session with you two, I could use something a damn sight more powerful than coffee."

As the two men stepped out onto the sidewalk, Pope said, "I am afraid that strong drink is forbidden to a man of my convictions, sir. Though I certainly understand your need at this juncture for just such a stimulant."

"Coffee it is, then."

"Fine," said Pope, as he fell in step with the tall lawman.

As the two men strode down the street, they made a fine contrast. Longarm, over six feet tall, was at least a head taller than Pope. The tall lawman was wearing a somewhat battered snuff-brown Stetson and a worn brown tweed suit and vest with a black string tie knotted at the neck of his light blue shirt. His cordovan leather boots—low-heeled army issue—had none of the sheen of Pope's boots. Longarm's face was ruddy, tanned to the shade of well-cured tobacco leaf, and he sported a stylish longhorn mustache, its greased tips flaring dramatically. At the moment, his somber eyes were set in a grimly

12

serious face that should have given all those who glanced at him the sense of a storm brewing.

Pope, however, seemed totally unaware of Longarm's simmering mood. The scientist was dressed in a flashy, fringed buckskin outfit, an immaculate broad-brimmed sombrero and finely tooled leather boots. Pope's face was florid and most of it was hidden behind a full, well-clipped beard. His eyes were hazel, and glowed now with a hectic, excited light as he kept pace with the long-striding lawman with an eager, hopping stride of his own.

Longarm sensed Pope's eagerness to chat; but for the moment, this was the last thing Longarm wanted. He had to sort out in his mind what he should do with this fool hopping along beside him. Only a child would have goaded Stewart the way Pope had. But then, both men struck Longarm as petty little antagonists in a world that was far bigger and a whole hell of a lot more dangerous than either of them had the wit to realize.

"We can get coffee in here, Pope," Longarm told his companion as they turned a corner and entered a small, unpretentious restaurant. "This be all right?"

"This will do nicely," Pope responded eagerly.

They found a table in a corner. Longarm sat down with his back to the wall and watched Pope carefully remove his hat and place it on the chair beside him. Then Pope took out his pipe, filled it, tamped it, and lit it with a sulfur match. Once he got it going to his satisfaction, he leaned back contentedly, looking for all the world like a pleased volcano.

The waitress took their simple order and left. Pope smiled broadly at Longarm. "You have no idea, Deputy, how pleased I was at the way you handled Stewart."

"I didn't think much of the way *you* handled him, Pope."

The man's eyes squinted through his pipe smoke at Longarm. "Is that so?"

"You both reminded me of school kids squabbling over marbles."

Pope frowned slightly, considering Longarm's words. "Perhaps so, Deputy. You might say that, I am sure, since you do not know all that has gone before. Stewart is a charlatan, a man who takes credit for the insights and hard work of others. He uses his wealth to prevent others from advancing their careers—even though these others may be far more deserving."

"Such as yourself."

"Indeed, yes. And now this fraud is attempting to keep me from Dragon Bluff."

Longarm nodded and studied Pope carefully. "And how do you feel about this British expedition that's moving into the area?"

"Why, they are welcome to whatever they can get." Pope smiled then, and Longarm immediately caught his drift.

"I see," Longarm replied. "Like Stewart, you will not go out of your way to help these British scientists."

"I will not."

Their coffee arrived. Pope insisted on paying.

"Did you hear what I told Stewart?" Longarm asked Pope.

"I overheard everything, I assure you. But you see, Deputy, I have no doubt at all that my men will be able to get all the fossils I need from that bluff, despite either Sir Thomas or that fraud, Stewart."

"Your crew is tougher, is that it?"

"Yes."

"Where did you find such men?"

Pope smiled. "I do not like to divulge trade secrets, Deputy. I found them. They are tough. And I pay them well."

14

Longarm sipped his coffee, then leaned back in his chair to study the scientist. If Stewart was pompous and arrogant, this one was dangerously naive, completely unaware of the forces he was unleashing. To judge by the way Pope dressed, he seemed to be playing a role he relished, but not one he really understood. These two dragon hunters might be brilliant enough, but in things that mattered, they both seemed woefully ignorant. It was a damn good thing they were chasing the *bones* of dragons and not the real thing.

Longarm finished his coffee and got to his feet.

"Stay put, Pope," he said, as the scientist hastily gulped his coffee down. "I've got business that won't wait. But I want you to know that if I have to tangle with either of you fellows again, it'll be against my better judgment. And you ought to remember that the law won't take sides in your damn fool quarrels. You better think that over carefully."

Pope smiled back up at Longarm. The man seemed unwilling to take offense. "Deputy, I understand your position perfectly. Of course I did not expect you to take my side against Stewart. But if the law will simply keep that man in his place, it will be doing all that I—or Sir Thomas—could possibly ask for."

For a moment Longarm stood over the dragon hunter, studying him. Then, with a shrug, he bid the scientist goodbye and strode from the restaurant.

Longarm was pretty close to the federal courthouse by then. Soon he was elbowing his way through the swarm of chattering lawyers on the ground floor. He climbed the marble staircase and paused only momentarily in front of the big oak door whose gold-leaf lettering read, UNITED STATES MARSHAL, FIRST DISTRICT COURT OF COLORADO, before pushing his way inside.

The pale young clerk with his plastered-down, center-parted hair looked nervously up from his typewriter as Longarm strode toward him.

"Is the chief inside?" Longarm asked.

"Yes, sir, Mr. Long. He's been waiting for you."

At that moment the door to Marshal Vail's office was flung wide and Billy Vail stood in the doorway, an anxious frown on his face.

"Get in here, Longarm. You got a train to catch tonight. Did you find that scientist fellow, Stewart?"

"I found him, all right," Longarm replied, as he swept past Billy Vail and slumped into the man's red leather armchair.

A glance at the banjo clock on the wall told Longarm it was close to four o'clock. The train Vail was talking about left at six that evening. But Longarm was hoping that he would be able to talk the chief out of sending him to Dragon Bluff. This was a job for someone with a lot more patience than he had. Wallace, maybe.

As the heavyset Vail hustled around behind his desk, he glanced unhappily at Longarm. "I got another telegram from the State Department. *They* just got a cable from the British foreign office. Sir Thomas is having great difficulty—and the State Department wants to know what I'm doing about it."

"What's happened now?"

"Two wagonloads of fossil bones were lost. The telegram didn't say how, and I couldn't care less. What bothers me is, we've got another death, and there's little doubt that those Americans at the site are behind it. Longarm, our government welcomed these British scientists—actually invited them to come. Hell, there's eight miles of ridge and bluffs filled with them damn fossil bones. There's enough for everybody."

Longarm shrugged. "Maybe so, Billy. Say, how about you sending Wallace on this one? I met an-

16

other American fossil hunter when I went to see Stewart. His name is William Edward Pope, and he's as looney as Stewart when it comes to these fossils. Take my advice. Send Wallace. He's a lot more diplomatic than I am."

"You are the man I'm sending, Longarm. That's final."

There was an iron gleam in Marshal Vail's eye. Longarm met the older lawman's relentless gaze for a moment or two, then shrugged and accepted the inevitable. "All right, Billy. But how about giving me something more to go on than I have now?"

"What do you want to know?"

"What's the law on this kind of operation? Does anyone own that bluff? And who owns all them bones they're hauling out? Also, Stewart said something about Chief Yellow Horn of the Arapaho. First I heard he was this far south."

"The chief is in the area, all right."

"How close to the diggings?"

Vail smiled thinly. "Dragon Bluff is on the Indians' land."

Longarm groaned.

"As for the law, nearest I can figure," Vail went on, "is the bones belong to whoever digs the fool things up and ships them out of there."

"There's no such thing as claims or titles?"

"Not on this find."

"So it's every collector for himself."

"That's right."

"How many men have been killed so far? Not counting that gent you just told me about."

Vail pawed through the pile of documents on his cluttered desk, pulled forth a large folder, and flipped it open. He ran a finger down the first page, then looked with upraised, bushy eyebrows at Longarm.

"Three, so far," he said. "A driver of one of the

wagons, a digger, and one of the British fellows who was riding shotgun on one shipment of bones." Vail glanced back at the folder. "And one more. A rattlesnake got him. He was shoving his nose along the ground with a whiskbroom in his hand, when the rattler caught him. But of course there's nothing you can do about that sort of thing."

"I don't like this, Billy. Four people dead already. A damned war! Over bones!" He shook his head. "I wish you'd send Wallace."

"You be on that train tonight, Longarm. Keep those British scientists healthy, and get the State Department off my back."

Longarm got to his feet and looked bleakly down at Marshal Vail. "And if I can't?"

"Don't come back here," Vail growled.

As Longarm strode through the outer office, he reminded himself that Billy Vail had just been kidding.

Or *had* he?

The scream came from beyond the next ridge.

Leaning over his buckskin's straining neck, Longarm immediately spurred him up the steep slope. A second later Longarm topped the rise and saw the Arapaho—and the small wagon train they were plundering.

Again the woman's scream sounded, a long, wailing cry of despair and terror.

Longarm snaked his Winchester out of its boot and thundered down the long slope toward the Indians, levering a fresh cartridge into the firing chamber as he rode. The Indians saw him coming. For an instant they paused in their plunder, then broke for their own mounts and weapons. A clutch of Arapaho ran away from a group of white men—and one white woman—abandoning them in their haste to reach their ponies. Longarm saw the woman collapse to the ground.

Galloping closer, Longarm fired over the heads of the Indians. He wanted only to frighten them enough to send them on their way. There were at least a dozen braves—more than a match for a lone lawman. He had an idea. As he rode still closer and loosed another round over the Indians' heads, he twisted in his saddle and shouted back at the ridge he had just crested and waved his arm. There were no other riders behind him, but he hoped the Indians would not stop to find that out.

The ruse might have worked, but before Longarm could turn back around in his saddle, an Indian bullet struck the Winchester's butt, slamming it with numbing force into the back of his head. He was aware only of a punishing blow that sent him flying off his horse. The ridge he had been looking back at tipped crazily and exchanged places with the sky. He slammed heavily into the ground, and then was flung tumbling down the slope. He came to a halt against the side of boulder buried solidly into the ground.

He shook his head and peered around him. The solidity of the rock grew. He found that he was clutching it to him frantically. Its solid heft seemed to anchor his reeling senses as he hovered on the brink of consciousness. Gradually, the horizon stopped spinning about him and he became aware of the Arapahos charging madly up the slope toward him.

Still somewhat dazed, but determined to meet their charge on his feet, Longarm pushed himself erect, spread his legs wide to balance himself and awaited the Indians' charge. The Arapaho brave in the lead was the one that caught his attention. The Indian was waving an elaborately carved, brilliantly decorated coup stick, and as he rode he let loose a series of high, keening cries.

"A-he!" the brave shouted. "A-he! *I claim it!*"

Longarm knew what he was claiming. He had already counted Longarm out, and was now about to touch his enemy with his coup stick to prove his valor.

But Longarm had no intention of allowing that indignity. The sight of the onrushing brave helped marvelously to clear his head and concentrate his attention. At the last moment, as the Indian leaned over with his coup stick, Longarm snatched at it and grabbed its beaded end with both fists. Then, planting both feet firmly in the ground, he leaned back and yanked as the Indian swept past. The young brave was lifted from his pony's back and went sailing over Longarm's head.

Longarm threw down the coup stick and spun to face the Indian, who had landed on his feet like a great cat, crouching, ready to spring. Longarm clawed the .44 from his cross-draw rig and covered the brave. The young Indian straightened defiantly —and waited for Longarm to pull the trigger. Longarm smiled at the waiting brave and then calmly holstered the double-action .44-40. The Indian folded his arms across his dark chest and threw his head back defiantly, an insolent gleam in his black eyes.

By that time the rest of the war party had thundered down upon the two. Instantly, Longarm and the brave were encircled by the Arapaho band. Clouds of white dust billowed up as the Indians brought their ponies to a halt. One Indian—older and apparently wiser, and wearing a chief's bonnet —stepped down from his pony and strode imperiously toward Longarm.

"You have good sense for a white man," the chief informed Longarm coldly. "You did not shoot Black Horse."

"Would you be Yellow Horn, Chief of the Arapaho?"

The chief nodded gravely.

"I am Deputy U.S. Marshal Custis Long. I crave no trouble with Arapaho or their famous war chief, Yellow Horn. When I come upon your warriors just now, I fired over their heads to warn them. I heard a white woman's scream."

The chief nodded. "Yes. Foolish white girl. One of my braves examined her closely, to see how white she was." He smiled thinly. "He would like to take her, but he knows now that she screams like a foolish chicken when he comes near. It is too loud for his ears—and for the ears of this chief."

Yellow Horn turned to the brave that Longarm had unhorsed and waved him back onto his pony. The unhappy brave swept up his coup stick and flung himself onto the pony's back. Once astride the animal, he glared down at Longarm and said something to the chief.

Yellow Horn answered him with a sharp word, undoubtedly a rebuke. The brave spun his horse about and broke through the ring of impassive Indians. Not one of them, Longarm noted, had yet lowered their rifles—and it looked as if every brave had one. The chief looked back at Longarm.

"Black Horse says the next time he will shoot the lawman, and not bother to count coup. I think he is being foolish," Yellow Horn said, the shadow of a sigh in his speech, his eyes suddenly wistful. "He is a young brave and must show courage, must count coup—or no woman of our tribe will have him. It is the old way of our people. But the Arapaho have no more tribes to fight. Our Indian foes are in the agency of the white man's government. They sleep under thin blankets and eat bad agency beef. Now the white man comes to the Valley Where the Giants

21

Are Buried. It is sacred Arapaho land. But the white man does not care. He comes to take the giants away. Tell me, lawman. Why do white men always take what the Indians have? Even the bones hidden in the ground. We do not take what you have! We do not *want* what you have!"

"I guess that's the reason, Chief," Longarm said wearily. "The white men want what the Indian has —even the bones buried in the ground. Sounds crazy, I know. And maybe it is. But that's the way it is."

Yellow Horn was puzzled.

"And do you know what the white men do with these bones?" Longarm asked.

Yellow Horn shook his head.

"The White Men put them bones all together, so the giants can stand upright once again. I will take you to see this wonder someday."

The chief's eyes gleamed. "Yellow Horn would like very much to see such a thing. It would be good medicine!"

"Fine, Chief. It's a deal. Now, would you tell your braves to lower their rifles and let me get on my way? I took quite a spill back there, and it feels like a few bolts got knocked loose."

Yellow Horn nodded quickly. He turned and spoke sharply to his braves. The rifles were lowered at once. Then the chief mounted up. He looked down at Longarm. "You have promised Yellow Horn. You say you will show him the standing giants. He will not wait long to see this!"

He saluted Longarm with an upraised palm, pulled his pony around and led his band away at a sudden gallop.

As Longarm squinted through the dust at the departing Indians, he wondered how much time he had left before Yellow Horn and the rest of his feisty braves would call him on that somewhat rash promise. Longarm had had no idea just how taken with the prospect of seeing a rebuilt skeleton the chief would be, which only meant Longarm hadn't been able to think very clearly with all those rifle barrels pointing at his head.

He was thinking clearly now, however. Of course the Arapaho chief would be anxious to see one of the standing giants. It would give him great prestige with his tribe. And an agency chief didn't have all that many opportunities to gain prestige. Yellow Horn would be waiting impatiently for Longarm to deliver.

With a weary sigh, Longarm started back up the slope after his horse.

Chapter 2

Leading his horse, Longarm approached the wagons. Four teamsters were reloading them, hefting the blocks of stone containing the fossils that the Indians had obviously thrown from the wagons. One of the men left the others and walked to meet Longarm. The woman whose scream had alerted Longarm was nowhere in sight.

The teamster was mopping his florid, bewhiskered face with a red bandanna as he approached. He had a powerful gut that sagged over his belt, and broad, yellow braces swelling over the dark blue cotton shirt he wore. But the man did not look soft. He quite likely wasn't. He stuck his hand out and grinned. Longarm found the grip powerful.

"Thanks, mister," the teamster said. "When you came riding down off that ridge, I could hardly believe it. My name's Bill Reed."

"Custis Long," Longarm replied. "I'm a deputy U.S. marshal, out of Denver. Heard there's been some trouble in these parts. Guess I found out pretty quick there was."

"That you did, Marshal."

"That woman all right?"

They started to walk toward the wagons.

"She's hidin' right now in one of the wagons, covering herself up as best she can. That devil of an Indian ripped most of her dress from her. One of the men gave her a shirt, and she's fixin' her skirt."

24

"Who is she?"

"Her name's Denise Ashley. We call her Denny. She's a teamster. Took over from her Dad about four years ago. She's small but tough, and can swear as good as a man."

They reached the wagons and Bill Reed introduced Longarm to the three other teamsters. The men were all grateful for his timely intervention and thanked him. He watched as they went back then to reloading the wagons.

They were high-sided ore carts, really, resting on heavy, iron-rimmed wheels. The chunks of stone they were lifting back up into the trucks had a curious appearance; they were blindingly white, as if they had been made incredibly clean. He asked Reed about this.

"Them stones've been wrapped in rags that've been dipped in plaster of paris. The plaster keeps the stones from fracturing. Used to be, the rock'd break and that would ruin the bone inside. The plaster protects the stone—and the fossil. Pretty crazy ain't it? All this just to steal bones." Bill Reed shook his head.

"Who are you working for?"

"A man called Charles Ogden Stewart. He don't come out here too often, but when he does, he's a real son of a bitch. But he pays well, so we got no cause to complain. Not until them pesky Indians showed up, that is."

"I've met Mr. Stewart," Longarm replied. "A wealthy man, is he?"

"That's what I hear tell—and he's got an Eastern college behind him."

"How far is the dig?"

"About twenty miles. We're on our way to the Union Pacific tracks at Dog Wells."

Longarm nodded. He had just come from there. It was about sixteen miles east. At that moment a

25

girl stood up suddenly in one of the wagons, clambered up onto a particularly large block of stone, then jumped lightly to the ground.

Watching her, Bill Reed grinned. "Denny," he said, "I thought maybe you was gonna stay hid."

"I gave it some thought," the girl said, striding toward them.

She wore a buckskin skirt that reached her ankles, which were encased in high-topped boots. She had done some fixing about her waist, so that there was a semblance of a sash holding up the skirt. Over the blue cotton shirt that had been given her, she wore a black leather vest. A black bandanna was knotted at her throat. An abundance of thick, chestnut curls was just barely kept in place under the dark brown Stetson she wore.

She smiled at Longarm and held out her hand. Longarm took it and looked down into blue eyes, so dark they resembled blueberries shining in the sun. The rest of her face was just as friendly and open—and as lovely as the eyes. Abruptly, she smiled.

"You're tall enough, that's for sure," she said. "And I guess you're just about as foolhardy. And brave. Sure glad you heard that scream of mine. That cussed Indian wasn't a bit polite, if you get my meaning. A lady likes to be asked."

Longarm touched the rim of his Stetson. "My name's Custis Long, ma'am. Pleased to meet you."

"I told him your name, Denny," Bill Reed told her. "He's a deputy U.S. marshal, sent here from Denver."

Denny grinned mischievously up at Longarm. "That was a right smart idea. Glad Denver thought of it."

"Are you all right, Miss Ashley?" Longarm inquired.

"A few bruises is about it," she replied. "Like I say, a woman likes to be asked. And this fool Indian had no manners at all. Guess he was a mite hungry for a woman." She shuddered suddenly. "Hell's fire, they *all* looked that way."

"But that wasn't what they come for," Reed told Longarm. "Just an idea that occurred to them savages when they clapped eyes on Denny."

"And what was their reason for attacking, then?"

"Them fossils, Deputy," Denny said, squinting up at him. "They fear the bones, you know. They think they are the remains of huge serpents that had burrowed into the earth after the Great Spirit killed them with bolts of lightning."

"Now where'd you hear that story, Miss Ashley?"

"My father," she said. "He told me many years ago. He knew about these bones, and he was friendly with the Indians."

"They attacked the bones, then, because they were scared of them?"

"No. Because they don't want us taking these bones from their sacred ground. I watched the Indians when they first attacked the wagons. As soon as they began hurling the fossils from the wagons, their faces registered almost pure terror. But they kept at it because that Indian chief would not let them stop."

Longarm nodded. "His name is Yellow Horn, Denny. I promised him I'd show him one of the giants standing upright once again."

"Can you *do* that, Deputy?" Denny asked.

"If I can get him into Denver, I can."

Bill Reed smiled at Longarm. "Good luck, Deputy. That don't sound like such an easy thing—gettin' that wild Indian to Denver."

"Well, I just won't think about it for now. It sounded like a good idea at the time. At least it sure pleased Yellow Horn, got him to pull his braves off me. That's all I was thinking of at the moment. They looked pretty mean and they were all well armed."

"They were mean enough," agreed Denny. "I can surely testify to that."

Bill Reed shook his head. "No Indian was meant for an agency life, and that's a fact. They're just itchin' to break out, and any excuse'll serve, as far as I can see. That Yellow Horn's got his work cut out for him if he means to keep them braves from breaking out."

Denny looked at Bill. "Seems to me he ain't doing such a good job right now."

Bill looked up at Longarm. "We've had it for today, Deputy," he said. "When we finish putting them fossils back into our wagons, we're goin' to make camp. You're welcome to join us, Marshal."

"Thanks," said Longarm. "Much obliged."

Denny smiled up at Longarm. "Maybe you can give us a hand, Deputy? Those blocks of stone are pretty heavy."

"Why, of course," Longarm replied. "That'd be my pleasure, miss. Just as soon as I find a good place to picket my horse."

"I know a fine place," Denny said. "Plenty of grass and some water. Our wagons passed it not far back. I'll go with you."

"Lead the way, Miss Ashley."

Helping Denise place those rock chunks back into her wagon had been an interesting exercise, especially with Denise managing to keep so tantalizingly close while he labored, but it had been a fearsome chore, as well, and Longarm was glad his labors were completed. Generous portions of hardtack, bacon and fried potatoes, eaten while he hunkered down beside the campfire, had filled him to the point of bursting. He was now more than willing for sleep to take him. The next day, he hoped, would bring him to the dig at Dragon Bluff.

As he unrolled his soogan from the slicker he

always wrapped around it and spread the slicker for a groundcloth, he realized how sore his back and arms were from all that lifting and carrying. He shook his head. If it hadn't been for that look in those wide blue eyes of a very fetching young girl, he might have been a deal less sore and maybe a mite more eager to visit her this evening.

He unrolled his soogan and opened the flap, shucked off his boots and slipped out of his britches. Then he took off his shirt and vest, folding them both neatly beside him on the grass. Before he was through with the vest, he took from it his watch, wound it, then examined keenly the watch fob attached to the watch by a fine gold-washed chain. The fob was in fact a double-barreled .44-caliber derringer. He kept it in the right-hand pocket of his vest—a deadly surprise to many in the past who had concluded that Longarm was without further armament after losing his Colt Model T. Satisfied that the small, deadly weapon was in fine working order, he tucked it gently under the folded vest alongside his watch. Then he placed his hat beside the folded clothes. He glanced then at his horse, picketed near the stream. Satisfied that all was well, he rolled into his soogan.

He was placing his .44 under his Stetson, beside the bedroll, when he heard a twig snap in the darkness below him. Alert at once, he lay perfectly still while he tightened his grip around his Colt. There was another sound—closer, this time. A cloth or some fabric was brushing across a low bush. A moment later Longarm felt the shadow of someone fall over his recumbent frame. He waited a split second longer, then spun about, thrusting his Colt up into a very startled face.

The face of Denise Ashley.

The girl jumped back, alarmed, her dark eyes wide in sudden terror. She had the presence of mind, however, not to cry out. Instead, she dropped the clothing she was carrying and clapped both hands over her mouth.

That left her standing in the moonlight, stark naked, a pile of her clothing at her feet.

Longarm swiftly put the Colt back under his saddle and smiled up at the girl. "You're going to get a chill standing there like that."

"I know," she said. "As a matter of fact, Mr. Long, I'm already pretty chilly. But I hadn't planned on standing here like this, you see. I was hoping to find a much warmer welcome."

"Get over here," Longarm said, flipping back the fold of the soogan.

"No more guns?"

"Not the kind that hurt, Denny. But I warn you, I'm a pretty tired man. This has been a long day for me—what with Indians and fossils."

"I'm not an Indian, and I'm not a fossil," she said, dropping beside him in the soogan. "Now," she murmured. "Warm me up, Mr. Long!"

"Ladies I'm this friendly with generally get to call me Longarm," he told her as he pulled her obediently to him. At once her lips covered his face, his chest, his arms, then his stomach. He wanted to tell her that lugging those damn fossils around had taken the life out of him, but he didn't have the heart as her lips continued to play magically over the length of his body. Her tongue was a flame, igniting him. Soon, despite his almost overwhelming fatigue, he was not only erect, but was reaching out for her, pulling her in under him, then swinging himself astride her.

"Oh, yes!" she muttered savagely, "Yes! Now!"

She flung her legs wide and he plunged into her savagely, impaling her, driving her into the ground. With a shuddering moan of delight, she flung her arms around his neck and fastened her lips on his.

Their tongues embraced. All fatigue driven from him now, Longarm was no longer measuring the effect of his driving thrusts on this diminutive creature caught beneath him. He was being swept along by a wiser, deeper force. She met his thrusts with the same fierce, reckless abandon. Together, caught up in the fury of their lovemaking, they mounted to a climax. She flung up her legs and tightened them about his waist, never missing a beat. She squeezed, then rocked wildly up at him. He found himself laughing, his head thrown back. Then he was at his peak, plunging over the edge. Lifting his head still higher, he cried out exultantly . . .

"I was never with a man who laughed like that," she whispered, cuddling close, her warm cheek resting on his chest, her head tucked under his chin. "It's nice."

"Why?"

"This is fun, isn't it? It brings pleasure. To hear you laugh like that sent a shiver of delight through me—that I was making you so happy."

"That we were making each other happy."

"Yes, that is better." She tightened her arms about him in a gentle, warm squeeze. "You are very good, Longarm. You bring a woman to life."

Longarm chuckled. That was just what this little kitten had done for him. Longarm was glad they had the same effect on each other.

She lifted her head from his chest, turned her face to his, and kissed him. It was a long, intense kiss. At the beginning of it, Longarm was too relaxed to consider the kiss as anything more than a thank-you for what had passed. But as the girl's lips began working hungrily against his, a fire grew in him and he found himself answering her kiss.

He began to roll onto her once again, but she pulled her lips from his and whispered fiercely, "No! Me on top! I want to ride you like a pony. Only it

31

will be slow, Longarm! It will drive you mad! I promise!"

Suiting actions to words, she suspended herself astride him and then lowered herself onto his erection. She did it with a sureness and gentleness that delighted him. As she came to rest, she wriggled her backside just a little and seemed to settle down inches lower. He found his shaft engulfed to its root by the enclosing, moist warmth of her. She began to rock slightly. Then, gradually, imperceptibly, she increased the pace of her rocking motion. Longarm leaned back and relaxed, the pleasure he felt mounting deliciously.

She looked down at him, smiling warmly. Pleasing him was pleasing her as well. Her tempo increased. Longarm wanted to reach up with his big hands and clasp them about her hips, to increase the depth and speed of the thrust. But he kept his arms at his side, forcing himself to let her set the pace. He saw her close her eyes and throw her head back. Her face hardened into a grimace of pleasure. Suddenly she reached down and grabbed both of his hands and crushed them against her breasts. He took hold of them, aware at once of her eagerly stiffening nipples.

By that time Longarm had lost himself in the fine frenzy of it. She was riding him now, not wildly, but caressingly—and with infinite skill. Each downward thrust of her body seemed to meld them into one complete, passionate entity. Each time she rose along his shaft, he felt the terror of losing her. Then she was plunging wildly down upon him once more, and he was thrusting up into her, driving just as hard.

Her climax came almost before he was aware of it. He heard her gasping cry, and then she was leaning forward, her breasts slamming into his chest, her tiny fists beating at him about his shoulders. He grabbed her wrists and held her, then flung both arms around her as he rose into her again and again, astonished at the repeated orgasms that exploded from his groin. He leaned back at last, her weight on him, aware of a sweet emptiness.

"Finished?" she whispered at last.

He ran his hand through the rich, dark tangle of her hair and laughed softly. She laughed with him, just as quietly. He did not know how long they lay like that when abruptly, like a startled animal, she lifted her head.

"What's wrong?" he asked.

"I heard something. Didn't you?"

"No."

She rolled off him and then got to her feet, a slender, pale shadow standing alertly beside him. He sat up. Yes, he heard it now, also.

Cries! Muffled shots!

"There!" Denny cried. "Hear that? Shooting!"

"Yellow Horn," Longarm muttered angrily. "He's come back, damn it!"

Swiftly Denny bent to pick up the garments she had discarded earlier. As she slipped into her clothes, Longarm swiftly tugged on his britches, buttoned up his shirt, then pulled on his boots. A moment later, fully dressed, he was standing by Denny, inspecting his Winchester. He glanced at Denny. She was completely dressed.

"Let's go," he said softly.

Longarm had camped almost a quarter of a mile from the teamsters' campsite. The light from the moon was not enough to keep them from stumbling occasionally, and by the time they neared the campsite both of them could see the fierce glow of burning wagons through the trees. With a gasp of dismay, Denny began to run. Longarm caught her from behind and pulled her back.

"Hold up!" he cried. "You don't want to go running out of cover into the light of those flames. That Indian might be waiting for you!"

Denny nodded quickly, immediately concerned. "Can you see?" she asked. "Is my wagon on fire, too?"

Carefully, Longarm peered out from the trees. They were still on a slight rise that overlooked the encampment. Not all the wagons were on fire, but each one had been overturned, their contents spilled out on the sandy ground. Longarm groaned involuntarily as he recalled having helped fill those same carts that afternoon.

But he saw no riders, no Indians. What he did see, however, disturbed him. Still bodies were scattered about the encampment, the garish light from the dancing flames playing over their prostrate forms.

Beside him, Denny gasped. "Are they dead?"

"Maybe not, Denny. You stay here. I'm going to circle around and come at the camp from behind those rocks. Wait for my signal. I'll fire twice into the air."

She nodded. "Hurry, Longarm. Please."

Longarm patted her on the arm and moved off through the trees.

The teamsters had corralled their horses behind the rocks. As Longarm approached the rocks, he came upon their sad, riddled carcasses. At once he knew he was not dealing with the depredations of Yellow Horn. The slaughter of these horses was simple butchery aimed only at one thing: stopping the teamsters from delivering their load of fossils. Longarm shook his head in dismay at this madness as he slipped past the still-warm bodies. All this fuss over gold or silver, he could imagine. But over ancient bones, fossils? It made no sense at all.

He came to the first blazing ore wagon and peered past it at one of the teamsters, who was lying facedown, a revolver in his outstretched hand. He was hatless, and the bald patch on the top of his head shone brightly in the flaming light. Crouching low, Longarm edged out from behind the burning wagon, then darted across the ground to the prostrate teamster.

"Hey!" Longarm said, nudging the fellow. "You all right?"

The teamster groaned and moved his head painfully. Bill Reed had introduced him simply as Dooley. "I been hit in the side. Think I busted a rib." He lifted his head to look at Longarm. "Them sons of bitches gone?"

"Looks like it. Who were they, Dooley? Yellow Horn's braves?"

"Not a bit of it. These damn Indians was white clear through. Pack of murderin' bastards! I think they killed Bucky."

"I'll go check the others."

Dooley nodded, swore softly, and pushed himself to a sitting position, hugging himself as if to make sure he wouldn't fall apart. Longarm found Bucky with a hole in his head. Bill Reed was on his feet, rifle in hand, looking warily about him in the darkness as Longarm approached.

"Denny," Bill said, as Longarm stopped beside him. "Is she all right, Long?"

"She's fine. Right now she's in that timber on the hill, keeping low."

"She can come out now. Them bastards is gone. They got done what they came to do, looks like."

"And what was that?"

"Stop this shipment of fossils, that's what. They killed all our horses and burned our wagons. Stewart's gonna be spittin' firecrackers when he hears this."

"You got any idea who's behind this?"

35

"Sure. Pope's gang. Sim Drucker and the rest of his gunslicks."

Longarm nodded. "You better see to Dooley. Bucky's dead. I don't know about your other man, Felcher."

"Check on him, will you, Long? I'll go see to Dooley. Last I knew, Felcher was racing for the rocks. He'd heard Pope's men shooting the horses."

Longarm left Bill Reed and went back to the rocks. He found Felcher's body halfway under a dead draft horse. His eyes were open wide, his mouth distorted in a silent scream. Longarm yanked off the man's buckskin jacket and threw it over the frozen face, then turned back to the timber to get Denny.

But again, as Longarm trudged through the chill darkness toward the timber, he found himself unable to comprehend how a battle over stone-encased fossil bones could bring out such madness. Longarm had seen men murdered for money, for power, for lust—but for *bones*? He sighed deeply, unable to fathom it, and unable to forget the look in Felcher's wide eyes. He imagined he could hear the teamster's silent scream.

Denny ran to him from the timber. He took her in his arms and held her. She lifted her face to his. "How . . . how bad is it, Longarm?"

"Pretty damn bad, Denny," he said.

He told her—everything.

"Oh, my God," she murmured, shocked, when he had finished. "What . . . what are we going to do?"

"Without your wagons and your horses?"

"Yes."

"Walk, looks like."

Together they turned and started down the slope to the campsite, which was still lit garishly by the flaming ore wagons.

• • •

Bill Reed had not been wounded. He had just hit the dirt as soon as the shooting began, content to play possum until the danger was over. It had been a wise course, at least for him. The two men spent the early-morning hours selecting an appropriate gravesite and burying Felcher and Bucky. Then, with Dooley aboard Longarm's buckskin, they began walking.

There was a religious settlement directly north of the encampment, and it was less than a couple of miles, according to Bill Reed. Dooley was still losing blood, and it was imperative that they reach the settlement before noon, Longarm figured, if Dooley was to have much of a chance of surviving. After a few miles, Denny got up on the horse behind Dooley and did her best to hold him upright while she took over the reins.

Well before noon, they found themselves in a lush, stream-watered valley. On the other side of the valley, tucked into the shadow of a towering bluff, Longarm could make out the beginnings of a small settlement. One or two huge barns were still under construction at various sites along the river. The valley itself had been turned into a vast checkerboard of cultivated fields. The settlement was undoubtedly off to a good start.

As they started down a long meadowland that extended as far as the tree-shaded stream, they saw someone in a farm wagon whipping his horses into a lather as he fled away from them across a narrow wooden bridge and headed through the cultivated fields toward the settlement. They had been spotted, it seemed, and the news was being brought to headquarters.

"Damn," said Longarm bitterly. "I wish that son of a bitch hadn't been in such of a hurry. Dooley could have been transferred to that wagon."

37

Longarm had stopped at the sight of the aroused farmer. He turned and looked up at Denny and the nearly unconscious Dooley. Denny had halted and was sitting aboard the buckskin with both arms wrapped around Dooley's sagging waist. Her arms were stained with the man's blood, despite the fact that Dooley's wound had been tightly bandaged in an effort to staunch the flow.

"Keep going," Longarm told her. "We can get some water from that stream, and maybe take another look at Dooley's wound."

"Will you take the reins, please?" Denny asked. "I need both hands to keep Dooley in the saddle."

Longarm took the reins from her and led his horse and its double burden after Bill Reed, grateful that now they were walking downhill toward the shade of the trees and the cool waters of the stream. He had an idea that Dooley would need both.

"Longarm," Denny said. "We've got visitors."

Longarm glanced up from the nearly unconscious Dooley and saw what appeared to be a well-armed and well-organized mob. At its head was a singularly imposing individual. The citizens of this new settlement, obviously, and their leader. They were marching across the wooden bridge, over which they had seen that other frantic farmer punishing his horses not too long before.

"What'll we do?" Bill Reed asked nervously. "They don't look too friendly, I'm thinking."

"They're not," agreed Denny. "I've heard they don't like us much."

"Why?" asked Longarm. "Have any of you people molested them?"

"It's not that," Bill Reed replied. "They think we're helping that professor we work for prove there ain't no truth in the Bible. Seems like digging up fossils goes against their teachin'. Ain't supposed

38

to be such big critters as that—long ago or now. After all, if it ain't in the Bible, accordin' to these here folks, it just blamed didn't happen."

"I see," Longarm said, turning back to the oncoming delegation. "I better go speak to that jasper with the big black hat and the long black overcoat. You folks stay put and let me handle him. There ain't no way people who claim to be speakin' from the Bible are goin' to let Dooley here bleed to death."

Longarm left the shade of the cottonwood under which they had taken refuge, and started across the fragrant meadowland toward the oncoming settlers. There were no womenfolk present, Longarm noted, which meant he could not count on their leavening presence. Every man was armed, including the white-bearded patriarch who led them.

As Longarm got closer to this man, his facial features became clearer and the first things Longarm noted were the glowering brow and the glittering eyes of the zealot that flashed arrogantly from underneath them. The leader carried himself proudly, striding with chest out toward Longarm. God was not only on this man's side, He was sitting on his shoulder, sounding trumpets in his ear.

When Longarm got to within thirty feet or so of the settlers, their leader pulled up and turned to his followers. He raised his hand as if he were blessing them, and told them he would see to this godless invader.

Then he turned to face Longarm, who had simply continued to advance toward him.

"Stop!" he cried to Longarm. As he called out, he raised his rifle, an old .45-70 Springfield conversion.

Longarm pulled up, unable to suppress the anger he felt at having someone throw down on him like that for no reason at all. He clamped his jaw shut,

39

however, and said nothing, waiting instead for the settlement's leader to speak.

"You and your ilk!" he called to Longarm. "Turn around and get out of this valley. You have no business here. You are not wanted. You are trespassing on private land!"

"That so? What's it called?"

"New Bethlehem!"

"And who might you be?"

"Reverend Thomas Dorr Wilson, New Bethlehem's founder and leader."

"We are not going back, Reverend. We have a wounded man here. He may die if he does not get seen to—and we figure your people can help him. I don't see how you can refuse—not if you are who you say you are."

"I'll have none of your tricks. Get out, I say! There is no place in New Bethlehem for the likes of you." He looked beyond Longarm, and his implacable expression hardened immeasurably. "I see you have a woman traveling alone with you! Dressed in a man's shirt, she is! A wanton! A hussy! I know of that woman. She does the work of men—and has the same freedom and license as those godless men who follow the blasphemous teaching of Stewart and men like him!"

Longarm was suddenly sick of this black-hatted zealot. He started toward him. "I don't like all this raving," he told the reverend. "Seems to me I might do better talking to your people myself."

At once the reverend lifted his rifle and sighted along its barrel. "One more step, mister, and I'll shoot."

"Hell you will, you old windbag. I'm the law in these parts! Put that rifle down or I'll take it from you and wrap it around your head! I told you just now I got a wounded man back there!"

40

The men behind Reverend Wilson brought up their rifles also, as Longarm continued his advance.

"Stand back!" Reverend Wilson cried, steadying his rifle. "I warn you! I'll shoot!"

"I told you," Longarm said, "I'm the only law in these parts! I'm Custis Long, a U.S. deputy marshal. Now put down that damn rifle!"

Reverend Wilson fired. The explosion of the bullet's heavy charge knocked him back a bit, and the rifle's barrel lifted into the air. All Longarm felt was his hat being flung back as the round cut through the top of the crown. He didn't bother to stop and go back for it, but kept on walking, his gunmetal eyes blazing with a cold fury.

"I'll fire again!" the reverend cried, astonished and obviously a little shaken at Longarm's continued approach.

Wilson took a hesitant step backward, and with shaking fingers started to reload hastily. Behind him, the settlers were backing up, and all of them were looking with a great deal of uncertainty at their leader. Longarm kept coming, aware that the reverend could not allow his followers to see him back down now—but aware also that the reverend had been shaken to his bootstraps when he had been forced to fire, only to have Longarm keep on coming. Longarm smiled.

"What's the matter, Reverend? Doesn't that Bible of yours have an answer for this sort of thing?"

Before the reverend could marshal his thoughts for an appropriate response, Longarm made a quick lunge, grabbed the rifle barrel and twisted the rifle from the man's grasp. As soon as he had a firm grip on the weapon, he turned, and in one sweeping motion flung the rifle into the center of the stream. Then he turned on the reverend, grabbed his coat lapels, and hauled him to within a few inches of his face.

41

"I'm going to ask you again, Reverend," he said, his voice low, but resonant with menace. "Are you going to let your people help my man?"

The reverend swallowed unhappily, then nodded almost imperceptibly. Longarm flung the man from him with such force that he fell to his knees. To Longarm's astonishment, he did not try to regain his feet, but instead stayed on his knees and flung his arms to the sky in a broad, supplicating gesture.

"Oh Lord!" he cried in a powerful but quavering voice, "forgive this your humble servant! My eyes were blinded by my concern for those whose lives you have entrusted to me! Pride consumed me! I put pride before my love of Jesus. Thy servant has failed thee! Forgive me, oh Lord! Let me have the wisdom to receive this man and his wounded comrade into our bosom! Forgive us, oh Lord! Forgive us!"

The settlers behind him caught his drift at once. They threw themselves down upon the ground, their rifles dropping by their sides, flung their arms skyward and began calling upon the Lord to forgive them as well.

Longarm scratched his thick head of dark brown hair and then stood for a moment, arms akimbo, as the impromptu church service gained momentum. Then, certain that he would have little more trouble with Reverend Wilson, he turned and started back to get his hat—and the wounded Dooley.

Chapter 3

Pleased, Longarm patted Dooley on the arm and stepped back from the bed. Bill Reed, standing beside him, was relieved as well. He patted his sagging belly, then ran his thumbs up under his suspenders.

"He's goin' to be all right, Longarm," the teamster said.

"Maybe so," said Dooley, smiling weakly. "But I sure feel light-headed. Like I was on a high lonesome."

"Mr. Dooley has lost a lot of blood, I am afraid," said Mrs. Newton, as she entered the bedroom, a warm bowl of something mouth-watering in her hands. "What he needs now is nourishment."

Longarm looked back at Dooley, whose dark curls framed his pale, drawn face. At sight of the woman, his eyes lit. Mrs. Newton was right, Longarm realized. What Dooley needed now was rest and nourishment. And Longarm was willing to leave that up to Mrs. Newton. She was the only one of the settlers who had insisted—despite her husband's fierce objections—that she had no choice but to take Dooley into her home and do what she could for him. She was a lean, hawk-faced woman, but there was a gentleness and a softness about her that was not lost on Longarm.

"Thank you, Mrs. Newton," Longarm said. "You're taking good care of Dooley."

"Well, you're the one that took out that bullet

last night, Mr. Long. I never saw a steadier hand. Now it is my turn."

Longarm nodded, turned to Bill Reed and left the bedroom with him. Not long after they had settled at the kitchen table, the woman left the bedroom, an empty bowl in her hand, a warm smile on her craggy face. Denny was at the kitchen stove, bent over a huge soup kettle. At sight of Mrs. Newton, she grabbed up the ladle, and in a moment Mrs. Newton was returning to the bedroom with another steaming bowl.

"How about us, Denny?" said Bill Reed. "That smells pretty damn good."

She laughed, and in a moment the two men were sampling the soup while they discussed their options. With their horses and wagons gone, Bill Reed, Dooley and Denny were out of business—and that meant that Charles Ogden Stewart, their employer, had no means of carting his fossils to the Union Pacific railroad in Dog Wells. Whoever had been behind that night raid had done an effective job of stopping Stewart—at least for now. And that same person had also been responsible for the deaths of two teamsters and the serious wounding of a third. As Longarm discussed the matter with Bill Reed and Denny, he came to the obvious conclusion: William Edward Pope was the gent responsible for that raid.

What remained now was for Longarm to gain what proof he would need to collar the cocky little paleontologist. But that would have to wait until he made connections with that British expedition. And when he asked the two what they knew about the paleontologist from England, he got an immediate response.

"I know the feller," said Bill Reed, running his thumbs up the insides of his braces. "Yessir, I sure

44

do. He's an odd one, he is. But he sure knows how to live in the wilderness, he does."

"Maybe you'd better explain that for Longarm," Denny suggested.

"Well, that blamed Englishman and his party don't visit the wilderness. They bring all the luxuries of civilization with them. They have little privies they set up in back of their tents. And not only that, but bathtubs too, if you can believe it. Their tents are more like houses than tents. And they have tables and chairs and people to wait on them."

Denny broke in then. "Not only to wait on them," she said, "but also to bring them their tea in the afternoon."

"That's right," said Bill Reed. "Their tea in the afternoon! And all their diggers have to drop their little pickaxes and whiskbrooms and join them. And it's not only tea, it's little cakes and cookies too. You never saw the like, Mr. Long."

"You visited them?"

"Yes, I did. Denny did too. They were advertising for help to carry their fossils to Dog Wells. We would have taken the job, but Stewart got wind of it and offered us more than the Englishman thought was fair. Not long after, they pulled up stakes and went looking someplace else for fossils. Stewart was mighty happy to see them go, I can tell you that."

"He was out here?"

"He came fast enough when he got word them Englishmen was here. But he's gone back to Denver now."

"He'll be back soon, though," said Denny, a sly grin on her pert face.

Bill Reed turned to her. "How come, Denny?"

"That Englishman has found another place to dig. That's what I heard. And this place has bones even bigger than the ones we've been hauling."

45

"How do you know this?" Longarm asked.

Denny's face clouded. Frowning, she said, "Bucky told me about it. He was pulling out of Dragon Bluff after he delivered this last load of fossils to Dog Wells. He was going to work for the Englishman." She shook her head sadly. " 'Course, he won't be doing that now."

"Denny, where was this other dig? Do you know?"

She knit her brows in concentration. "Around here somewhere, I think. But I wasn't sure where. Bucky said something about a pine bluff, but I don't know where in tarnation that is."

Bill Reed's eyebrows shot up. "Sure you do, Denny!"

"What do you mean?" she asked, surprised.

"Hell," Bill said emphatically, "that's where we are now! Take a look at that bluff southwest of this settlement."

"You mean—?"

Bill Reed nodded sagely, then looked at Longarm and grinned. "That's what it's called. Pine Bluff, and this here valley is Pine Bluff Valley. Leastways, that was what they used to call it before this damn New Bethlehem crowd barged in here and took over."

Mrs. Newton came out of the bedroom, a slight smile on her gaunt face. She closed the door softly behind her, then caught Longarm's eyes. Her smile broadened.

"How is he, Mrs. Newton?" Longarm asked.

"Asleep," she said, obviously pleased. "Never knew a man didn't like my herb soup."

"That's right," seconded Bill Reed. "Longarm and I just finished a bowl. It sure does warm a man right down to his bootstraps."

The woman blushed. "I'm right pleased you had

some." Suddenly it seemed, she didn't know what to do with her hands. She brushed them down along her black skirt to dry them. Then her hands flew nervously to the thick pile of rich auburn hair that was bound in braids about her head like a massive crown.

To give the woman some breathing room, Longarm asked, "Will Dooley be all right?"

"Oh, yes. He's a strong man. And his wound is clean and already healing. He's broken a rib, but that'll mend soon enough." She noticed something and frowned. "My, you men have no coffee," she cried, startled. She almost ran to the stove to put the coffee on.

She was filling the coffeepot at the sink pump when her husband entered.

Longarm had had his fill of Mexico in years past. One thing he had never liked much was the enthusiasm the locals had for the bullfights. But he'd gone to a few, and now, as he watched Calvin Newton enter his kitchen, he was reminded of the entrance of the bull into the bullring. The man seemed to sniff the air as he brought himself to a halt and glared ominously around him, first to his wife at the pump, then at Longarm, Bill Reed and Denny at the table. Nothing his eyes struck seemed to please him.

His stature was short but powerful; his head seemed to rest directly on his broad shoulders without the advantage of a neck. The sleeves of his coarse, black shirt were rolled up and his arms seemed to be a mass of powerful musculature. His waist was a mite thick, but solid. It did not sag; and as he stood there, he planted his short, bow legs far apart, and eyed Bill Reed and Denny with a cold, implacable gaze.

"There's a wagon and two horses outside for you

47

and your friend in there," he barked powerfully. "Take it and get out of here. Now."

"Calvin!" his wife cried softly, aghast.

He focused a withering gaze on her. "You've done enough already, woman!" he told her with brutal directness. "It was you who insisted that these godless heathen find refuge under my roof. It is you who have made me the object of pity. I have suffered your insolence for the last time! This is my home! And under its roof, you will obey—or get out! Is that clear?"

Crushed, the poor woman could only nod her head dumbly, her hand still frozen on the pump handle.

Longarm got to his feet quickly, embarrassed for the woman. He wanted to say something to help her. And he really wanted to come back at the fellow for his behavior, but one look at his round, piggish face, the small, mean eyes and the thick, brutal lips, and he knew it was hopeless. Calvin Newton didn't know any better. And he had undoubtedly picked himself a religion that was on his side in the matter.

Denny and Bill Reed also got to their feet, each of them glancing uncertainly up at Longarm. He understood their confusion. Was Dooley well enough to travel in the back of a wagon all the way to Dog Wells?

Longarm looked across the kitchen at Carrie Newton. "What about it, Mrs. Newton?" he asked gently. "Is Dooley well enough to travel?"

"He's . . . he's much better, Mr. Long. If Mr. Reed and Miss Ashley are careful, he maybe could make it. But . . ." she glanced almost furtively over at her glowering husband— "it would be very painful for him, I'm thinking."

"Then you think he could make it."

She nodded unhappily. She obviously did not like

48

the idea, but saw no way at the moment to deny her husband's demand.

Bill Reed cleared his throat. "If you folks will sell us some provisions for the journey, Miss Ashley and I'll be on our way before noon—and we'll take Dooley with us. He may be wounded and the ride might well hurt him some, but old Dooley wouldn't want to stay here under this roof and cause Mrs. Newton any unpleasantness." Bill Reed was looking coldly at Calvin Newton when he said this. Then he looked at Mrs. Newton and his face softened. "But I sure want to thank you, Mrs. Newton, for all you done. It was right kind of you. An angel of mercy you was, and that's a fact. It's been a pleasure knowing you."

"Thank you, Mr. Reed," she said, tears suddenly appearing in the corners of her eyes.

At that, Denny broke from the table, rushed to the woman's side and took her in her arms. As Denny comforted the woman and held her protectively, she turned and glared with undisguised fury at Calvin Newton.

But the man only straightened defiantly under Denny's gaze and swung his attention back to Longarm and Bill Reed. "Good! It's settled, then. I'll expect the whole passel of you out of this house by noon. If you'll give me a list of what you think you'll need, I'll go to the storehouse and see what I can find. I assure you, the price will be reasonable."

A moment later, with Bill Reed's penciled list in his hand, the man vanished out the door. Only then did Mrs. Newton break down completely. To escape her sobs, Bill Reed and Longarm stepped outside on the low porch. Wordlessly, Longarm handed the teamster one of his cheroots, took one for himself, then lit both cigars with a quick snap of a match head against his thumbnail. Sucking the smoke into his lungs, Longarm took a deep, unhappy breath.

49

It sure as hell was a pity what some women had to go through, just to have a man around the house.

The sound of the wagon taking Dooley to Dog Wells had only just faded in the distance when Longarm strode to the barn and set about saddling the buckskin. He had just about finished cinching up the saddle when he heard hurried footsteps coming across the yard. He turned to see Mrs. Newton burst into the barn. She looked distraught. Her hair, no longer tightly bound in braids, streamed out wildly behind her as she ran. The neck of her blouse was open, and it looked to Longarm as if all the buttons had popped loose.

"Mr. Long!" she cried, throwing herself into his arms. "You must take me from here!"

As gently as he could, Longarm took her arms and pushed her from him so that he could look down into her wide, tearful eyes. As the same time he saw the rapidly discoloring welt over her left cheekbone. "Mrs. Newton," he told her softly. "You know I can't do such a thing. You are a married woman. This is your home!"

"Oh, please!"

"Study on it a moment, Mrs. Newton. Ask yourself what you're asking me to do!"

"Asking *you* to do?" She seemed confused. It was obvious that she had not thought through completely what she was proposing to Longarm.

"Yes," Longarm replied, still keeping his voice gentle. "You are asking me to run away with another man's wife."

"I can no longer be a wife to that man!" she spat with sudden, bitter venom, pushing herself away from Longarm and straightening up to her full height.

"Perhaps that's how you feel now, ma'am," Longarm persisted reasonably. "But maybe you should give yourself time to think on this. You might feel different after all this unpleasantness has passed."

She placed her hand up to her cheekbone and looked at him closely. It was as if she were peering at him through a dirty windowpane and could not see him clearly. "I . . . I might feel different, you say. Unpleasantness, you call it! You are like *them*! You are *one* of them!"

"Now, ma'am, I don't know what you expected of me. I am a lawman. That's what I do, so I guess that's what I am. And I ain't much more than that, I'm afraid. I got some old-fashioned ideas, maybe— and one of them I been able to hold to pretty good: I don't run off with married women. If that makes me one of them, then I guess I plead guilty."

"Well said, Marshal!"

Longarm spun to see Reverend Wilson push through a side door. Behind him came Mrs. Newton's glowering husband.

"You must forgive this poor, benighted woman," Reverend Wilson said.

Mrs. Newton shrank as the reverend strode closer to her. Longarm saw not merely fear in her eyes, but terror—the kind he might see in the eyes of a small animal caught inexorably in some cruel trap. Triumphant in his scorn, her husband pulled up beside the reverend, his arms folded over his massive chest, his legs set wide.

"Carrie Newton is an evil woman, Marshal," Reverend Wilson said thunderously. "Calvin has tried heroically to wring the evil out of her—to instill in her the appropriate virtues, and to make of her a true servant of God. He has striven mightily, I say —but alas, he is working with material even Jesus Christ himself would call incorrigible!"

As this awesome indictment struck her, Carrie Newton gasped, then sank to her knees, her head bowed forward into her hands. Great, wracking sobs

51

tore from her throat. "No," she moaned, shaking her head from side to side. "Oh, no! That is not true."

But the reverend had the bit in his teeth now. There was a Bible in his hand, his finger holding a place. He flipped open the Bible and in sonorous tones, calculated to strike terror into the heart of any true believer, began to read from it over the weeping woman.

" 'For the lips of a strange woman drop as an honeycomb,' " he thundered ominously. " 'And her mouth is smoother than oil!' "

The reverend paused to let that sink in. Carrie Newton's head had sunk lower. She was no longer weeping. She was moaning instead.

"No, no," Carrie whimpered. "It is not true, I tell you. It is not true!"

Reverend Wilson stepped back and bellowed down at her, "Strange woman, listen! I am reading from the Holy Book!"

Carrie, her gaunt face streaked and dirty from her tears, glanced beseechingly up at Wilson. "Please, Reverend. Do not read that. It is not true! I am not such a woman!"

"Aha!" Wilson cried, pleased that he had forced her to deny her evil. He seemed to lick his chops at the spectacle. Triumphantly, he went back to the Bible and continued to read. " 'But the strange woman's end is bitter as wormwood, sharp as a two-edged sword! Her feet go down to death! Her steps take hold on hell!' "

He clapped the Bible shut. It sounded like the clap of doom in that dim barn. Longarm saw Carrie's narrow shoulders jump with terror. Stepping back to better view his handiwork, Reverend Wilson turned to Calvin Newton and with a generous sweep of his hand presented the wailing woman on the floor back to her righteous husband. The man was in a positive glow as a result of his good works this day. Longarm got the distinct impression, however, that he would have felt even better if Carrie had crawled across that filthy barn floor and planted kisses on his feet. He would willingly have allowed her that abasement.

Calvin approached his wife. "Get up!" he said to her.

"Calvin!" she moaned, wincing away from him.

"Get up, I said! I forgive you!"

Stumbling slightly, occasional sad sobs breaking involuntarily from her, Carrie Newton pulled herself erect, a look of abject misery on her tearstained face. Pathetically, like a blind old dog reaching out with its paws, she reached out for her husband.

With the back of his hand he slapped her so brutally that she was flung back with stunning force. She slammed into the side of a stall, then slid, barely conscious, to the straw-littered floor of the barn.

Nodding with approval, Reverend Wilson smiled upon his follower. "I will leave you to finish the disciplining of your wife, Calvin. See to it that she transgresses no further, else for both of you, it will mean expulsion from New Bethlehem!"

With that threat hanging in the air, he turned about and strode swiftly out through the side door.

As his footsteps faded, Calvin approached his semiconscious wife. "Get up!" he said.

She opened her eyes and stared uncomprehendingly up at her husband.

"Stand up!" Calvin thundered.

She began to stir valiantly, but her senses were obviously still reeling. With a heavy curse, Calvin kicked her, hard, sending her spinning over the floor. He started after her swiftly, no doubt ready to kick her a second time.

By that time Longarm had had enough. With three quick strides, he overtook Calvin, grabbed the man

53

by the shoulder and spun him around. Before Calvin understood what Longarm was about, the lawman punched him in the face. The sledgehammer blow caught him flush on his jaw. Longarm heard the man's jawbone crack from the impact as the fellow piled backward to the floor. Calvin tried to get up, his mouth working furiously—and then he grabbed his face with both his hands and began to moan.

Longarm realized he had broken the man's jaw.

He stepped past the prostrate man and knelt beside Carrie Newton. All this had not happened, he realized perfectly well, just because she had insisted on caring for the wounded teamster. But that action —that insistence on helping a fellow human being— was what had brought matters to a head between her and her husband. And now, if he rode out of here and left her to the fury of her injured husband, there was little doubt in Longarm's mind that he would kill her. His rage would feed upon itself, and soon she would no longer be able even to moan for mercy —and when he was done with her finally, the breath of life would have been thrashed out of her.

"Carrie," he said softly. "Carrie, can you get up?"

She nodded slightly and opened her eyes. In a whisper he could barely hear, she said, "You called me Carrie."

"Yes," he said, smiling at her. "I don't like 'Mrs. Newton,' somehow."

She straightened herself, wincing slightly. Then she brushed her hair out of her eyes. "I . . . I don't like it either, Mr. Long."

"Call me Longarm. You still want to ride out with me?"

She closed her eyes, as if she could hardly believe what she had heard. Her eyes still closed, she nodded her head. "Oh, yes," she murmured. "Yes, *please,* Longarm."

"Get what things you'll need. Not much. They

will have to fit behind your saddle. I'll find a horse and saddle it for you."

She nodded eagerly and got painfully to her feet. Already, Longarm noted, the side of her face where her husband had struck her was swelling and purpling. With a fearful glance past Longarm at her still-prostrate husband, she turned and hurried from the barn. Longarm turned and looked down at Calvin. The man was still on his back, holding his jaw with both hands, his eyes fixed with murderous intensity on Longarm.

"You'll be all right," Longarm told him. "Just bandage your jaw shut and keep it shut. Leave enough of an opening so you can use a straw. You'll lose some weight, maybe, but you'll survive."

The man started to say something, then yelped painfully and shut both eyes, tears of rage welling from them. As Longarm left him, he found he felt no remorse whatsoever for having injured the man so painfully.

Before they rode out, Longarm and Carrie helped Calvin into the house, where, under Longarm's direction, Carrie bound her husband's jaw tightly and made him reasonably comfortable. Riding from the settlement, they encountered some hostility in the form of outraged stares; and before they left the place entirely, a very surprised and disconcerted Reverend Wilson overtook them and began berating Carrie for her unseemly conduct. Longarm pulled up and advised the reverend that he was once again letting his pride get in the way of his good sense. The reverend reined in without another word and let them ride out.

With the settlement an hour's ride behind them, the distant pine bluffs that rimmed the valley became a rugged escarpment looming so high that it almost shut out the sky. They followed the river from the valley as it coursed along the base of the bluff, turning slowly north into a wide canyon. Longarm was looking for signs of the Englishman Denny and Bill Reed had told him about. From the looks of the pine-clad bluffs on both sides of them, this might well be the country the British expedition was exploring in its search for more fossils. Pine Bluff, Bill Reed had told them. All well and good, Longarm mused as he rode, his head flung back while he peered up at the red, striated walls of sandstone. But *which* Pine Bluff?

They rounded a bend in the canyon and found themselves on a broad flat, a further valley below them. And hard against one towering wall, they found the British.

As they rode closer, Longarm remembered Bill Reed's description of them, and chuckled. The old teamster had not exaggerated. There were big tents and small tents, and behind each tent was a curtained bathtub or privy. Cases of provisions and equipment were piled neatly about the perimeter of the camp, and the many horses and mules were safely tucked away in a rope corral. The general appearance of the camp was impressive. There was no litter; no harnesses were thrown loosely about. Everything seemed in fine order, with neat piles everywhere.

"How are you going to explain me?" Carrie asked nervously.

Longarm glanced at her and smiled. "I hadn't given that much thought, Carrie."

She blushed. "Well, maybe you should."

He nodded. Carrie was wearing a rough blue woolen shirt and a long black skirt with petticoats. But she was not wearing a corset; this fact was obvious from the way her breasts swelled against the shirt, which she wore open at the neck. Her hair she wore down, and its long, luxurious tresses extended past her shoulders. There was everything in her dress to suggest a wanton female, but nothing in her manner.

"I'll try the truth, Carrie. How's that?"

She smiled, transforming her plain, angular features into beauty. "Yes, Longarm," she said. "I think that would be a fine idea. How does the side of my face look?"

"Still a mite purple and swollen, but the ride seems to have done you good."

"It has done me more than that, Longarm."

He smiled and looked back at the camp.

The Englishman in charge was waiting for them at the perimeter of the camp, arms akimbo, a smile on his face. Behind him was a small army of associates, a few of whom had the rough-hewn solidity of teamsters. Longarm pulled up alongside the Englishman, dismounted, helped Carrie to dismount, then turned to the fellow and stuck out his hand.

As the Englishman shook it, Longarm said, "I'm Deputy U.S. Marshal Long. I am hoping you are Sir Thomas Dorset."

"At your service, Deputy," the man replied. "I must say I am rather astonished. Have I committed some crime, to be accosted in the middle of this fabled land by a law officer?"

"The American State Department sent me, but I can explain that later. This is Mrs. Newton. She's had a long ride and she's a bit weary. Is there anyone here who could show her to some water and see that she has a chance to freshen up?"

"Oh, that's all right, Longarm," Carrie protested feebly. "I'm fine."

"Welcome, Mrs. Newton," the Englishman said, bowing gallantly. "My sister will be delighted to assist you—and to have someone of your gender to keep her company. I am afraid she is famished for female companionship! You have come as a wel-

57

come surprise!" Sir Thomas turned to a small, alert-looking young man. "Jeffrey, will you fetch Isadora, please?"

Jeffrey was off like a shot. Sir Thomas, smiling warmly, turned back to Longarm. "Come, Deputy. My tent is not far. We'll have some extra chairs set out. Would you care to join me in a drink?"

"My whistle is a bit dry, now that you mention it. Thank you."

As Longarm and Sir Thomas started toward his tent, a tall, lean, red-haired young woman hurried toward them.

"Ah," said Sir Thomas, halting. "Allow me to present my sister Isadora, Deputy."

The young woman halted in front of Longarm, her green eyes flashing with intelligence and—Longarm could not help but notice—a disarming and quite flattering curiosity about him. She was wearing jodhpurs, a white silk blouse, and a black kerchief at her neck.

"Isadora," said Sir Thomas, "we have two guests, Mrs. Newton and U.S. Deputy Custis Long."

"It's a pleasure to meet you, Mr. Long," she replied, boldly holding out her long, delicate hand to him.

Longarm took the offered hand and shook it, trying his best to meet the directness of her gaze with an appraisal just as direct. "A pleasure, ma'am," Longarm told her.

"And this is Mrs. Newton, Isadora," said Sir Thomas, clearing his throat to catch Isadora's attention. "Perhaps she would not mind sharing your tent with you. I'll leave her in your hands."

Isadora turned her attention to Carrie Newton, her imperious gaze softening at once. Smiling warmly, she opened her arms to Carrie. "How nice!" she said. "Someone for company! Lost among all

58

these brutes, you have no idea how pleased I am to see another woman."

With her arm draped fondly over Carrie's shoulder, Isadora led Carrie off toward a more secluded tent situated amidst a grove of young poplars in the bend of the stream that ran past the campsite. The two seemed like old friends. Longarm was grateful for Isadora's instant and warm acceptance of the older and somewhat bedraggled woman. He knew that women could be like this with each other, but it always surprised him when he saw it.

As Longarm and Sir Thomas continued toward his tent, Longarm looked the Englishman over. His manners, like those of his sister, were impeccable. Longarm felt truly welcome. It was not going to be difficult, Longarm felt, to do what he could to protect the man from the barbarities that rival paleontologists had already visited upon each other as well as this Englishman.

Sir Thomas was almost as tall as Longarm. He was not built as huskily, however. He was slim and almost as willowy as his sister. Yet there was nothing feminine in his manner. His dark hair was thick and close-cropped. His face was lean, angular, and clean-shaven except for a thin, meticulously barbered mustache. His dark eyes, like those of his sister, were piercing and unflinching. Also, like his sister, he wore riding breeches. His shirt was dark cotton, and the bandanna knotted about his neck was red. He wore no hat, but as Longarm reached the Englishman's tent, he glimpsed a pith helmet resting on the seat of a canvas chair.

While they were approaching the camp table that had been set up in front of Sir Thomas's tent, the alert Jeffrey—it was obvious to Longarm, now, that he was the Englishman's manservant—hurried ahead of them into the tent and came out unfolding a camp chair for Longarm. Then, while Longarm and

Sir Thomas made themselves comfortable about the table, Jeffrey brought out a decanter of Scotch and two glasses on a silver tray and placed the tray on the table.

"Excellent, Jeffrey," Sir Thomas told his servant. "Thank you. This should serve nicely to wet the deputy's whistle, I dare say."

As Jeffrey left them, Sir Thomas poured two fingers of Scotch, neat, into Longarm's glass, then poured himself an equal amount. "Cheers," said Sir Thomas, raising his glass to Longarm.

"Cheers," repeated the big lawman as he took up his own drink.

The Scotch was a bit mellow for Longarm's taste, which ran to the more pungent bite of Maryland rye. He didn't think it would be polite for him to fetch the bottle he carried in his saddlebag, however, so he settled back and let the pale amber liquor burn its way—rather pleasantly, he was surprised to note—down into his gut. He looked over the encampment, pleased to have found the British expedition so easily, and pleased, too, to have found it in such excellent order. The teamsters and the other members of the Englishman's team were going about their work quietly and efficiently. There was about this encampment no sense of danger at all. An outing—a pleasant outing in the American wilderness—was all it appeared to be to Longarm. He was immensely relieved.

Remembering Billy Vail's tale of alarm and murder and the State Department's frantic wires to Denver, Longarm could only question the judgment of the State Department, or at least of the petty functionary who had relayed—without bothering to seek confirmation—the British government's false alarms. There might have been a few unfortunate deaths, but certainly there had been no warfare to the extent of those reports. And everything in the

60

camp was obviously under tight and efficient control.

"That woman with you, Deputy," Sir Thomas said. "She has a different name than you do, but you referred to her as missus. She is a . . . friend of yours?"

"I guess you'd be calling her a damsel in distress. Carrie Newton's a woman who's just run away from her husband. And the reason he's not following her is because I had to break his jaw when he wouldn't stop beating on the poor woman. She's from that settlement further back in the valley. She's finished with it and her husband, and I'm simply helping her to get away."

"My word! Helping her to get away, you say. How bluntly you put it. You mean, rather, that you are running away with another man's wife."

"That's about the size of it, I guess." Longarm took out two cheroots, passed one to Sir Thomas and kept one for himself. He struck a sulfur match and lit both his and Sir Thomas's cheroots. Then he took a deep drag and sat back contentedly in his chair. "But I didn't take the woman for myself," Longarm continued. "I helped her get away to save her from a brutal husband. There's nothing between us, Sir Thomas, except that, and I would be right pleased if you and your sister would extend to her every courtesy. She is not a cheap or a petty woman, and she deserves a whole hell of a lot more than she's been getting."

"How did you happen to run across her, if I may ask? This is quite unusual, you must admit."

Longarm took another sip of the excellent Scotch and told the Englishman of the events that had led him to seek shelter with the Newtons in the settlement. When Longarm had finished, Sir Thomas nodded.

"I see," he said, pursing his lips thoughtfully. "She

went against her husband in order to help you save your man Dooley. She is a brave woman, judging from your account of her husband. She will be extended every courtesy, Deputy. That's a promise."

"Call me Longarm," the lawman suggested. "And thank you. I knew you were a gentleman."

"And of course I was pretty sure that I too was dealing with a gentleman. You will, I hope, forgive my curiosity concerning this woman."

"Don't give it a thought, Sir Thomas."

"And now, Longarm, what could the State Department possibly want with me? You promised me an explanation, if you will recall."

"I remember." Longarm finished his Scotch, stuck the cheroot back into his mouth and took a few puffs. "It seems your government has got my government very upset. A war was going on—or something close to it—between you and some American . . . whatchamacallits."

"Paleontologists?" Sir Thomas suggested with a slight but uncondescending smile.

"Right," Longarm replied, smiling slightly also. "According to the reports, four men were already dead." Longarm shook his head, snorting softly in derision at the report.

"Quite right, Longarm. Five men in all. It has not been pleasant, not at all."

"You mean it *has* been that bad?"

"It has been difficult, I must admit." Sir Thomas finished his drink.

"But, my God, Sir Thomas, this encampment is as calm as a church meeting. I don't see guards. Your men don't look proddy. Carrie and I rode up to your camp without being stopped by any lookouts. If it's as bad as you say, why in tarnation haven't you taken any precautions?"

"Oh, my dear man, we have. We have!"

"Show me!"

"Draw your weapon, Longarm. Carefully."

"What?"

"Do as I say, Longarm."

Longarm reached across his belly, carefully, and pulled his double-action Colt from its waxed, heat-hardened holster. He did this swiftly as well as carefully, in one single, fluid motion.

"Now get up, Longarm. Carefully. And then extend your weapon and cover me as I get to my feet as well. Is that clear?"

"Clear enough, but I sure as hell wish you'd tell me what this is all about."

"You'll know soon enough," Sir Thomas said as he got to his feet, stepped away from the table, and slowly raised both hands over his head.

The moment Sir Thomas's hands stopped moving, a distant rifle shot echoed in the canyon, and at almost the same instant the gun in Longarm's hand went flying. In a rapid chorus thereafter, a series of rifle shots came from the trees and bushes surrounding them; and with each came the whine of ricocheting bullets, all of them close enough to make Longarm wince. Simultaneously, armed men burst from cover and began running toward Longarm and Sir Thomas.

Holding up his hand, palm out, to halt the onrushing men, Sir Thomas called, "Stop! It's all right! Just a demonstration! Get back to your posts."

Shaking his head, Longarm retrieved his Colt and examined it unhappily. There was a slight nick in the barrel where the slug had glanced off it. Outside of that, there was no damage at all. That was one hell of a marksman, whoever the hell he was. Longarm shuddered and pulled back the flap of his frock coat to drop the Colt back into its holster. Then he looked into the smiling face of Sir Thomas.

"That was a damn fool thing to do, Sir Thomas,"

Longarm said. "I might have got killed. Or *you* might have."

"You wanted me to show you what precautions I have taken." He smiled. "I just have. But don't fret. You were in no real danger. My men have orders to fire only warning shots at first."

Longarm shrugged wearily and sat back down in the canvas chair and reached for the Scotch. "All right. You showed me. Now join me in another drink, Sir Thomas. I think I need it."

Sir Thomas laughed.

Chapter 4

As soon as Longarm finished his second drink, he asked Sir Thomas for an explanation, then leaned back to listen.

In a voice that revealed little of the anger he must have felt, Sir Thomas explained that on two occasions—after he had been visited first by Ogden Stewart and then by William Pope—armed men had attacked his teamsters. Sir Thomas went on to verify the losses Vail had mentioned, including the deaths of two teamsters, one of Sir Thomas's diggers, and a man he had hired on as a guard. There was no doubt in Sir Thomas's mind as to who had engineered these attacks, or why. In both cases, he was certain, the two American paleontologists, Pope and Stewart, were responsible.

When the Englishman had finished, Longarm nodded and said, "That was why you had those jaspers sitting out there with their rifles pointing at me?"

"I admit, it was a drastic precaution. But as I said, each time I got a visit before from an American—unannounced, that is—it led to trouble of one kind or another. That gentleman Pope, for instance, seemed quite arrogant in his boast that his men would be able to stop me. It was not long after his visit—that very night, in fact—that two of our wagons were driven off in the night and a teamster killed when he tried to stop them. When my lookouts told me *you* were riding up, I thought I would arrange an object lesson, in the event that you too might have come here to threaten this expedition or try to stop it." He smiled. "So your plea for some demonstration of my defenses was, as it happened, quite easy to arrange."

Longarm smiled thinly and pulled on his cheroot. "You'd already set me up."

"Yes."

"There's just one thing I'd like you to explain for me, Sir Thomas."

"Fire away, Longarm."

"What's all this fuss—hell, downright shooting warfare—over bones? I could understand it if you were digging for gold or silver. But *bones*? You men are supposed to be scientists, intelligent men. Educated men. And here you are, acting like gangsters, hijacking shipments of bones, killing people in the night. What's going on here, anyway?"

"Yes," Sir Thomas said, nodding his head. "I can understand your confusion, Longarm. I share it, to a certain extent. You are quite right. Scientists are supposed to be intelligent. Such men are not supposed to do such things."

"Then why *do* they?"

"Because they are desperate. Because, as I see it, their lives depend on maintaining what we call priority."

"Priority?"

"They have to establish by objective proof that they are the first either to have named a new subspecies or to have unearthed and fitted together such a subspecies. As a result, they can name the beast, and the name they give it will remain—and their renown will be such that thereafter doors will be opened for them, so to speak, in the scientific community. In short, Longarm, their livelihood will be assured. They will be awarded needed funds and

66

given the positions in scientific bodies that will enable them to prosper, not only as human beings, but also as scientists. You say it is not gold or silver we seek? Quite right. But it is something infinitely more valuable—to a scientist." He looked carefully at Longarm. "Does that make sense to you? Can you understand why that might be true?"

"Yes," Longarm replied thoughtfully. "I guess I can understand that, all right. A man's reputation has always been worth money. Look at what Will Cody has been able to do with it. I doubt if he can keep track of what Ned Buntline's written about him, and maybe the man's beginning to believe half of it himself. But it don't matter; it makes him a fine living, and right now that's the important thing."

"Precisely. A scientist's reputation can secure for him lifelong fame, even a kind of immortality. Dean William Buckland, for instance, is famous for, among other notable accomplishments, his discovery, description, and naming of the *Megalosaurus*."

"Mega *what*?"

"Sir Thomas laughed. "*Megalosaurus,* Longarm. It is a genus of dinosaurs. All scientifically described animals and plants, fossil and recent, belong to a genera and to a species. The generic name *megalosaurus* indicates a category that may include several species of dinosaur. *Megalosaurus cuvieri,* for instance, is named in honor of the great French anatomist and paleontologist Georges Cuvier." He smiled. "So you see how it works."

Longarm chuckled. "And what is it that you are looking for, Sir Thomas?"

"I am in no need of funds, Longarm. So I suppose I am looking for fame instead. I could be seeking it in worse endeavors, I am sure. Primarily," he said, leaning forward with sudden eagerness, "I am interested in whether or not the smaller dinosaurs

67

with teeth, which I frankly define as carnivorous, actually preyed upon the larger herbivores. The bone of a herbivorous dinosaur bearing the marks of a smaller, carnivorous dinosaur would effectively prove my contention that, indeed, the smaller dinosaurs could and did prey on the larger."

Longarm's brow knitted into a frown as he carefully shaped an unfamiliar word: "Herbivore . . . ?"

"Plant-eating, Longarm, versus meat-eating."

"And if you did find such a bone, what would *that* prove?"

Sir Thomas's eyes lit up as he contemplated Longarm's question, and again Longarm was struck by the apparent childlike quality of these scientists. Grown men they were, and yet there was so much about them of the wide-eyed child.

"It might just give us a clue," Sir Thomas said, "as to what happened to these giants that dominated our planet for so long. They vanished, you know, almost overnight, geologically speaking. Perhaps these smaller, more vicious, meat-eating dinosaurs overran the world, feeding on the larger, slower-witted giants who were content to munch on leaves and vegetables from morning till night."

His eyes still thoughtful, his mind evidently still engrossed in this possibility and its implications, Sir Thomas reached over and absently filled Longarm's glass. Without a word to the scientist, Longarm took the glass, leaned back, and sipped it. All this talk of giant dragons roaming the earth and getting chewed up by smaller dragons was enough to give a grown man a bellyache.

And nightmares for sure.

It was dark, and Longarm had found himself a place for his soogan, close in under the cliff wall, a spot bedded with pine needles and protected by an overhanging shelf of rock. Sir Thomas had offered him a tent in the camp, but Longarm had insisted on finding his own spot. Past experience had proved to him the wisdom of locating himself away from the hornet's nest whenever trouble was afoot.

He had just finished unrolling the soogan onto his slicker and had already pulled off his boots in anticipation of a quiet smoke when he heard soft footsteps approaching through the pines.

In the act of snapping his sulfur match alight with his fingernail, he dropped the match and swiftly, silently withdrew his Colt from its holster. Aiming it in the direction from which the light, barely audible footsteps were coming, he waited. The darkness in front of him shimmered and broke—and out of it stepped a transformed Carrie Newton. Her gaunt figure had been transformed by a long, white nightdress into something flowing, giving her form a kind of insubstantial loveliness. Her auburn hair, incredibly long, had been combed out so it extended down her back and fell across her breasts, a shimmering flow of dark tresses. Her eyes had become luminous, spectral in their beauty.

She came to a halt before him without uttering a word. Longarm put away his Colt and cleared his throat nervously. He was anxious not to hurt the woman's feelings. And of course he might have her reason for this visit all wrong—though he sure as hell didn't think so.

"What's the matter, Longarm?" she asked. "Are you angry with me for coming to you like this?"

"Carrie," Longarm began uncertainly, "I didn't take you from New Bethlehem because I wanted you for myself. What I mean is, you can go back to your tent without feeling you've disappointed me."

"Go back? But why?"

"You don't have to think you got to pay me for what I did."

She dropped to her knees before him, her eyes

69

transfixing him. She was furious with him, and in that instant Longarm remembered a maxim he had always tried to follow: never take a woman against her will, but never refuse a woman when she *is* willing. And then he saw the tears in her eyes, tears of frustration as well as rage.

"Oh, damn you, Longarm!" she said vehemently.

Longarm hated to admit it to himself, but he was shocked at her language. "Carrie," he protested, "I'm just trying to do the right thing. You're a married woman."

"I see," she replied. "And you don't feel you should take . . . advantage of me. Is that it?"

When she put it like that, it *did* sound kind of silly, but he shrugged and said, "I guess that's it, Carrie."

"You're lying!"

"Carrie," Longarm said gently, "you'd best go back to your tent. Like I said before, this ain't why I took you from that settlement."

"Longarm! Don't you think I have enough sense to know that? You did it because you are the man you are—a gentleman. You took me away because you knew what awaited me in that house if my husband were to get his hands on me again. I came out here tonight because I . . ."

She couldn't go on. Her voice broke and she turned her head away from him. In the moonlight, he saw the gleam of tears on her gaunt cheeks—and realized then why he was acting like this, so damned righteous. The woman was not attractive to him. He had seen her used terribly by the man who was her husband, and he felt only pity for her, nothing more. As he realized this, he felt a sudden pang of shame. At least he could make the effort to see in her something more than that.

He reached out and took her gently in his arms. She resisted at first, then collapsed into him, still weeping softly. He rested his hand on her hair, then began stroking the long tresses. She stopped weeping at last, and looked up at him. Her eyes were still swimming in tears and her nose was red from the crying. He kissed her eyes shut and pulled her still closer to him. Gradually, the tiny sobs that occasionally broke from her ceased entirely and she snuggled against him, seeming almost to grow into his body.

"I came out here tonight," she told him in a soft, lovely voice that warmed him strangely, "because I needed you. Just the way sometimes, I imagine, you need a woman. Was that so terrible?"

"No," he replied, kissing her on the lips this time, gently, easily, tasting the salt of her tears. "There's nothing wrong with that, Carrie."

She returned his kiss passionately, then swiftly unbuttoned the front of her nightdress. As it fell away from her and she pressed herself against him, he was astonished at the warmth and fullness of her breasts. It kindled an answering warmth within him. He flung wide the soogan's flap and threw it over them both. A moment later he had covered her nakedness with his own . . .

Later, much later, she stood before him in her nightdress, a spectral figure once more.

"That was lovely," she told him softly, leaning her head for an instant against his chest. "A gentleman you are, Longarm. A *very* gentle, kind man. I had begun to lose hope that such men still existed."

Longarm was at a loss as to how to reply. He had not often been called a gentleman by the women to whom he had made love in the past. His lips brushed her forehead as she stepped away from him and glided into the darkness. As her pale figure was swallowed up by the night, he felt a momentary chill. He shook it off and stood quietly for a moment, recalling her caresses, the surprising passion he had been able to kindle in her, her words of endearment. And of course she had been right.

There was nothing terrible about her need for him, nothing wrong with the love they had shared this night—nothing wrong at all.

Chapter 5

When Longarm, leading his horse, returned to Sir Thomas's campsite the next morning, he found that the Englishman was way ahead of him. The man had broken camp by the first light of dawn, it appeared, and there were only two members of the expedition still on the site: an old teamster patiently hitching his mules to a heavily laden, canvas-topped wagon, and the cook, who was still busy packing provisions back into his chuckwagon.

The fellow brightened when he saw Longarm approaching, and hailed the lawman cheerfully. The cook was a tall, sinewy fellow with a long, gray, scraggly beard and wild, red-rimmed eyes. A black, high-peaked sombrero never seemed to leave his head, no matter what the circumstances.

"Sir Thomas told me to save your breakfast," he told Longarm cheerfully.

"That was decent of him."

A scrupulously clean man, the cook washed his long, gnarled hands in a cooking pot of steaming hot water as Longarm settled by the warm coals of the morning campfire. Wiping his hands hastily on his apron, the cook served Longarm a platter of hot biscuits, eggs and bacon. Not only were the biscuits hot, but the coffee was almost scalding, just the way Longarm liked it in the morning.

Finishing up his breakfast quickly, Longarm asked the cook why Sir Thomas had been in such an all-fired hurry to get moving this morning. The big fellow paused and then drowned a small wildflower with an accurate shot of tobacco juice and looked at Longarm. His eyes narrowed. "Didn't he tell you yesterday? You two was talkin' up a storm. Thought sure he'd of told you all about it."

"All about what?"

"One of his young assistants has found some fossils in the side of a canyon wall up yonder about ten miles. Sir Thomas was all set to break camp yesterday, soon's he heard; but then you showed up."

"I see. Up the canyon, you say?"

"Yup. Ten miles or so. Just follow that narrow stream, otherwise you'll get lost. That young assistant says there's lots of other canyons branching off this one. He called it something fearsome—a labathing, or some such word."

"A labyrinth?"

"Yep. That's it, all right." He grinned at Longarm, revealing almost black, tobacco-stained teeth. "Looks like you federal lawmen are almost as smart as an Englishman."

"Looks like it, Cookie. Thanks for the breakfast."

As Longarm mounted and started up the canyon, he wondered why Sir Thomas had not told him about his assistant's discovery. And then he chuckled as he answered his own question. Sir Thomas still did not trust Longarm. He was, after all, an American lawman—and the two men who had given him most of his trouble so far were also Americans. The wily Englishman had no choice but to play his cards close to his vest.

Sir Thomas's assistant was right, Longarm noted, as he followed the stream up the canyon. The steep-sided canyons branching off this main canyon were inviting, no doubt, but they surely did present a baffling, winding course to his eyes. That was what

74

they were, all right: treacherous, scorpion-infested labyrinths. A rider could easily get lost in such a maze of twisting, turning avenues of rock.

Over the years, Longarm was sure, this particular stretch of badlands must have claimed its share of prospectors and outlaws.

He did not want to punish his horse. As a result, it was the middle of the afternoon when Longarm overtook Sir Thomas, who had reached the spot his assistant had found and was making camp under a massive rock wall, well over a hundred feet high. Along the top of its rocky bluff ran a thin stand of pine. Sir Thomas had come upon the Pine Bluff he had left Charles Ogden Stewart's dig to find.

As Longarm rode into camp, he was greeted by an almost jubilant Sir Thomas. Jeffrey took Longarm's horse while Longarm joined Sir Thomas, who wanted him to meet the young man whose discovery had brought them to this canyon—and this spectacular find.

"Meet Tim Dinsdale, Longarm!" Sir Thomas said, beaming at the young man who was standing in front of his tent. "He's the one who first heard of this marvelous find—and traced it."

Tim and Longarm shook hands. Tim was grinning shyly. "Pleased to meet you, Mr. Long," he said.

"Call me Longarm, Tim," Longarm told the young man.

He looked quite young to Longarm, a very sunburned, flaxen-haired stripling. Yet his eyes burned with the same exciting intensity as did Sir Thomas's. They were both hooked on the same pipe, Longarm realized, and it gave them quite an enthusiasm for doing what they had to do in order to succeed.

"He's been searching for this particular canyon

for more than a week now," Sir Thomas explained. "But I had faith in him. I knew he would find it."

Tim tipped his head and squinted through the late afternoon sunlight at Longarm. "We only hope Stewart and that other one don't find this place too."

"No fear of that, Tim," said Sir Thomas. "Besides, we are here first."

"I'm afraid the law don't recognize any such thing as priority, Sir Thomas," Longarm explained. "It's not like a gold strike where you can stake out a claim. After all," he finished with a grin, "they're just bones."

"Ah, but what bones!" Sir Thomas cried. "Come! Let us show you!"

"I was hoping you would," Longarm remarked as the three started off, heading for the towering wall of rock. "I hear all this talk about a find, but I don't see much."

"You will," Sir Thomas promised. "You will."

A full hour later, after a long, hot scramble up a steep, heavily timbered slope, they came to a halt before the rock wall. It had been cut as cleanly as if a giant meat cleaver had done the job. Only the meat cleaver had had to make more than one stroke to penetrate the rock completely. There was a series of steplike ridges; Longarm counted four of them altogether. Soon the three men had clambered up the steep rock to the first cactus-littered ledge.

"Look, Longarm," Sir Thomas said, pointing up at the wall of rock. "Look closely at that strata. See it, the glint of fossil bone?"

And then Longarm saw it—a jagged, sawtoothed ridge running east and west along the strata. "What the hell *is* that?"

Sir Thomas turned at once to Tim. "Tell him what you think, Tim."

Pleased that Sir Thomas had asked him to explain what it was to Longarm, Tim cleared his throat eagerly. "Mr. Long, that's the exposed vertebrae of a very large dinosaur, and it's *in articulation!*"

Longarm grinned at the young man. "That's good, is it?"

"Of course! This joining together of the bones in their proper relationship means that this just might be a *complete* skeleton."

"I see. And all you have to do is dig away all that rock to get to it."

"Yes, Longarm," said Sir Thomas. "It is quite a task. Quarrying for dinosaur bones is a difficult, time-consuming job. But well worth it. I feel sure the results of this dig will be—well, spectacular!"

Tim grinned with pleasure. The man was evidently immensely proud of his discovery and more than eager to begin work on this cliff. But it was a job Longarm was glad *he* was not going to have to undertake. Hacking away at that solid wall of rock with pickaxes would be a hot, miserable job. And it would take time. At least the rest of this summer, Longarm realized suddenly.

During their walk to this cliff, Sir Thomas had explained what lay ahead for their expedition, once they began to work. Longarm wondered if Billy Vail had realized how long his deputy was going to be absent from Denver. Digging out this dragon could take almost as long as it took to build the pyramids —and Longarm would have to watch over the expedition members like a mother hen all that while.

"Guess you gents better get busy," Longarm drawled, shaking his head in wonder at the awesome task ahead of Sir Thomas and his men. "I don't want to spend the winter in this here country. Gets pretty cold."

Sir Thomas laughed. "I promise you, Longarm," he said, "we will *not* be here that long. If this dinosaur is as complete as I think it is, and if it is a

Laosaurus, as I have every reason to believe it might be—well, then, we might be on our way out of this canyon before August."

"I sure hope so," said Longarm, as he and the others turned their backs on the cliffside and started carefully down off the ledge. "It gets cold in the winter, just like I said—but these badlands turn into a shriveling hell in August."

"I will keep that in mind," said Sir Thomas, as the three plunged into the timber below the bluff.

By the time they left the timber and started across the meadow, on the far side of which Sir Thomas had set up camp, it was late in the afternoon. From the direction of the camp, Longarm heard the sound of tent stakes being driven into the hard-baked ground. He imagined he could also smell the beginning of the supper meal. Cookie had arrived finally, it seemed. Sure enough, as Longarm and the others waded across the swift, shallow stream that fronted the camp, he saw the tall figure of the cook standing beside his chuckwagon.

He also saw Isadora Dorset talking to the cook, so urgently, in fact, that the cook had put down a large biscuit tray and was pointing at the three men as they neared the outer perimeter of the camp.

When she turned and saw Longarm, Isadora began immediately to hurry toward him. It was not her brother or Tim she sought. This was obvious from the beginning. Longarm was the one she appeared almost desperate to see.

When she got within hailing distance, she cried out, "Longarm! I must speak to you!"

He waved to her and kept going. But as the three men approached her, Isadora waved her brother and Tim past her.

"Longarm is the one I want," she told her brother anxiously. "Just Longarm. It's . . . personal."

"By all means, Isadora," said her brother, with a smile. He winked cheerfully at Longarm as he and Tim continued on to the camp.

Longarm held up and looked down at Isadora's distraught features. Something was wrong, terribly wrong. A faint uneasiness stirred within him. "What is it, Isadora? What's happened?"

"I don't know." She stepped closer, glanced quickly about her, and said, "Didn't Carrie visit you last night?"

Longarm almost blushed. "Yes," he said. "She did."

"Well, where is she *now*?"

"My God, Isadora. Isn't she with you?"

"She never returned to my tent, Longarm! I thought she had stayed with you. When she didn't show up at the camp in your company, I thought she might have ridden with Cookie. But she was not with him, either. Oh, Longarm! I'm frightened! Could she have gotten lost in that darkness and wandered off?"

The question answered itself. Of course she could have, and there was no doubt in Longarm's mind that this was exactly what had happened. That meant he had to ride back down the canyon, backtracking all the way to the camp—and then pick up her trail. He glanced at the sky and cursed silently. He had, at the most, three hours of daylight left.

"I'm going after her right now," he told Isadora. "I want Cookie to pack me some provisions while I go see to my horse."

She hesitated, obviously even more distraught now, because she saw in Longarm's manner just how serious he considered matters to be. Her worst fears were being confirmed.

"Isadora!" snapped Longarm. "I'll be no good without provisions. Cookie will know what to pack for me. Hurry!"

Without a word, Isadora spun on her heel and, with the reckless abandon of a small girl, ran toward the chuckwagon.

Longarm was not able to get back to the previous campsite before darkness fell. He made a dry camp in the canyon, slept fitfully until dawn, then rode out, chewing on the tough, stringy pemmican that Cookie had come up with. He reached the campsite by midmorning and searched the area for sign of her. Nothing.

He didn't like that. It meant she had never gotten back to the camp at all. Carrie had become lost during the night and had stumbled off into a desolate, treacherous wilderness—and was still lost, perhaps in a panic by now, her feet bruised and perhaps bloody, her nightdress torn. The picture these thoughts painted for Longarm was too unpleasant to contemplate, and Longarm thrust it resolutely from his mind and returned to the spot where he had put down his own bedroll that night.

Off his horse, he searched the ground around his camp for her footprints. But pine needles carpeted the ground and her light feet had made no impression at all. She had appeared almost like an apparition to him as she stole out of the pines that night, and now, in searching for signs of her passage, he realized he might just as well be trying to track a ghost.

He picketed his horse on the edge of a bright park, then began working his way back and forth down the slope on foot. He was in timber all the way, and was hoping that that long nightdress she was wearing might have caught on something, a twig or a branch, anything that would give him some indication of the direction she might have taken.

He was almost at the foot of the slope when he saw—in a patch of bare, soft ground—the heavy imprint of a man's boot. He knelt to study it more closely, then got up and retraced a path directly up through the timber toward his camp. He was rewarded almost immediately. Across a damp, level stretch of ground, he saw four more prints, the heels of the man's boots sinking in quite deeply with each stride. He followed the trail swiftly into the pines above the tracks, keeping his head up, his eyes level.

He had nearly reached his campsite when he found what he was afraid he was going to find. On the tip of a sharp, thornlike branch sticking out from a lodgepole pine, he saw a tiny patch of white fabric. He plucked it from the branch and examined it carefully. A dark stain had coagulated on one edge of it. He rubbed the fabric between his thumb and forefinger. There was no doubt, none whatsoever. This fabric had come from Carrie's nightdress, and the dark stain on it was dried blood.

Calvin Newton, broken jaw and all, had come after his wife.

When Longarm found the spot where Calvin had tethered his horse, he realized how bad it was for Carrie. Calvin had ridden out into the canyon and across the stream to the other side. But Carrie did not have a horse. From the sign Calvin left, it was clear—frighteningly clear—how Carrie was traveling.

She was on foot—being dragged, more than likely, by a rope attached to Calvin's saddle horn. The imprint of her stumbling footprints, and in some cases the heavy print her entire body made as it impacted on the soft ground, were vivid proof of her husband's brutal impatience. That no one had heard her call out meant that Calvin had gagged her, either by wrapping a bandanna around her mouth or by stuffing a portion of her nightdress in her mouth. Again, Longarm found the picture his imagination presented to him infuriating. Only he could not wipe the image from his mind, this time. For now he had to see clearly, read every sign if he was going to track this man and take Carrie from him.

It soon became obvious that Calvin was not taking her back with him to the settlement in the valley. That realization worried Longarm even more; it meant that what Calvin intended as punishment for his wife was something that even the stern code of his brethren would not have allowed. What, then, did this son of a bitch have in mind, Longarm asked himself as he rode up the canyon, wincing at every sign of Carrie's cruel passage.

Longarm followed their trail into one of the branching, labyrinthine canyons he had noted the day before as he rode up the main canyon. He wondered. Had Calvin been peering out at him, Carrie crumpled semiconscious at his feet, as Longarm rode past? Might she have seen him and tried to call out? Longarm thrust the scene from his mind and continued up the narrow, winding canyon.

He glimpsed the first sign of Carrie's blood on the trail an hour into the canyon. He dismounted and studied the dark smear that extended across a flat rock, and came to the conclusion that Carrie must have been dragged across its face. Further up the trail, a portion of her nightdress, no longer white, was fluttering pathetically from the bloody thorn of a prickly pear. As he flung himself from his horse and snatched the piece of fabric from the cactus, he realized in that instant what Calvin Newton had in mind.

He was dragging his wife after him for the sole purpose of leaving a trail that Longarm would find virtually impossible *not* to follow.

Calvin Newton wanted Longarm, and he was using his wife as bait.

Chapter 6

Despite Calvin's intentions, Longarm reached a fork in the canyon and was unable to find any sign that would tell him for sure which branch the man had taken. Since the canyon to his left was the broadest, Longarm took that one. After more than a mile, he realized he had made the wrong guess and back-tracked to the other canyon. He had not gone far this time when he saw in the distance a ledge above the canyon floor massive enough to hold a miner's shack. Beside the shack Longarm saw the gaping hole of a mineshaft. From the looks of it, Longarm concluded it was still in operation.

When he rode closer, he found a narrow but well-worn trail that led up to the ledge. He followed it and reined in at last before the shack. Without dismounting, he called, "Hello, the house!"

There was no response, except for a faint echo that seemed to come from the mineshaft. Longarm shifted wearily in his saddle. The squeak of its leather in the late-afternoon heat emphasized the disquieting silence that hung over the shack and the mine entrance. It resembled the silence, Longarm felt vaguely, that sometimes follows a terrible struggle—or battle.

Dismounting cautiously, he snaked the Winchester out of its boot and advanced to the house. Pulling up in front of the door, he called again, "Hello, the house!"

The silence stank of menace. Longarm advanced lightly to the shack's door. It hung on sagging leather hinges. With the barrel of his Winchester, he nudged it open, then stepped inside.

The owner had floored the shack with rough planks; they sagged as Longarm stepped into the one-room cabin. A scratched and battered deal table stood in the center of the room. A cot was hard against a rear wall, the straw of the mattress's ticking protruding. A filthy pillow without a pillowcase was on the floor beside the cot. An old army blanket lay rumpled on the bed. A low table served as a sink. On it he saw a wooden bucket with tin dishes and flatware poking out of it. A potbellied stove was near the low table, and sitting on top of it was a coffeepot. Sacks of potatoes and other provisions had been thrown into a far corner. From one sack, footsteps of flour led almost as far as the bucketful of dishes.

It had the look of a recently used room. Its owner had left abruptly, intending to return almost immediately. There were too many items that would have been taken if the owner had intended a long trip from these premises: a bedroll in one corner; a gleaming, well-cared-for Winchester hanging on the wall over the cot; a worn but serviceable saddle in one corner. He walked over to the stove. It was cold. He picked up the coffeepot and peered into it. The coffee had boiled away, leaving a black mess on the bottom of the pot.

Longarm glanced quickly around him, peering carefully at everything. There was no sign of trouble, no evidence of a hasty exit, of an alarm of any kind. The prospector who worked this mine had simply stepped casually out for a minute—and then failed to come back.

What did the fellow mine? Gold? Silver? If so, where were the results of his labor? And then Longarm saw how the flooring near the cot appeared to be uneven—out of line—when compared with the other planking. He strode over, reached between the planks and lifted. One came easily. The nails were for show only. Reaching under, he felt many small pouches, selected one and pulled it out. Untying the drawstring, he poured gold dust into his palm, examined it for a moment in the shack's dim light, then returned the gold dust to the pouch and the pouch to its hiding place. Replacing the flooring, he stood up. No man would leave such a treasure willingly.

Longarm left the shack, stood in the doorway, and called out once again. Nothing. He glanced at the opening to the mine, shrugged and headed for it. An accident, perhaps. Rotten timbers collapsing on him. A miner working alone was in constant danger of such a thing. But as Longarm felt the clammy darkness fall over him, he knew that whatever had happened to this miner had been no accident. Everything was too neat and well cared for. This fellow had a place for everything and everything in its place. The wheelbarrows, the hoists, the pickaxes—all were well worn, but each item was stored or parked neatly. Accidents did not often happen to such men.

What *had* happened to this man was, more than likely, Calvin Newton.

Damp cobwebs brushed against his cheeks. Once or twice, a crossbeam cracked his forehead. The inky darkness became complete. He decided to go back for a lantern. Turning, his boot struck something yielding. Another boot. The *toe* of another boot. It had sprung back at his touch, the way a foot would if the sinews were still strong, the muscles still alive. He reached down quickly and grabbed at the boot. Then his hand touched the man's shin. Peering carefully into the gloomy alcove, he saw the pale

85

glow of a face. It was so dim, Longarm felt for a moment that he might be looking at his own reflection in a dark pool.

Swiftly, Longarm moved into the alcove, reached down, and grabbed the man under the shoulders. In a moment he had him sitting up. A tight bandage had been wound many times around his mouth; it was so tight, Longarm realized as he unwound it, that it was a wonder the man was still able to breathe. He could not talk, only groan. But when Longarm made an attempt to lift the man so as to carry him out, the fellow's groans became curses and he cried out.

Longarm swiftly eased the man back onto the ground. "What is it? Something broken?"

"My ribs," the fellow gasped. "Busted. Untie my hands and feet. I can walk out, I think."

But so tightly had the man's feet and hands been bound that as soon as the blood began rushing into them, the fellow muttered savagely about the fiery pins and needles that stung his hands and feet. Longarm removed the man's heavy boots and massaged his feet and ankles, while the miner rubbed his hands furiously.

"My name's Alf Riley," the miner said. "Who're you, mister?"

"Name's Custis Long. I'm a lawman, a deputy U.S. marshal."

"I'm right glad to meet you, Marshal."

"Who did this to you?"

"Blamed if I know what his name is—a blackguard with a dirty bandage wrapped around his jaw. Meanest son of a bitch I ever met, next to an Apache I tangled with when I still had all my teeth. Yessir, a real devil in the flesh, he was."

"His name was Calvin Newton. He was alone?"

"Didn't say that. And he wasn't. He had a woman with him. That's how I got this busted pair of ribs.

86

I tried to help her. He had her on the end of a rope when I first caught sight of them coming up the canyon. He was hauling her the way an Indian hauls a captive back to camp. You know, before he turns him over to the squaws."

"Yes," Longarm said tonelessly, "I know."

"So I hid behind a rock and came up behind the bastard and told him to get off his horse. But he spooked his horse and drew on me before I could fire up at him. I was a mite slow, I reckon."

"You underestimated him."

"That I did."

Longarm pulled back. "Can you make it now?"

"Reckon so," Riley said, pulling on his boots and then hoisting himself slowly upright.

Longarm helped him, and a moment later Riley hobbled out of the mine's entrance. The man halted and shook his head in wonder. Though every movement was obviously quite painful for him, he turned himself slowly around, blinking happily in the brilliant sunshine as he took in the canyon's towering walls, the blue sky overhead. Alf Riley was very glad to be alive.

"Never thought this damn canyon could look so beautiful, Marshal," Riley said. "Didn't think I'd ever clap eyes on it again. Thought I was a goner. Couldn't move, couldn't cry out. Just sit there in that pocket and die."

Riley reached out to Longarm for support, and the two men headed for the shack. Riley was in his late fifties, Longarm judged. He was not bearded, but a white stubble covered his face, and what hair he had left was as insubstantial as tufts of cotton batting. Not much over five feet in height, the little man was nevertheless quite lean and obviously fit. And even though he was in great pain as he walked into his shack, his pale blue eyes were alight with pleasure to find himself once again in his humble living quarters. There was, after all, no place like home.

"You better rest on that cot," said Longarm. "I'll put the coffee on."

"Now, you don't need to do that, Marshal!"

"Call me Longarm, Riley. And yes, I do need to do that. Sit down and relax. I know how to make coffee. And wait'll you taste my son-of-a-bitch stew."

Riley protested only slightly, and as soon as Longarm had put the coffee on, he tore a bedsheet into strips and bound Riley's ribs as tightly as the old man could stand it. When Longarm had finished, Riley lay back down on the cot and, with a sigh, closed his eyes, a contented smile on his face.

It was close to sundown when Longarm, on Riley's suggestion, took two chairs out onto the ledge so that the two could enjoy the sunset. Riley had been most appreciative of Longarm's stew; and as the miner settled carefully into a battered wooden chair beside him, the tall lawman handed him a cheroot. The two lit up. For the past hour or so, Longarm had been trying not to think of Carrie and what she must be going through, but now he felt he could no longer deny his concern.

"The woman," he began. "You saw her, Riley. How was she holding up?"

"Not good. Not good at all. Soon as he kicked me silly and then dumped me into the mine, he moved on. Didn't give her a chance to rest up any. He said a queer thing, though, before he left me. Said he didn't think I'd be alone for long."

Longarm worked his cheroot around in his mouth. "That's about what I've been figuring, Riley. He's leaving a trail for me to follow. He knew I'd soon be passing your place."

"But he didn't know you'd find me like you did."

"No, he didn't. But then, I don't think that worried him all that much."

"Nope. It sure as hell didn't."

"But the woman—she was on her feet, able to walk?"

"Just about. And she seemed pretty feisty too, like she wasn't going to let the bastard make her beg. But she was all tore up, Longarm. A pitiful sight, it was."

"You say he spoke to you. He has a broken jaw. That's why he wears that bandage around his head and chin."

"He talks, all right. But you can just barely understand him, and he don't move his lips hardly at all." Riley shook his head as he recalled. "It sure made him sound queer. And I didn't like his eyes none, neither. They was the eyes of a man who don't need alcohol anymore. He's already riding a high lonesome—without booze. He's a crazy man, Longarm. Plumb crazy."

"That don't excuse him any."

"I didn't say it did. But its goin' to make it tough for you to bring him in, I'm thinking."

"Yes," Longarm agreed. He got to his feet then, and tossed the remains of his cheroot into the canyon. The sun had already gone down and the mountain chill was setting in. Longarm was anxious to get an early start the next day. He turned and looked down at Riley. "Think I'll turn in. I've put my bedroll behind your door, and I'll sleep with my .44 under my pillow. I'd appreciate it if you slept with a weapon too. That son of a bitch knows I'm after him and he just might double back."

Riley grunted a little and pushed himself to his feet. "That's a good idea, Longarm," he said grimly. "I'll sleep cradling my Winchester. And I hope he *does* come back. Nothing I'd like better than to ventilate that rattlesnake."

The two men turned and headed back to the cabin.

But Calvin Newton did not double back; and as the first rays of sunlight touched the rim of the canyon wall high above Longarm, he mounted up, waved goodbye to Alf Riley, and rode on up the brightening canyon—aware now for sure that he was expected—that up ahead of him a madman with a near-dead woman was waiting to kill him.

True to the pattern he had established, Newton left signs that Longarm could not mistake: hoofprints in the soft ground bordering the narrow stream that cut through the canyon; the bare footprints of a woman; long furrows caused by someone being dragged along; then the stumbling, tragic footprints once again. At last, close to noon, he found a large, torn portion of her nightdress, bloodied and filthy, hanging on a scrub pine that was growing out of the canyon wall. It had been placed there deliberately.

He kept riding past the spot, his eyes now lifted, his Winchester in his hand. Cautiously he guided his horse around a bend in the canyon, his eyes searching the canyon's rim now—both sides of it. He was looking for movement of any kind—a dark, scurrying shape against the sky, perhaps, or the tell-tale glint of sunlight on metal.

He pulled up suddenly, groaning aloud.

What his eyes had found instead was the figure of a naked woman hanging by her neck.

His eyes riveted to that terrible sight, he rode toward her—as an irrational compulsion to climb to that rim and cut her down from the pine tree swept aside all caution. Too late, he caught the flash of sunlight on a rifle barrel above him to his left. The report came just as he flung himself forward over his horse's neck and spurred the animal to a sudden gallop. The bullet ricocheted among the rocks behind him. The sound urged him to greater speed. A second shot sent a round buzzing just ahead of him. A third shot ricocheted some distance behind him. Longarm spurred his horse on, glancing back only once at the now dim figure standing on the canyon rim behind him.

He rode on until the twisting canyon's walls hid him completely from Calvin, then dismounted rapidly, sending his horse toward a patch of grass with a smart whack on the rump. His Winchester at the ready, Longarm crossed to the far side of the canyon, found a game trail that led to the canyon's rim, and started up. His decision to stay on his horse and keep riding had been the result of his estimate of Calvin Newton's accuracy with a rifle butt tucked under a broken jaw. He had guessed right; Calvin's aim had not been very good.

As Longarm struggled up the narrow game trail, he hoped Calvin's aim would remain poor.

Longarm moved along the ridge for a good hundred yards before he caught sight of Carrie's body in the distance. From this angle, he could see that she was dangling out over the rim. He saw something else, as well. The rope was not around her neck. Longarm crouched lower and moved back from the rim, away from the canyon. Great boulders blocked his path. He circuited them swiftly, keeping low. Carrie was no longer in view. He changed direction and began moving parallel with the canyon. He kept going in this direction for another fifty feet, then circled back toward the rim. Coming to a ledge flanked by pine, he slowed and peered through them and found an unobstructed view of the canyon, the trail along the rim—and Carrie.

Longarm winced at what he saw.

Carrie was trembling pitifully, and it was obvious

91

why. The rope had been passed around her chest, knotted in the back, and then drawn up around her chin before being tied to the branch of the pine. It was a tough, gnarled pine—a bristlecone—and its roots were firmly fastened into this tough, unflinching canyon wall. But it extended out over the canyon, and with every movement Carrie involuntarily made, she could see the canyon floor far below, twisting dizzingly under her. And the position of her neck and head due to the angle of the taut rope must have been an excruciating torment. Strangulation might have been kinder. It was a wonder that she still lived—if, indeed, her occasional trembling *was* assurance of that. He had seen a horse shuddering in that fashion long after a bullet had plundered its skull . . .

Longarm shook this last grisly thought from his mind and looked carefully around. Calvin was nowhere in sight. That figured. Carrie had been strung up there as bait. And Longarm was the animal Calvin was waiting to trap. Calvin knew Longarm had seen Carrie and would have to come back, if only to cut her down.

The bastard had him, Longarm realized. No. The bastard had Carrie—and that was worse.

Longarm stole out of the pines, still keeping low, dropped behind a boulder, then moved around it toward the rim. Within ten feet of the rim, he halted and waited, hoping for some sign that Calvin was in the vicinity. He heard and saw nothing, though of course that did not mean much. Calvin was obviously just as patient as Longarm.

Only Longarm could not afford to be patient much longer. The sight of Carrie—dangling out over the canyon, twisting slowly, trembling—was getting to him. He had an instinct for this sort of thing, and Carrie did not look as if she could last much longer.

Longarm crept still closer to the rim, then flattened himself and looked to the left and then to the right. Nothing. He waited. The gnarled trunk of the bristlecone was less than five feet from him. Carrie's head and shoulders, as she dangled out beyond the rim, were even with his. If she continued to turn, her eyes would meet his. Then, off to his left, a rock wren, startled by something, darted up from behind a low boulder and flew out over the canyon, scolding as it went.

That was all the sign Longarm needed. Calvin was behind that boulder. Longarm had already levered a fresh round into his Winchester's chamber. Quickly swinging up his rifle, he straightened, aimed, and fired over the boulder at something dark that was hastily dodging away. Longarm raced toward the boulder, levering swiftly and firing as he went. Calvin disappeared into a splash of pine just beyond an upthrust of red rock.

Swiftly, Longarm turned and raced back to Carrie. Laying down his rifle, he took out his pocket knife, then crawled out onto the pine tree, got a firm grip on the rope just above Carrie's head, and cut the rope free of the branch. Carrie was not heavy, yet the sudden pull of her dead weight gave Longarm a momentary scare; he was almost pulled from the pine tree. But he hung on and worked his way backward off the pine until he was standing on the canyon rim. Then he hauled Carrie up beside him.

Her eyes were closed, and she did not move as he untied the rope.

"Carrie," he murmured softly, urgently. "Carrie!"

He felt her drawn, dust-white face. There was no warmth. For a moment he thought he had rescued a dead woman. Then she groaned. It seemed to come from deep within her. Still her eyes remained closed, her face immobile.

He was about to call her name again, when he heard running boots behind him. He got to his feet

93

and whirled in time to see Calvin Newton, his rifle held over his head like a club, charging him with all the fury of a maddened bull. Longarm threw up his arm as the rifle's butt came crashing down. He was painfully shaken by the blow as Calvin rammed him and sent him stumbling back. The heel of his foot struck a low boulder. He felt himself falling backward—into space.

Almost immediately, his back slammed with numbing force onto a hard, flat surface. The breath was knocked out of him, but he managed to reach out and turn his head to see what had caught him. A ledge. His breath returning, he saw what it was that kept the ledge in place: the tensile strength of the bristlecone pine's coiled, arthritic roots.

Calvin's mad, bandaged face appeared above the rim. He was infuriated to see Longarm staring up at him from less than ten feet away. He had expected much more. Longarm reached swiftly across his belly and in under the flap of his frock coat. He was pulling his Colt free when Calvin's first unsteady rifle shot blasted down at him. The round ricocheted off the ledge, causing a small explosion of rock shards to dig into the side of Longarm's face.

Longarm fired up at Calvin. The round seemed to explode the filthy bandage that held his jaw together. The rifle clattered from his hands and he staggered back, out of sight. Holstering his weapon, Longarm reached out for the pine's roots, secured a firm grip, and hauled himself back up onto the canyon's rim.

Calvin was gone, his rifle remaining where he had dropped it.

Longarm's left forearm was pretty sore where Calvin's rifle had crashed down upon it. But fortunately it was not broken. Longarm moved to Carrie's side. She was still unconscious. He slapped her gently. She groaned, but did not move or open her eyes. She was alive—just barely.

Longarm left her to see to the woman's deranged husband. He could not take a chance on another frenzied attack, especially not if he was going to take Carrie back down that narrow game trail to his horse. Calvin's footprints were not difficult to follow, and soon Longarm was aware of the dark bloodstains that accompanied the man's tracks. He was wounded badly, judging from the amount of blood.

He lost Calvin's trail among some rocks, but kept going. The trail led down into a tortured land of gullies and washes, the only vegetation scrub pine and juniper. The dark entrance of a narrow canyon beckoned to him across a small salt flat. It looked like a good enough place to retreat to and lick your wounds. And halfway across the flat, he saw the dim imprint of Calvin's boots. The man was still losing blood, Longarm noted. He moved faster, then, keeping low. Calvin had left his rifle back on the ridge, but Longarm did not know if he carried a sidearm. He was within a few feet of the canyon's entrance when a shot from the canyon exploded dirt at his feet. Calvin had a sidearm.

Longarm darted to one side until he was out of sight of anyone inside the canyon's mouth. Then he continued toward the canyon, hugging the rocks as he moved. When Longarm was within a few feet of the canyon's mouth, Calvin shouted out to him.

"Hold on, Marshal!" he cried. "I'm a wounded man! I'll throw out my weapon and come peaceably!"

"Do it, then!"

An instant later, Calvin's sixgun hurtled through the air and landed just in front of the canyon's entrance. Longarm waited for Calvin to emerge.

When he didn't, Longarm crouched lower and cried, "Come on out of there, Calvin. I won't shoot."

"I know that, damn you!" the man cried. "But I'm a wounded man, Marshal! You shot me in my face. I've lost sight in one eye! I . . . I need help!"

His revolver still held in front of him, Longarm straightened somewhat and entered the canyon. Almost at once there was an explosion of hoofs. A large, powerful form bore down on him. Longarm tried to jump back, but he was too late as the horse's flaring nostrils and bulging eyes brushed his face and the animal's massive chest sent him hurtling back against the canyon's wall. Dazed, Longarm could only manage a single shot at the disappearing rider. He raced out of the canyon in time to catch a glimpse of Calvin looking back at him. The man's face was a grotesque mess of bandages and blood. He did indeed look as if he had lost the use of one eye, perhaps even the entire right side of his face. But that one glimpse was all Longarm got as the man galloped around a massive boulder and disappeared. The sound of his horse's pounding hooves gradually faded.

Longarm went back into the canyon for his hat, then brushed himself off, wearily certain that he would have no more trouble from Calvin Newton—at least for a while.

Chapter 7

Carrie was barely conscious when Longarm returned to her, and had lapsed back into unconsciousness by the time they arrived back at Riley's place. While Longarm eased Carrie gently off his horse, Riley— wincing from the discomfort of his cracked ribs— hustled from his shack to give Longarm what help he could.

As Longarm lay Carrie gently down on Riley's cot, Riley brought in fresh water from his well, and dipping some wash towels into the ice-cold water, he placed a cold compress on Carrie's forehead. Then he sponged away the dirt and grime that had encrusted her battered features. The cold water did the trick. Carrie opened her eyes and looked with wonder at Riley's grizzled face, poised so closely over hers.

The wonder turned to panic, however, until she turned her head and saw Longarm. He reached out and took her hand gently. "It's all right, Carrie," he told her. "You're with friends now. Your husband's gone."

"Gone?"

"He was wounded pretty bad the last I saw of him, and he was riding hard to get away. He won't bother you anymore, I'm thinking."

She looked at him for a long moment, as if she found it difficult to believe, then lay back down and closed her eyes, her gaunt, battered features calm.

She looked at peace for the first time in a long while.

Longarm nodded to Riley, indicating that they should leave her be for the moment, and left the cot. Riley followed him to the doorway.

"I've got a passel of Englishmen digging bones out of a mountainside back there," Longarm told Riley. "I think maybe I ought to get back to them and see what mischief they got themselves into. You think you can take care of Carrie for me? She's in no condition to ride, and she's really got no place to go."

"Sure, Longarm. I can take care of her, I guess."

"Feed her, Riley. Get some food into her. I'll be back for her as soon as I can get away."

The grizzled miner grinned at Longarm. "Don't you worry none, Longarm. I'll have her as plump as a spring chicken in no time."

Longarm clapped on his hat and moved through the doorway. "Good," he said. "I knew I could count on you. And keep an eye out for that lunatic of a husband. Like I told Carrie, he was wounded pretty bad, but he's just crazy enough to circle back here looking for his wife. You think you can handle that?"

"Longarm," Riley said, "do you have any idea how happy I would be to get my hands on that son of a bitch? I'll keep my eyes peeled. And I'll be hoping he shows."

Longarm bid Riley goodbye, then strode to his horse and mounted up. With a single wave to the miner, he nudged the buckskin toward the narrow trail that led back down to the canyon. Once he reached its floor, he glanced back at the ledge.

Riley was standing in full view with his Winchester cradled in his arms. He waved to Longarm and disappeared.

● ● ●

The echoing rattle of distant rifle fire alerted Longarm long before he reached Sir Thomas's camp. Longarm promptly left the canyon floor and toiled up a steep game trail, dismounting and leading the buckskin most of the way. His approach to Pine Bluff was from the north, and he was riding the buckskin again when he caught sight of the first outlaw, or rather of the thin tendril of smoke that curled up from the rocks where the fellow had holed up.

Dismounting swiftly, Longarm snatched his rifle from its boot and, as silently as a big cat, crept up a flat boulder to get a better view of the sniper. The man was prone behind a cinderlike stone of volcanic origin. As Longarm watched, the sniper lifted his rifle to his cheek and fired down into the encampment below. Longarm heard the heavy *thwack* as the bullet found its target—most likely one of the ore wagons, from the sound of it. There was a half-hearted rattle of return fire from the canyon below, and immediately other outlaws in the rocks opened up, most of them coming from Longarm's right.

The sniper chuckled and levered a fresh cartridge into his Winchester's chamber. Longarm swore softly to himself as he studied the mountainside leading down to the sniper. There were several ravines cutting between them and a stand of pinyon that clung to a gravel slope. Longarm dropped from the rock and glided swiftly down the slope, keeping the pine between him and the rifleman. Slipping through the thin stand, he knelt behind a granite upthrust, lifted the rifle and drew a bead on the sniper, whose attention was riveted on the confusion and dismay he and his fellows were creating in the camp below.

"Having fun, mister?" Longarm drawled.

He spoke just loudly enough to be heard by the sniper; he did not want to alert this fellow's henchmen.

Without moving or turning his head, the man said, "Who the hell wants to know?"

"Put down the rifle," Longarm told him, just as quietly.

"Give me a good reason."

"I've got a rifle aimed at the back of your head, you stupid asshole."

Carefully, the sniper placed his rifle down on the ground beside him, then rolled over so he could get a better look at Longarm. The fellow had a mean, beaten face. Someone a long time back must have stepped on his nose. It was thin, but seemed to have been bent almost flat. The eyes were a pale blue, the lips bloodless and set in a pocked face. He was not clean in dress or in person. The only thing bright about him was the Bull Durham tag dangling from the pocket of his greasy leather vest.

He wore his gun tied down, gunfighter-fashion, in an oiled, flapless holster.

"Get up," Longarm told the man, as he moved out from behind the granite and picked his way down the slope toward the fellow. "Keep your hands in plain sight and don't make no sudden moves."

"You ain't heard the last of this," the man told Longarm. "I got men all around here in these rocks. You'd better put that rifle away and hightail it out of here."

"Can't do that," replied Longarm. "People like you are my business."

"Damn it! You the law?" The fellow got sullenly to his feet.

"Turn around, friend," Longarm said softly. "Face away from me. Use your left hand to unbuckle your belt."

The man grinned. "I don't care if you are the law. We was just funnin', is all. A joke. Like to watch them limeys jump some. No harm in that."

"I told you to drop that belt," Longarm repeated, thumb-cocking the Winchester. "Do it. Now."

"I told you, lawman. I got friends. All around me in these rocks. You don't scare me. What'll you do? Shoot? I'll bet my boys have spotted you already."

Longarm brought the rifle up deliberately and squeezed the trigger, putting a neat, small hole through the crown of the man's hat, a black Stetson with a wide, flat brim.

The man swept the hat off his head. His pale blue eyes were blazing. "I said it before, lawman. You ain't heard the last of this."

"You going to drop that gunbelt? I can aim a mite closer. Make a nice hollow sound, the bullet would, going through that empty head of yours."

The gunman regarded Longarm, darted forward, carefully, then forced himself to smile as he turned around and unbuckled the gunbelt. Longarm swept it up, then grabbed the man's rifle. The fellow watched him sullenly.

"You be careful of them weapons, mister," he told Longarm. "That's all good hardware, a .44-40 Winchester and a new Smith & Wesson revolver."

"You're right," Longarm agreed casually. "These are fine weapons."

As he spoke, he heaved the rifle and gunbelt, holster and all, out over the lip of the canyon. As they disappeared from sight, Longarm thought the man was going to throw himself after them. He turned back to Longarm then, beside himself.

"Okay," said Longarm. "Just settle down. The only way you're going to get any of that hardware back is by going down to that camp with me. Let's go!"

The man looked wildly about him, obviously frantic to know where that gang he had been boasting about was. But Longarm had no inclination to wait. He motioned with the barrel of his rifle.

101

"You heard me," he told the gunman softly. "Get a move on, down that trail."

"My horse," the man rasped, furious. "I got to get my horse."

"Later."

Abruptly the man grinned, exposing ferretlike teeth. It was all the warning Longarm needed. With the barrel of his Winchester, he struck the fellow in front of him to the ground, then whirled and was in time to pick off a fellow standing on a rock. The fellow had been taking deliberate aim with a carbine —too deliberate, as it turned out. His carbine discharged harmlessly as he staggered back out of sight.

This was not the end of Longarm's troubles, however. Even as Longarm took aim at another gunman scrambling down the slope toward him, the fellow he had just disarmed slammed into him. Longarm had half expected the move, and was braced, but the maniacal force of his attacker was something he could not have been prepared to withstand. As Longarm buckled momentarily, a wild blow from his attacker caught him on the side of his head and knocked him to the ground. In a burst of almost womanish fury, the fellow jumped onto Longarm and began flailing away madly at the astonished lawman. It was Longarm's astonishment that allowed the situation to deteriorate.

When he did make his move, it was too late. The sniper had flung Longarm's rifle away, and the one Longarm had seen racing down the slope toward them had joined his attacker. Both men then proceeded to kick at Longarm's prostrate body. Nevertheless, he managed to scramble to his feet. He then knocked the second man off balance, and a desperate roundhouse right to the sniper's chops sent him ass over teakettle; but before Longarm could follow that up by drawing his Colt, the second one struck him from behind and kicked the weapon out of his hand.

Flat on his back, dazed, Longarm found himself looking up at two hard-breathing outlaws, both of whom were glaring down at him with such maniacal fury that Longarm would have found it comical if he didn't know what such men were capable of doing to another human being when they found themselves aroused in this fashion.

"He's mine," gasped the fellow with the pocked face. "I'm going to kick him into jelly beans. I'm going to make him beg for his mama!" His yellow, ferretlike teeth gleamed for a moment in his face, and he took a step closer to Longarm.

Longarm tried to brace himself, but the sniper's kick was expertly placed and driven home with a will. Gasping from the pain, Longarm coiled up like a big worm that had been stepped on—and reached quickly into his vest pocket for his derringer. A second kick, just as vicious, snapped Longarm back over onto his back, grimacing from the explosion of pain.

"Let me have a go at him," cried the sniper's companion. He was a bearded, round-faced, round-bellied man with tiny black eyes. His eyes snapped eagerly at the sport as he aimed a kick at Longarm's groin.

As the fellow brought his foot back, Longarm fired up at him, catching him below his belt buckle. The .44 slug did considerable damage to the man's gut as it propelled him violently back. Longarm jumped to his feet and saw the man clutching at his bowels, a look of pure, deathly horror on his face. While the man sank to his knees and then toppled onto his side, Longarm swung around swiftly to face the sniper.

But the man had already turned tail and was halfway up the slope. Longarm had no faith in his derringer at that range, and by the time he retrieved his rifle, the sniper had disappeared into the rocks. A moment later, Longarm heard rapid hoofbeats as the man spurred his animal furiously away.

Longarm looked back at the round-bellied man. He was sitting up, his back to a boulder, staring straight ahead. A thin trickle of blood was streaming from one corner of his mouth. His face was the color of an old newspaper. Both of his pudgy hands were clutching at the hole in his gut, while coils of gray, blood-flecked intestines surged through his fingers with each breath the man took.

A man gutshot was not a pretty sight, and Longarm had to force himself to remember that this poor son of a bitch in front of him had, only a moment before, been ready to kick Longarm's balls up into his bicuspids. Longarm went down on one knee beside the man.

"Can you talk, old son?" he asked, as gently as he could.

"No, you bastard," the man gasped. "I can't. I'm dyin'. Can't you see that?"

"I see it, all right. I'm sorry. If I'd had the time, I would've aimed higher. What's your name?"

"Bronski," the man gasped, coughing softly.

"Who was that fellow just run off and left you?"

"Chuck Ballenger."

"And where might I find him when he comes to light?"

"Dog Wells," the man gasped. "The Red Dog Saloon." The man coughed, each convulsion causing still more of his gut to push out through his clutching fingers. With tears in his eyes, Bronski said, "He's sweet on Marge Tucker."

"Want me to get him for you?"

"Yes. Catch the son of a bitch. He left me here to die!"

"You'll live," Longarm said, knowing it was a barefaced lie. "What's Ballenger up to?"

"He was onto them limeys. It ain't bones they's after. It's gold! And they ain't filed any claim on this here mountain. He'll be back to get that gold." The man coughed violently. "You gonna help me, you bastard? I can't live if I don't get help! Go on down to that camp and find me a doc!"

Longarm stood up. "I'll do that, Bronski. I'll go on down to the camp below us and get help for you."

"Thanks," the man said.

He grabbed his glistening entrails a little tighter, let his head fall back against the rock, and closed his eyes. Longarm waited a moment or two, then bent closer. Bronski's squirming guts were still, his hands cold. He was dead.

Longarm left Bronski for the buzzards already circling overhead and went searching for the outlaw he had shot off the rock. He didn't find him, only his rifle and a bloodstain on the side of a rock. So that was one down and still two to go. And, like Bronski said, Chuck Ballenger would be back. The lure of gold would be enough—more than enough—to draw him back to this canyon.

Longarm found his horse and rode down the steep trail and entered the encampment not long after. As soon as he was sighted, word flew ahead of him, and before he had reached Sir Thomas's tent, Isadora and Sir Thomas had hurried to greet him. Anguish and distress were imprinted clearly on their faces. Longarm's worst fears had been realized, he guessed. Another of Sir Thomas's people had been hurt.

"Was it you chased them off?" Isadora cried.

Longarm nodded. "Heard the shots when I was riding up. Came up on them from behind."

"I knew it!" cried Sir Thomas. "As soon as the shooting stopped and then I heard that other firing

105

after. It sounded like a gunfight! By Jove, Longarm! It's a lucky thing you're all right! How many of the blighters were there?"

"Three that I know of. One's up there still."

"You mean . . . ?" asked Isadora, her brows knitting, her hand up to her mouth.

"Yes," Longarm replied. "I left him for the vultures." Longarm looked then at Sir Thomas. "Are any of your men hurt?"

"One," Sir Thomas replied. "Tim. The young tiger tried to climb up after them."

"How badly is he hurt?"

From behind Longarm came Tim's cheerful voice. "It's nothing, Longarm. A flesh wound."

Longarm spun about, relieved. "Where?"

"My left arm," Tim said, laughing. "Now I won't be able to wield a pick, not for a while, anyway." He said this last glancing over at Sir Thomas, a smile on his face.

"As long as it's your left arm, Tim," Sir Thomas said, laughing gently, "you can still write. I'll find work for you. Cataloguing should begin soon. And I'd like to see some sketches of this one before we get too far along." He grinned at Tim, and Longarm could see at once how pleased Sir Thomas was that Tim had come out of this latest scrape with nothing seriously wrong.

"No problem there, Sir Thomas," Tim replied easily. "I've already started a few sketches."

Tim was using a huge red bandanna for a sling. He seemed quite pleased with himself, as a matter of fact. There was a reckless gleam still in his eyes, and Longarm wondered how much of that bravado was the result of Isadora's presence. A beautiful woman could always grow a stripling up real quick.

"Who fixed you up?" Longarm asked.

"I did," said Isadora. "The wound was a mess, but it's clean now, and I shall keep it that way."

Longarm bowed to her slightly, and smiled. "Remind me to get a flesh wound as soon as possible."

Isadora's green, cat's eyes glowed with sudden warmth. "Why, Longarm. I didn't know you had even noticed me. Please! Be my guest. As soon as you get a flesh wound, I want to be the very first to know."

"Don't worry," Longarm replied. "You will be."

Isadora became suddenly serious. "But Longarm, what became of Carrie? Didn't you find her?"

"I found her, but that's a long story." He glanced at Sir Thomas. "This camp still too disorganized to rustle up some vittles, Sir Thomas? All that shooting and riding has left a big hole in my stomach."

Sir Thomas nodded decisively. "We'll be able to fill that hole soon, Longarm. As soon as I find Cookie. The last I saw, he was lying flat under his chuckwagon, a large pot over his head."

They all laughed at that, and as Longarm started into Sir Thomas's tent with Isadora at his side, he found himself promising the tall, green-eyed redhead that he would be glad to tell her all about Carrie as soon as he got the chance, but that she would just have to wait. On top of the recent unpleasantness he had had to contend with, recounting her story was just too much. He hoped she would understand. She said she did, but he could tell that her curiosity was already killing her.

Dusk had turned rapidly into a dark, moonless night. Tim was in his tent, close to a lighted kerosene lantern, as he worked on his sketches for Sir Thomas, who was in his tent also, packing a few of the small fossils they had found lying at the foot of the cliff. Longarm was sitting on a log in front of the campfire. Behind him, Cookie was still banging pans and muttering unhappily to himself as he kneaded the dough for the next morning's biscuits.

107

The hole in Longarm's stomach had been filled to his satisfaction, and at the moment he was showing no willpower at all as he smoked one of his cheroots.

"May I have one, Longarm?" Isadora asked, materializing beside him.

"I'm surprised at you, Isadora. Don't tell me you are addicted to such a filthy habit."

"Can you ever forgive me, Longarm?" she asked, sitting down beside him on the log.

For answer, Longarm fished a cheroot out of the inside pocket of his frock coat and handed it to her. He watched, somewhat amused, as Isadora unwrapped the cheroot, then quite daintily but effectively bit off the tip. He had a sulfur match waiting. He cracked it to life with his thumbnail. She lit the cheroot, then leaned back contentedly, inhaling deeply, expertly. Longarm was convinced. This wasn't a show for his benefit. The woman really found comfort in the filthy weed.

Isadora glanced over at him. "I don't often get a chance to do this, Longarm. Do you approve?"

"It's a mighty nice way of relaxin', and I don't see why the men have to keep all the good things to themselves."

"Very well put, Longarm," she replied, her eyes gleaming in the firelight.

Longarm looked closely at Sir Thomas's sister. There was no doubt about it. None at all. She was a most fetching woman. Beautiful. Yes. That was the word. He liked the way the firelight heightened the glow of her cheeks.

"Now, tell me, Longarm. I want to know what happened to Carrie."

"You know, I reckon, that she came up to visit me."

"I do indeed, Longarm," she said. "In fact, I was the one who encouraged her. I told her you were a

108

gentleman. And I knew you would understand a woman—this woman, especially."

"Yes," Longarm said, aware that he was blushing faintly. "Well, she left me and started back to your tent—but never got there."

Isadora took the cheroot out of her mouth and leaned closer. "I was sure of that much, Longarm. But what happened?"

Longarm told her. Everything. He finished up his account with his recollection of Alf standing on the ledge in front of his cabin, his rifle cradled in his arms, eager to have Carrie's husband show up just once more.

"What about that awful man?" Isadora asked anxiously. "Do you think Carrie's husband *will* come back?"

"He seems to be a man so filled with bile that nothing short of death will stop him. As I told you, he's fearfully wounded. But sometimes a wounded animal can cause considerable more trouble than one in good health."

She shuddered. "You talk of him as if he *were* an animal."

"That's just what he is, Isadora. An animal. That's what any man is. The most dangerous animal in the world. At least, that's the way I've found them."

"What are you going to do about those men who just attacked us?"

"Leave here first thing in the morning and see if I can trace Calvin Newton or Chuck Ballenger. I'm just hoping I don't catch up to those two rats when they're in the same damn corner. I might not get off so easy if I do."

"First thing in the morning, Longarm?"

He looked at her. "Yup. First thing."

She leaned her head against his shoulder. "I hope

you will forgive my boldness, Longarm," she whispered softly. "But there is really no reason at all why you should sleep tonight under the cold night sky. There's room in my tent."

From behind them, Tim's voice cut through the stillness. "Isadora!" he called. "Have you seen Longarm?"

"I'm over here, Tim," Longarm called. "Isadora's with me."

At the sound of Tim's progress toward them, Longarm smiled at Isadora. "I think," he said, "that there *is* one good reason to keep me out of your tent tonight. Tim. I don't think he'd understand."

Isadora nodded. Sighing slightly, she took one last drag on her cheroot and dropped it into the fire. Then she straightened up to wait for Tim to reach them, and in a soft whisper reminded Longarm that there would be other nights just as inviting as this one.

Chapter 8

Close to five o'clock the following day, the country broke downward into rolling dunes of sand and clay gulches. Longarm crossed a shallow creek, pausing long enough to allow his buckskin to have a short drink, reached a road, and continued on it toward Dog Wells.

His shadow ran before him longer and longer as the sun dipped behind him. Five hundred feet into the desert floor, Longarm turned to catch the last violent splash of flame as the sun dropped below the dark hills out of which he had just ridden. The cool wind came soon after, like a benediction. As dusk blanketed the world, he rounded a bend in the road and saw Dog Wells in the distance.

The town sat on a bench, facing the desert. It was little more than a double row of buildings on either side of the main street, with the Union Pacific feeder line, its station, water tower, and sidings just visible in the dusk on the other side of town. His buckskin's hooves thundered on the plank bridge that carried him over a creek. He rode into Dog Wells, past single-story frame houses squatting forlornly along the road. Through windows coated with dust, their faint lantern light bloomed yellowly. Halfway down the street, Longarm met the chief intersection in Dog Wells. On its four corners sat a hotel, a livery stable, and two saloons. Over the saloon next to the livery, a weathered sign read: TEXICAN. The saloon catty-corner across the intersection from it was the RED DOG.

Longarm dismounted in front of the livery stable. An oldtimer whom Longarm recognized drifted out of the darkness of the doorway and peered closely at Longarm's tall, alkali-dusted figure.

"Back, are you?" the fellow asked.

"Yup. Good horse."

"I told you he was a good one. Third stall back."

Longarm gave the buckskin a small drink at the street trough, removed his gear, and hung it up. He stood a moment in the stall, his hand resting gently on the buckskin's sweat-gummed back. He was studying his next move. Denise Ashley and Bill Reed might still be in Dog Wells, taking care of Dooley. If so, they might be able to help him locate this Chuck Ballenger, since Ballenger on the loose was a real threat to Sir Thomas and his expedition. Gold fever was a difficult sickness to shake.

Longarm left the livery stable and started up the street to the Texican. On the way, he paused in the darkness to light up a cheroot. As he sucked in the smoke, he looked quickly, warily around him. The cheroot gave him little pleasure as the smoke from it struck his parched mouth. He stopped alongside a trough's feedpipe and let the water roll into his throat and fill his belly. Then he continued on to the Texican and pushed through the batwings.

This was suppertime, which meant slack business for the saloon. He advanced to the bar and took his Maryland rye neat and quick, saw no sign of Bill Reed, and left. He stood under the porch roof in front of the saloon and looked across at the Red Dog Saloon. That dying man, Bronski, had mentioned a Marge Tucker at the same time he had spoken of the saloon. Longarm continued to smoke the cheroot to cover his idleness as he looked the town over—and watched the men passing on both sides of the street. He just might get real lucky and maybe spot Ballenger entering or leaving the Red Dog.

As he stood there, he caught a sudden odor of food from the hotel across the street. Its effect on him was so sharp and immediate that an ache began in the corners of his jaws. He decided his search for Bill Reed would just have to wait. He crossed the street to the hotel and signed the register and climbed a set of narrow stairs to a second-floor room in the back. He took off his frock coat and shirt and filled the washbowl from the pitcher. As he washed his face, he felt the mask of alkali dust crack. His skin beneath the alkali dust burned as the rough soap cleaned it.

A moment later he was back downstairs, standing in the doorway of the hotel's dining room, searching for an empty table. He caught sight of one in a far corner, advanced to it, and within a few minutes had finished ordering his supper from a clean, chubby young lady who seemed as efficient as she was cheerful. He sat back then, his muscles loose, enjoying the luxury of having someone else rustle up his meal. It was also good to get out of the saddle. He finished his cheroot and was about to light another one when his better sense talked him out of it. His meal arrived and he ate ravenously. When its remains were removed, he leaned back in his seat, belched contentedly, and decided he would like to sit awhile longer. He ordered a third cup of coffee.

He was sipping the coffee contentedly when he found himself growing slowly more alert. Like an animal who had just caught a scent on the wind, he stiffened instinctively. He put down the cup of coffee and looked around at the other men in the dining room.

They were almost all, without exception, hard,

113

sullen men, their laughter more like the snarl of caged animals. They had followed him with their eyes when he entered the dining room earlier. At the time, their coldly appraising looks had made him feel he was being touched by unclean hands. Used to such apraisals from the men he spent so much time chasing, he had shrugged it off. Now, however, as he looked carefully about him, he realized that he should have paid better attention.

But what was causing the hair on the back of his neck to stand up now? On his earlier trip to Dog Wells, he had not generated anything like this fierce hostility, even though he had made no effort to hide the fact that he was a federal officer. What made the big difference this time?

Almost as soon as he asked himself this question, he had his answer. If he had not been so hungry when he first entered this dining room, or so contented after his meal, he might have had it a whole hell of a lot sooner. A very unhappy gunslick, sitting at a corner table well to Longarm's left, was watching him with the cold, unblinking eyes of a rattler. And the moment Longarm saw the sling that held the gunslick's right arm, he knew where he had seen this jasper before: he was the rifleman Longarm had shot from that boulder a moment before Chuck Ballenger plowed into him. Though Longarm had caught only that one split-second glance, it had been enough. Longarm had a tendency to remember very well any man he tracked on the other side of his gunsight.

As soon as recognition flashed in Longarm's eyes, the gunslick bolted to his feet. He was so eager for a clear path to Longarm, he kicked a chair out of his way. The fellow had flat, dead eyes, and a scar that ran down his right cheek like a dirty piece of string that pulled the corner of his mouth down into a perpetual sneer. His left hand had been resting inside the sling. It came out now, holding a long-barreled Peacemaker.

"You son of a bitch," he said to Longarm. "I'm right glad you paid a visit to Dog Wells. I been waitin' for you. So has Chuck." The man smiled then, but the scar would allow only one side of his face to join in the hilarity.

There was a slow, methodical emptying of the dining room all this while, with not one single diner counseling the fellow with the busted arm to mend his ways or offering any aid or comfort to Longarm. They had been waiting for this confrontation, evidently, since the moment Longarm first entered the hotel dining room. A few licked their lips as they left. Though obviously unhappy that they were going to miss the action, they had complete faith in the gunslick's ability to cut Longarm down. One of the last to leave the room grinned wolfishly back at the two of them and said, "Kill the bastard, Slant! He's a federal officer. We don't need none of his kind in these parts."

Longarm looked back at the gunslick. His name was Slant, it seemed. Longarm did not have to ask why.

"I'm taking you to see Chuck," Slant said. "I don't want him to miss this. You killed Bronski, you bastard, and you're goin' to pay for it."

"Let's go, then," said Longarm. "Chuck's just the man I want to see."

Slant walked up close to Longarm. "I don't like you, lawman!" he hissed. "I don't like you none a-tall."

"That's a real shame, Slant. You sure do make me feel bad when you tell me that."

With a vicious swipe, Slant caught Longarm on the side of his head with the Peacemaker's barrel. It sent Longarm reeling across a table. His head ringing like a blacksmith's anvil, he brought the

115

table and dishes and silverware down with him as he crashed to the floor. He got a glimpse of the waitress as he rolled groggily off the crockery. She was cowering in the kitchen doorway, terrified. There was to be no help from that quarter.

A kick from behind sent Longarm's shoulder into the wall. At that moment he had been drawing his Colt from his cross-draw rig. When he slammed into the wall, he lost the Colt. It clattered away from him. With a cry of triumph, Slant moved in close to Longarm and kicked him a second time, his boot digging viciously into Longarm's side, just under the ribs. At once Longarm flung both arms around the man's right foot and then rolled swiftly over. Slant went down with a cry. Looking up from the floor, Longarm caught a glimpse of the man's left hand striking the edge of a table and losing the Peacemaker.

Longarm scrambled to his feet. Slant had landed on his torn-up shoulder and was in great pain. Longarm kicked Slant's Peacemaker across the room, retrieved his own weapon, and leveled it at the unhappy gunslick.

"Get up, Slant. I don't care how bad that hurts. You promised to take me to see Chuck Ballenger, and I intend for you to do that. Now!"

Slant got slowly to his feet, kicking a chair out of his way in his fury at this turnabout. Keeping his revolver trained on Slant, Longarm called the waitress over to him. She came out of the kitchen slowly, warily—her eyes as big as saucers.

"Yes, sir?" she asked in a tiny, frightened voice.

"How much do I owe you, ma'am? For my supper, I mean. It was a very fine bit of cooking, and you be sure to tell the cook that."

Astonished, the waitress nodded slowly and told him his meal was seventy-five cents. As Longarm counted out the change into her palm, he reminded her that he wanted her to compliment the cook. The girl nodded slowly a second time, then abruptly turned and darted like a frightened deer back into the kitchen. Then Longarm nodded curtly to Slant.

Slant turned and led the way from the dining room, through the hotel lobby and out into the street. A large crowd had gathered, and Longarm thought he heard a vast, collective gasp of dismay when Slant appeared on the walk in front of the hotel, with Longarm behind him, the lawman's Colt a foot from Slant's back. The townspeople slunk quickly back into the shadows. In a twinkling, it seemed, the boardwalks and street were deserted.

That didn't fool Longarm. In the darkness, guns were drawn and cold eyes were watching him, calculating when the best time would be to start slinging lead. Dog Wells, Longarm now realized, was one of those Western towns where the chief industry was giving aid and comfort to men and gangs on the dodge, or to ambitious gunslingers who had not yet made the post office's rogues' gallery. If the West were a cesspool, and they wanted to empty it, this town would be the place where they would pull the plug.

"Slant," Longarm barked. "Hold up."

"What's the matter, Marshal? Don't you want to find Chuck?"

"Never mind that. I want you to tell your friends who might be watching that the first sign I get that they're unfriendly, I'll pull this trigger. Ever see the hole a .44 slug makes in a man's back, Slant?"

"I seen it," the man replied sullenly. "Plenty of times."

"I figured you might have. Go ahead, give a shout."

"All you men out there!" Slant yelled. "This lawman's got a Colt in my back, and he's one trigger-happy lawman. So back off! Me and Chuck can handle this guy without no help from any of you!"

"You already done fine, looks like!" some leather-lunged fan of Slant's yelled from the shadows of an alley.

Slant turned back to Longarm. "Let's get this over with, Marshal. If Chuck ain't heard the commotion by this time, he must be with his woman."

"Get moving."

Slant turned back around and led Longarm into the Red Dog Saloon. The two men marched through a silent, vastly amused crowd of men, up a flight of stairs, and down a long hallway. In front of a door, Slant hesitated. He had a pretty good idea what game was being played on the other side of the door and was reluctant to disturb it.

"Go ahead, knock!" barked Longarm.

Slant knocked softly.

"Who the hell is it?" Chuck Ballenger called.

"It's me! Slant!"

"Go on downstairs! I'm busy!"

Longarm heard a woman's giggle at that, followed by the sound of a slap against a well-padded backside, most likely. A shriek of delight followed.

"Chuck," Slant called unhappily. "This is important!"

"So is this, you meathead! Leave me alone!"

Longarm stepped closer, shoved the barrel of his Colt deep into Slant's back, and then pounded loudly on the door. That did it. A furious oath exploded from Chuck. Longarm heard a tiny cry of dismay from the girl, followed by the heavy tread of approaching bare feet. The door was flung open, and Longarm stuck the barrel of his revolver into Ballenger's face.

"This is a double-action, Ballenger," Longarm told him. "Back up!"

118

Longarm took Slant by the shirt and flung him into the room, then marched in after him, keeping the Colt's muzzle just under Ballenger's nose. Stumbling before Longarm, Ballenger kept his feet only with difficulty. The man was a sight. He didn't see the need to wash often, so his lank nakedness had an unclean, maggotty quality to it.

The woman in the bed was also naked. She was generously endowed and at Longarm's unceremonious entrance, she had snatched up a silken bedspread and covered as much of her as she could get away with, which did not leave much to Longarm's imagination. She had long blonde hair that splashed off her ivory shoulders and covered some of her milky-white breasts; their large dark nipples peeked through the golden tresses like frightened eyes.

"How dare you!" she cried, without too much conviction. His gun frightened her. "This is my room! You have no right to come in here like this!"

Longarm smiled at her. "How *should* I come in?"

She pulled the bedspread up further, covering her breasts. Longarm thought he saw a gleam of excitement in her eyes. Despite appearances, she was obviously enjoying Ballenger's discomfiture.

Slant and Ballenger were standing together in front of the bed. Both men were furious, but wary as well. "Damn you, mister!" Ballenger said. "You ain't heard the end of this!"

"You keep saying that," Longarm told him.

"What the hell do you want? We cleared out of that canyon, didn't we?"

"Sure. You cleared out. But you made it plain enough you were coming back. All that gold down there had you in a real sweat. Remember?"

"Sure. I remember. I couldn't believe them crazy limeys were after bones. But I learned different. It ain't gold they's after, it's bones, all right."

119

"Sure," broke in Slant. "We just learned about them. We was all mixed up, Marshal. If we'd'a knowed it wasn't gold them Englishmen was after, we would've let them be."

"We just made a mistake, Marshal," said Chuck. "There ain't no reason for you to come after us. Hell, there ain't nothin' we can do with bones. And that's a fact."

We learned our lesson, Marshal," said Slant. "You don't have to worry none about us. Not anymore."

Longarm feasted his eyes on the two men. One was a pockmarked, mean-looking jasper with bloodless lips and pale eyes, standing—or cringing—before Longarm, clothed in nothing more elegant than his own sallow, dirt-encrusted skin; the other one, his face set in a perpetual sneer, was watching him with the cold, dead eyes of a rattler. Neither man was a pretty sight, or a comforting one—and as Longarm had reason to know, they both liked to use their feet on someone who was down. Real sports, both of them.

"So you want me to forget all about that shooting in the canyon, your sniping at the expedition members," Longarm said reasonably. "There isn't any gold there, so you're willing to cut your losses and let bygones be bygones."

Chuck Ballenger's eyes lit. "Why, sure, Marshal! That's it! You said it yourself. Let bygones be bygones."

"I'm sure willin'," chimed in Slant.

"Well, I'm not," said Longarm. "I'm taking you two downstairs to the lockup. The local constable can hold you until I'm ready to come back for you. It'll be a long wait, but you two can use the time to figure out a proper defense. Saying you made a mistake isn't going to do it, I'm afraid."

"Defense? Marshal, you can't mean that!" Ballenger cried. "You already took my rifle and my sixgun—and killed poor Bronski. And you wounded Slant here just fearful! Ain't we suffered enough?"

"Not quite."

"What's the charge, Marshal?" demanded Slant. "We ain't done nothin' you can hold us for!"

"What makes you think you can get away with firing at members of a British expedition, wounding one of their members and damaging equipment, then attacking a federal officer with intent to kill?"

"It was all a mistake!" insisted Ballenger.

"Get dressed, Ballenger—or I'll march you down in your birthday suit. After that, Marge won't be the only one in town who knows what you look like with your clothes off."

"Which is dirty," snapped the girl. "Very dirty."

As the sullen Ballenger sat on the edge of the bed and began to pull on his drawers, Longarm, his gun still trained on the two men, glanced at the girl in the bed. "We haven't been formally introduced," he said. "I'm Custis Long."

She was a pretty girl, perhaps a little hard—and a moment before, eyeing Chuck Ballenger, her eyes had gone mean. They were alight now, however, as she replied, "My name is Marge Tucker. I own the Red Dog."

Longarm nodded. "I figured."

"You really going to pen up this animal?"

She spoke with a contempt that startled Ballenger. In the act of pulling on his boots, the gunman froze and looked at Marge, astonished.

"I really am, Marge. Him and his sidekick."

"Good," she said. "Beddin' Chuck has not been all that pleasant. Like you said, Custis, he's a mean one and likes to use his feet. His hands, too. All this time I had to let on I liked it." She looked coldly, maliciously at Ballenger, and smiled. "The truth is it felt like I was in bed with a big white worm."

121

Fully dressed now, Ballenger turned and leaped onto the bed, wrapping one arm around Marge's neck as he scooted up behind her. Then Longarm saw the knife. With a brutal upward thrust, Ballenger brought the blade under Marge's chin, breaking the flesh. Uttering a startled, painful cry, Marge began to struggle. The knife went in deeper. Instantly the blade was covered with blood.

"I'll kill her, Marshal! I don't think much of this whore. Don't you think I do! I'd just as soon kill her as not if you don't let me and Slant out of here!"

"Go ahead," Longarm commanded, stepping quickly aside. "Get out of here! Both of you!"

Slant fled out the door. Ballenger kept Marge in front of him, snatched his gunbelt and holster from the back of a chair, and followed after Slant, still dragging the naked woman with him. Longarm waited a decent interval, then raced to the door. As he stepped through the doorway, a shot from the head of the stairwell sent a slug into the doorjamb just above his head. Longarm ducked back into the room for a moment, then, crouching low, darted down the hallway to the stairwell.

As he started down the stairs, he heard a man's startled cry and the sound of a chair overturning in the saloon below. A woman's high, piercing scream cut the air. When it died, a wild uproar of shouts and angry cries erupted from the saloon. By the time Longarm reached the saloon, he was just in time to see Marge being dragged, still struggling, out through the bat wings.

As he burst out of the saloon a moment later, a shot from the first of two horsemen galloping down the street splintered the slats of the open bat wing. Longarm raised his Colt to return the fire, but thought better of it as he caught sight of Marge's pale nakedness flanking the dark figure of the lead rider.

He raced out into the street and aimed again, this time at the trailing rider. Longarm fired twice. His second round took Slant square in the back. Slant flung up his one good arm and spun backward off the horse.

Longarm raced down the dark street toward the fallen gunslick. As he pulled up to examine the man, he heard a faint scream. Glancing up, he saw Marge's pale form striking the road just outside of town, then heard the sudden thunder of Ballenger's horse as it crossed the plank bridge.

Slant was not moving. From the position of his body, Longarm was pretty certain the fellow would not soon move again. He left Slant's body to the crowd that was streaming from both saloons and the hotel, and trotted down the street toward Marge's body, huddled, naked and pitiful, in the dust of the road.

She did not stir until Longarm was within a few feet of her. Then she rolled over onto her hands and knees and glared up at him. Even in the darkness, he could see what a bloody mess she was. Both breasts were dark from the blood that had streamed from her neck wound.

"Damn it, Marshal!" she cried. "Don't just stand there! Throw your coat over me!"

Pleased to see that her wounds were more bloody than serious, he chuckled and shrugged out of his frock coat. As he threw it over her back, she got to her feet and wrapped it around her. Never before this moment had Longarm's humble frock coat covered such lascivious splendor, even if she was a mite bloody at the moment.

"Now what?" Longarm asked her. "You planning on walking back to the Red Dog dressed like that?"

"If you were a gentleman, you'd carry me back!"

"If you were a lady, you wouldn't be in such a fix."

"Don't you think I know that? All right, then," she said, striding defiantly past him, her long, silky legs flashing in the night, "you're no gentleman and I'm no lady. Goodnight! I'll have your coat cleaned and returned to you in the morning."

Longarm caught up to her and swung her almost effortlessly into his arms. She wrapped both arms around his neck and leaned her head against his chest. The warmth of her was intoxicating, but Longarm told himself he was not going to let it color his judgment of this tough little blonde. She snuggled closer into his arms. Ahead of Longarm, the crowd was surging down the street to meet them.

"Now what, Marge?"

"Just keep right on walking. If any of those gorillas say a word, I'll cut them off, and they know it. And then tomorrow, Marshal, we're going after that son of a bitch."

"Just me, Marge."

"No," she said with finality. "I know where Chuck's heading."

"You can tell me. It's going to be a long, hard ride over very rough ground. It's my job, and I'll handle it. Alone."

She hugged him tighter as the crowd of men began to surge around them, the men's eyes gleaming excitedly in the darkness. They were seeing more of Marge Tucker than most of them would ever see again. Marge was right. The men kept their comments reasonably solicitous as Longarm carried her through their ranks.

As Longarm neared the Red Dog, Marge whispered in his ear, "I'm going after that son of a bitch, with or without you. You want to come along?"

Longarm knew when he had a lousy hand. He

124

shrugged mentally and threw his cards in. "All right, Marge. We'll leave first thing in the morning."

"Of course," she murmured, her head snuggling up under his chin. "We've got other business tonight."

Chapter 9

When Longarm returned to his hotel the next morning, he found Bill Reed and Denise Ashley waiting for him in the lobby. Bill was still mopping his beefy face with a large red bandanna. And Denny's eyes still reminded Longarm of blueberries in the sun, only as the two of them hurried across the small lobby toward him, Longarm thought he caught a hint of disapproval in those wide blue eyes.

As soon as they finished their greetings, Longarm asked, "How's Dooley?"

"He's dead," said Bill Reed bitterly, thrusting his large stomach out angrily. "That long ride here in that wagon opened his wound up again."

"We tried to keep it clean, Longarm," Denny said, "but there's no doctor in this terrible place, and pretty soon the wound got worse. Bill tried to clean it out with whiskey, but it just got worse."

"He was burning up so bad at the last of it," Bill said, "I figured he already had both feet planted in hell."

"It's all that man's fault," said Denny. "Mr. Newton. He drove us out of his house, made us take that long wagon ride to this place. The ride really shook Dooley up something terrible."

"I'd like to meet up with that man again someday," said Bill Reed.

"I'd like to meet that fellow again, myself," Longarm admitted mildly.

"Denny and I, we saw you last night, Longarm. Shooting down that fellow Slant."

"And then carrying that woman back," said Denny, watching Longarm closely. "She is a very notorious woman, from what I hear."

"Yes," Longarm said. "I suppose she is, Denny. But you ain't supposed to judge a book by the cover that's on it. Ain't that true?"

"Not really," said Denny, "because I don't think a person who can't judge others by appearances is very smart. We really *do* look like what we are, Longarm."

Longarm didn't much like the drift of that. "Well," he said, to change the subject, "what are you two up to now?"

"We need new wagons and stock to go back to hauling bones for that professor Stewart. But we don't have either—and no money to buy them," said Bill Reed.

"We're out of business, Longarm," said Denny.

"Broke. Stone broke," seconded Bill Reed. "And that's the long and the short of it, I'm afraid."

"Maybe not."

"What do you mean?"

"That Englishman, the one you described to me so well, you remember? Tea in the afternoon? Tents with all the comforts of home? Well, I found their dig and I can tell you how to get there. He's had some bad luck—that's why I was sent out here, don't forget—and I'm sure he could use you both to drive his ore wagons. You tell him I sent you, and it will be all right."

Denny looked at Bill Reed. It was obvious that the two had become more than friends. "But we were hoping we might be able to get that Professor Stewart to pay for new wagons and stock, weren't we, Bill?"

"That's right," agreed Bill, with an ironic smile. "But then we'd be working for Stewart again—and you know what happened the last time. I think it would be safer for us to try our luck with this Englishman. At least he's got Longarm on his side." He looked at Longarm. "Ain't that right, Longarm?"

"I suppose that's one way of looking at it."

Denny smiled up at Longarm. "I guess it is. You tell us how to get to this Englishman's dig, and we'll go there." She frowned suddenly. "But aren't you going back with us?"

"That jasper I shot last night—Slant. He had a sidekick. That was the rider who dumped Marge Tucker and rode out. When I tracked those two to this town, I was hoping they were the ones behind that gang that shot up your wagons. Well, what Marge told me convinced me that Ballenger had nothing to do with it. But she also convinced me that Ballenger knows where that gang is. So we're going after Ballenger this morning."

"*We?*"

Longarm looked down at Denny and shrugged. "The lady insists. She don't like Ballenger any more than I do. And she has a few ideas where to find him."

"Well," said Denny, her wide blue eyes alight with mischief, "if you don't find Ballenger, I am sure you won't die of boredom."

Longarm laughed. "Join me in breakfast, you two. I'll give you directions for getting to that Englishman's dig."

"As long as you're buying, Longarm," laughed Bill Reed, "lead the way."

Late that same afternoon, Marge and Longarm topped a gentle rise. Marge pulled up and pointed to a dark ridge directly ahead of them on the far side of a desert flat.

"On the other side of that ridge," she told Longarm, "there's a small valley. He's got a cabin at the

128

end of the valley. A shack, really. Chuck wanted me to live out there with him and keep house." She glanced at him. "Can you imagine? The only way I could clean that pigsty would be to burn it."

"You think he's there?"

"It's a good bet. It's where he goes to lick his wounds. And after the lovely way you handled him last night, he's got wounds to lick."

Longarm nodded and urged his horse down the slope. "Let's go," he said. "There's an Englishman back there I don't want to leave for too long."

"An Englishman?" Marge asked, using her riding crop to keep her horse alongside his. "There's no woman back there waiting for you? Just an Englishman?"

Longarm laughed. "I'm on an assignment, Marge. And my assignment is to protect that Englishman from assorted desperadoes, such as Chuck Ballenger—and also from jealous fellow scientists." He shook his head wearily. "That ain't to mention Chief Yellow Horn and his Arapahos."

"I see," she said. "With all that, you have no time for permanent attachments."

"The only permanent attachment I have is to the badge I carry in my wallet."

"It is nice for you to say that, Longarm. After last night, especially."

"Nothing personal, Marge."

"Of course, Longarm. I understand. After all, a woman in my . . . profession understands that before she understands anything else."

"I never thought of it like that," Longarm admitted. "But I guess that's true."

Marge was riding a powerful roan gelding. Longarm had taken out the buckskin again. The two horses were a match for each other, and the riders were too, Longarm realized. Marge was not riding sidesaddle, but astride. She forked the roan as naturally as any man would. She had fashioned herself a long split skirt and was wearing it with a white blouse and a black, buttonless vest. Her hat was a black, flat-crowned sombrero with a wide, flat brim. The black hat contrasted nicely with the bright luster of her long golden hair.

"Do you still like what you see, Longarm?" she asked, as she caught his appraising glance.

Longarm smiled. "I still like what I see."

By the time they crossed the flat and rode into the badlands on the other side, the sun was getting low. Longarm was anxious to reach the valley Marge had told him about before dark. Marge was pretty certain they would reach it long before then, but it didn't look that way as they guided their horses through the narrow arroyos and across the treacherous washes and gullies that cut across their trail.

Only when darkness covered the landscape like a smothering blanket, and they could ride no further on their nearly spent horses, did Marge finally admit to Longarm that she was lost.

As Longarm reached up to help her down, she said, "I'm sorry, Longarm. Once I rode into this broken country, I completely lost my bearings. One gulley or wash looks so much like any other."

He smiled. "Not if it's your home ground, it don't."

"Well, this land is not my home ground, obviously." She looked around her at the dark landscape. The darkness had transformed the boulders and mountains that rose on all sides into hulking, menacing shapes. Longarm saw her shudder.

"The thing is," Longarm said, "Chuck Ballenger could be anywhere in these hills. His valley could be over that next ridge. Right?"

"It might be."

"So we got to figure he could have seen us coming. This is his country, not ours. He might be out there now, waiting for us to bed down for the night."

"Longarm! Do you have to say things like that?"

"Nope. I don't have to. Not unless it's true, that is. I figure we'd best make a dry camp, then set up dummy sleepers in our bedrolls and keep watch."

"Oh, Longarm! I'm so tired."

"It was your idea to come along. You can do what you want. But I intend to live through the night."

She trembled slightly. "Damn you," she whispered. "So do I! But you make it all sound so grim."

Longarm looked down at her and shook his head. "Marge, don't you understand what kind of an animal you're dealing with? This Chuck Ballenger is one of the meanest pieces of offal I've come across in a long, long time."

"Oh," she said, laughing nervously. "I've always been able to handle his kind."

"In bed, Marge. Yes. That's *your* territory. But now you're outside. In *his* world, in that part of the jungle that *he* owns. You're out of your element now. He's *in* his."

She moved closer to him in the darkness and put her arms around his waist and rested her head against his chest. "Take care of me, Longarm. The way you did last night."

Longarm chucked softly and stroked her long silken hair. "First we'll have to light a campfire, eat, and set up our dummies."

"I'll help," she told him with sudden cheerfulness. She pushed away and looked up at him. "You'll see. Even over a campfire, I'm a fine cook."

"I'm sure of it," Longarm told her. "I'll go gather firewood. We'll want a good fire if those sleeping dummies are to work proper. A man can't be fooled by something he can't see."

They could see the campfire clearly from the ledge. Longarm had picketed the horses far down the canyon and had filled both saddle blankets with boulders and placed them around the campfire. As they looked down now, they could see how the dancing flames caused the canyon wall alongside the fire to shimmer and jump in its trembling glow. The two dummies looked just fine. As an added touch, Longarm had used their saddles for pillows and placed their hats down beside each bedroll.

"They look so real," Marge whispered. "As if that's really us down there."

"That's the way it is supposed to look," he replied.

"Do you think it'll work?"

"Sure, if Ballenger didn't see us setting the trap."

"Oh, Longarm," she sighed. "You're such a Gloomy Gus." She snuggled close to him. "Of course it'll work."

"It won't if we don't shut up," he whispered, kissing her full on the lips.

"Mmmm," she murmured. "All right. Let's let our bodies do all the talking."

They were both in Longarm's sleeping bag, naked. He had let the warmth of her kindle him during their short conversation. Now, as she pressed herself against him, she made a small sound of delight. She could feel how big he'd grown. In a fierce burst of enthusiasm, she pushed him down flat on his back and mounted him, enclosing his shaft with an almost savage downward thrust.

The enveloping warmth of her charged him with a delight that almost intoxicated him. It swarmed up his loins until he could almost taste it. She fell forward onto him, her magnificent breasts crushing their

132

warmth onto his chest, her lips fastening hungrily, devouringly upon his. Her tongue began to work in feverish mimicking of his own wild, upward thrusting.

There was no longer any attempt on his part to hold back for her, something he always tried to do out of consideration for his partners; this time he was thinking only of himself, while she hung onto his wildly bucking torso with a low, continuous squeal of delight. His climax came in a fierce, annihilating rush that dizzied him, emptied him. But gasping in the enjoyment of it, he found she was now just as determined to gain her climax as well. She kept going and would not release him.

He wanted to tell her that it was no use, that he was spent; but to his amazement, he found himself growing within her. She squealed softly and flung herself up and back, her blonde hair flying out, momentarily framing her pale flower of a face in its golden penumbra. She was grimacing with the urgency of her need, and despite the wetness of her, she managed to hold his resurgent erection with a force that delighted him. Caught up now once again, he began to drive up to meet her every thrust, grinding his pubic bone against hers. He ran his hands up and down her spine. He could feel her muscles tensing under the warm, silken skin.

He was back at his peak, riding the crest now— aware that he was deliciously out of control. He got a firm grip on each of her hip bones and began slamming her hard down upon him, imparting increased momentum to each of her thrusts. Her groans told him this was exactly what she wanted. She leaned back, shuddered, grew rigid. Flinging her head back still further, she let out a tiny cry. At that moment he too climaxed, pulsing helplessly up into her as she rocked, groaning, back and forth.

At last she collapsed forward onto his chest. She

was sobbing softly. Surprised, he kissed away the tears on her cheeks. Her lips found his and this time her kiss, though not without passion, was soft and warm, filling him not only with passion, but a sweet tenderness as well.

"You see how it can be, Longarm?" she gasped softly, tiny sobs still coming from her. "It was good last night, but not like this."

"No," Longarm whispered. "It was not like this."

"You see now why I wanted to come with you after that filthy man. I wanted to see him taken, yes. And I wanted to be able to help you do that. But I also wanted more of you. Do you understand? You are a man on the move. You will never come my way again, I know. So now I take what I can—as long as I can!"

With a fierce cry she was on him again, her lips on his no longer warm, but cruel and molten with the fire of her need for him. Her tongue probed like something alive, deeply into his mouth. The smell of her became heavy with the hot musk of her desire. He could smell it in her panting breath and found himself rolling over onto her. It had an amazing effect on him. He sprang to life again. Aroused now beyond anything he had experienced in a long, long time, he took charge, lifting her buttocks with his big, rough hands and slamming her in under him.

Both of them had become pure animal now, lust incarnate, unhitched from all traces, wild, unrestrained . . .

It was like the peace that came after a good fight or a good drunk—only better, far better. Longarm stretched his long limbs luxuriantly. He was as empty as a spent revolver sitting on a shelf. There was no smoke or fire left in his chambers or his barrel. He was clean of urgency, drained of all tension. Marge slept in the crook of his arm, her golden tresses spread over his naked chest like perfumed silk.

What was that?

He groaned inwardly, every muscle in his long frame tensing. And then he heard the tiny clicking sound again, and knew exactly from where the sound was coming.

His trap was being sprung!

Pulling hastily out from under Marge, he leaned over the ledge and peered down at the campfire. He thought he saw Ballenger's shadow moving toward it, but he could not be sure. On his feet in an instant, he plucked his Colt out of its holster where it lay beside the bedroll, then glided on swift, bare feet down off the ledge, heading for the campfire below. Again he thought he saw Ballenger, but as he got closer to the campfire, it proved to be only a shadow thrown against the canyon wall by the still-busy flames.

On the canyon floor now, he moved swiftly through the darkness toward the campfire. Again he heard that curious click of metal on stone coming from the direction of the campfire. There was no doubt of its direction now. He slowed down, then halted, confused. There was no one by the fire. Not a soul. The two dummy sleepers were in plain sight, unmolested. The leaping firelight had played tricks on him all the way.

As he stood crouched, irresolute, the campfire exploded in a burst of sparks. A round ricocheted off the canyon wall just above him. Another explosion followed, and then another. Longarm flung himself to the ground as the bullets buzzed like deranged hornets all around him. He swore and ducked his head down.

He knew now what he had been hearing. Someone —Chuck Ballenger, most likely—had been tossing cartridges into the fire. The object, obviously, must have been to make Longarm think Ballenger was coming from that direction.

Which meant Chuck Ballenger *wasn't* coming from that direction!

"Longarm!" Marge cried from the ledge. "What's going on down there? Are you all right?"

"Get off that ledge!" Longarm called back. "Ballenger's up there somewhere!"

As if to prove that assertion, Marge's sudden, furious scream cut through the night. Longarm saw two figures struggling on the ledge, one of them Marge, her long blonde hair flying, her pale, naked figure standing out starkly against the darker figure of her attacker.

"Thanks for bringing her!" Ballenger cried. "I'll know just how to use her!"

Cursing, Longarm scrambled to his feet. The cartridges Ballenger had tossed into the fire had all been expended by this time, but as Longarm started to run toward the path leading back up to the ledge, Ballenger fired down at him. The bullets whined dangerously close. Longarm was forced to take cover, not daring to fire back for fear of hitting Marge. A moment later, after the firing from the ledge had stopped, he darted from cover and began climbing back to the ledge—only to hear the distant hoofbeats of a galloping horse as Ballenger spurred away through the night.

Marge was now Chuck Ballenger's captive. And Longarm had delivered her to him.

Chapter 10

Longarm pulled up, dropped the reins of Marge's horse, and dismounted. He was high in the badlands, following Ballenger's sign. Sharp prints were visible in a sandy wash, and Longarm went down on one knee to examine them closely.

Yes. It was Ballenger's horse, all right. The animal was laboring under the weight of two riders and had already thrown a shoe. But it was a powerful beast, and its stride was still strong.

Longarm mounted up, still leading Marge's roan, and urged the buckskin on. It had already been a long day after a sleepless night, and he was tired. He was still furious with himself, seething inwardly at how neatly Ballenger had tricked him. The gunslick had been way ahad of him, had toyed with the two of them the way a cat does with a mouse. Only this time there had been two mice.

Ballenger's sign led up a gradual slope that brought Longarm into a lovely park area. In the slanting rays of the sun, the tall grass—festooned here and there with blue and red wildflowers—was a warming sight. But Longarm took precious little comfort in the beauty of the park as he followed the bent grass and clear sign that showed him how swiftly Ballenger had crossed this sward.

Beyond the park, Ballenger's tracks followed a descending path that took Longarm out at last on the other side of a compact stand of scrub pine. The pine grew along the crest of a ridge, which shouldered higher and higher. Along this ridge, Longarm found a game trail and followed it. He found himself enjoying a spectacular view of the badlands. Far down to his right he caught a river's gleaming band of silver as it wound through the narrow canyons below. Every once in a while, Longarm glimpsed Ballenger's sign. The gunslick's animal was slowing some, but still moving along steadily. Longarm was certain, now, that he was close to that valley Marge had told him about.

He shook his head. He had been a fool to let Marge talk him into serving as his guide. It was obvious that she could never have found this valley of Ballenger's.

Abruptly, the trail ahead of him appeared to drop out of sight. He pulled up and then gently coaxed his horse to the lip of the ridge. As soon as he neared the edge, he found the trail again, swinging off to his left, winding close around a huge boulder. He caught sight of Ballenger's fresh tracks, as well.

The trail dropped swiftly then, almost too steeply, before leveling off. He was turning in his saddle to glance back at Marge's feisty roan when he caught a brief glimpse of a green land far below, surrounded on all sides by precipitous walls. Jutting fingers of rock closed off the view. But Longarm knew now that he was on the right trail, that before sunset he would be in Chuck Ballenger's valley.

Only it did not work out that way.

The game trail vanished on a smooth, rocky ledge that had nothing beyond it but a swift mountain stream piling headlong between two smooth canyon walls. Longarm urged his buckskin off the ledge and into the stream bed. He rode on down through the damp canyon for more than a mile, the swift water swirling up around the buckskin's legs, almost brushing its belly at times. At last the can-

138

yon's walls fell away. Longarm left the stream and found no trail and no sign of Ballenger's tracks.

By this time the sun had gone down. With the canyon walls leaning over him, increasing the gloom, Longarm was forced to admit to himself that he would not find Ballenger's valley this day. He found himself a spot well-hidden among some boulders and made camp, promising himself to get an early start the next day.

He found it difficult to sleep, however, despite having ridden most of the day. He kept thinking of Marge in the hands of Chuck Ballenger. She had been in the man's arms before; and it was a situation, as she had made clear to him, with which she was quite competent to deal. It had been, after all, her profession before she became the Red Dog's owner. But somehow this fact seemed to give Longarm no comfort at all.

In the clear light of morning, Longarm took a good look around his campsite and realized at once that he must have gone well south of that valley he had glimpsed from the game trail. But to be on the safe side, he rode still further down the canyon, looking for Ballenger's tracks. He found no sign.

Satisfied, he turned back into the stream. This time, as he struggled up through the rushing water, his eyes searched carefully the walls on both sides. In less than a mile, he caught the slight fold of rock behind which a narrow trail could be glimpsed. He rode into it and soon found himself in a narrow arroyo that allowed passage through it only grudgingly. Presently, Longarm came out onto a grassy sward overlooking the valley he had caught sight of yesterday.

He took a quick look around. It was the beginning of a bright day, and he had little doubt that Chuck Ballenger would be on the lookout for him. Spotting

139

a clump of alders to his left, Longarm rode over to it, dismounted, and led both horses into its cover. Then he pulled his Winchester from its boot, checked its load, and stole from the timber, scouting for a spot from which he could observe the valley undetected. It didn't take him long to find a spot behind a clump of juniper which gave him an almost unobstructed view of the valley.

The shack was where Marge had told him it would be—beyond a stream at the far end of the valley, sitting on a bench halfway up a slope and well in among a stand of cottonwood. Just as Marge had described the place to him, the cabin was a miserable, single-room affair with a crooked stovepipe for a chimney. The outhouse leaned precariously over its noisome pit, the barn was at best a makeshift lean-to, and there was no corral for the horses, of which there were six, all of them grazing in the flat below the shack.

Longarm studied the layout for a while, then decided his best bet would be to work around behind the cabin and approach through the cottonwoods. He pushed back through the juniper and glided off, heading for the timber above him. He figured he should make it to the cottonwoods within two hours. As he set off, he wondered about all that horseflesh grazing in the flat.

Approaching the single window at the rear of the cabin, Longarm found out where those horses had come from. Chuck Ballenger had visitors. He could hear their drunken voices clearly and the occasional sound of chairs scraping. A tattered piece of oiled paper served as a windowpane. Longarm had little difficulty seeing into the room.

A card game was in progress. Five men were around the table. Marge, dressed in dirty Levi's and a torn shirt and with nothing on her feet, was doing her best to serve them whatever they wanted, which appeared, for the most part, to be more liquor. Even as Longarm peered into the room, one of the cardplayers flung an empty whiskey bottle out through the open front door, yelling for more hooch as he did so.

Longarm pulled back from the window to study his next move. It was obvious that Ballenger had great faith in the supposed inaccessibility of his hidden valley. He had posted no guards, and did not now act like a man who expected a visit from a determined federal lawman. Good. That meant Longarm at least had the element of surprise in his favor.

But if he counted on surprise alone and stepped into the cabin blasting away, it would be disastrous for Marge. If she was not winged by a stray bullet, it was certain Ballenger would again use her as a shield. Longarm had to get Marge out of that cabin before making any kind of play. Furthermore, who in tarnation were these other jaspers? They had the stamp and the smell of men on the run. Were they part of Ballenger's gang, or were they just another wild bunch who had stopped by to hole up with Ballenger for a while?

Longarm realized it didn't really matter. They were on the scene and would have to be dealt with—but it was Ballenger Longarm wanted, and without any injury to Marge.

He would just have to wait for his opportunity. The whiskey would befuddle their senses soon enough. Suddenly he heard someone in the cabin swear and insist loudly that he had to take a crap, that he wasn't going to wait on any son of a bitch who didn't know how to play his hand. There were hoots of derision at this, the sound of a chair scraping, and a moment later Longarm heard the fellow approaching the outhouse from the side of the cabin.

141

The fellow was grumbling unhappily to himself as he felt his way through the blinding sunlight to the privy. Longarm had little time to make his decision, but he made it and ducked quickly out of sight behind the privy a second before the card-player with the full load staggered into view around the corner of the shack, groping for the outhouse door.

Longarm heard the man's heavy breathing and felt the privy rock as the fellow yanked open the door and lurched inside. He listened as the man cursed off his tight Levi's. Then came a relieved silence.

Leaning his Winchester against the back of the privy, Longarm drew his Colt and moved swiftly around to the front of the little building and pulled open the door. The man sitting with his Levi's down around his ankles was a lean, bald fellow with a narrow red nose and mournful eyes. He was probably going to ask Longarm what the hell he wanted, but Longarm didn't give him the chance. He brought the Colt's barrel down sharply on the top of the man's skull. The fellow's eyes rolled up into his head as he collapsed forward into Longarm's arms. Longarm hefted the man up onto one shoulder; then he lifted the top of the bench. The rotted wood gave way and the nails holding the bench pulled free. Longarm flung the bench out of the privy and unloaded his burden into the pit, headfirst.

Longarm listened to the man's heavy breathing for a moment, then left the privy, snatched up his Winchester, and returned to the cabin window to await developments. After a short while, the waiting cardplayers grew restless. First one, then another, yelled out to their tardy comrade to hurry the hell up and get back in there and finish the game.

There was, of course, no response.

One of the men—it wasn't Ballenger—suggested

142

that Charlie might have fallen in. The man next to him remarked that this might improve the absent cardplayer's smell. The talk rambled some after that, until one of them demanded that Marge come closer so she could find out what a real man was like. A sharp retort from Marge put the man properly in his place, and Chuck Ballenger spoke up then to tell this worthy that Marge was his woman—as long as she kept her nose clean and stopped riding around the countryside naked. This brought raw, derisive laughter from the other three, but when the hilarity subsided, one of the men pushed his chair back impatiently and started for the door.

"Goddamnit," he said over his shoulder as he stepped out the doorway, "that poor son of a bitch *might* have fallen in, at that. He was drunk enough."

Longarm moved swiftly away from the window and was behind the privy when the second man approached it. Longarm heard the fellow pause, then swear softly when he found the bench on the ground in front of the privy. Then Longarm heard him pull open the door and step inside. As Longarm slipped around to the front of the outhouse, he heard the man's startled gasp as he looked down into the hole and saw Charlie's huddled form. He started to turn, perhaps to yell something to his comrades in the cabin, but before he could utter a sound, Longarm cracked him smartly from behind, then pitched him unceremoniously into the dark, fly-buzzing shithole alongside his friend.

A moment later, crouched on the other side of the cabin, Longarm watched the cabin's open doorway closely. Already an impatient cry to the second man had been made, and as Longarm watched, Chuck Ballenger and two other men poked their heads out, the three of them obviously puzzled.

"Find out what the hell's going on, Sim," said

143

Ballenger. "They couldn't *both* have fallen in. You go with him, Wally."

Longarm ducked his head back as Sim and Wally took out their sixguns, glanced warily around, then left the cabin and headed around to the outhouse. Chuck Ballenger had ducked back into the cabin, and Longarm could hear him talking to Marge. Longarm darted to the open doorway and slipped into the cabin, his Colt out in front of him.

His luck was holding.

Marge was just inside the door, and Ballenger, his back to Longarm, was reaching for his Winchester on a hook over his cot. At the sound of Longarm's entry, he turned, startled. Longarm stepped carefully in front of Marge to shield her.

"Leave that weapon on the wall, Chuck," Longarm said softly. "You won't need it now."

"Jesus!" the man said, astonished. "How the hell did you find this place?"

Longarm moved closer to Ballenger and kept his voice down. "That's not important. Unbuckle your gunbelt. Do it!"

Ballenger's holster and belt thumped to the floor.

"Now go to that window and tell those two men out back to come on in here. But peaceable, or I'll ventilate you first thing."

It was at that moment that the men outside began shouting. They had discovered where their two buddies were resting.

"Never mind that," Ballenger yelled to the two men as he poked his head out through the window. "We got ourselves a visitor! Come on back in here! And keep your guns in their holsters, or the son of a bitch'll shoot me!"

There was a short argument. Longarm started for the window. Suddenly Marge screamed and leaped for Longarm, both arms outstretched. As she

144

knocked Longarm aside, a sixgun roared from the open doorway. Longarm saw Marge buck as the slug took her in the back. He caught her with his left arm as he spun and snapped off two quick shots. The fellow in the doorway staggered back, dropping his gun, a red stain appearing on his right shoulder. As he turned and ran down the slope toward the horses in the flat, Longarm, still holding Marge up by one arm, spun back to face Ballenger.

The man had his knife out and was hurling himself at Longarm. Longarm fired twice into the man's midsection, catching him just above the bellybutton. Two neat holes appeared in his shirt. Ballenger stopped, sank to his knees, then buckled forward, the knife clattering to the floor, both hands clutching at his stomach.

Longarm carried Marge to the cot, then ducked his head out the rear window. He was just in time to see two very dirty, horrified gunslicks stumbling out of the privy. Longarm fired once over their heads and all three started running down the slope after the one Longarm had wounded.

Longarm hurried over to Marge. She was conscious and obviously in considerable pain. Longarm was sick at heart. He had not only come to this valley to get Ballenger, but also to rescue Marge. She had been right. She knew how to handle the likes of Chuck Ballenger, and would have survived if it had not been for Longarm's heroics. He took her hand. It was feverish. She looked up at him with bright, frightened eyes.

"I been hit bad, Longarm," she said.

"That bullet was meant for me, Marge. That was a fool thing to do."

She smiled wanly. "Don't scold me, Longarm," she said.

145

"I didn't mean to, Marge. What I meant to say was thanks."

"You're so solemn," she told him." Right now it hurts something fierce, but I'll be all right. Won't I?"

"Of course. But we'll have to stay here awhile, and I guess there's nothing for me to do but dig that slug out of your back."

"There's plenty of whiskey here, Longarm. Or don't you approve of a woman getting drunk?"

"That depends on the woman—and the circumstances." He got up and looked down at her.

The sheet under the girl was a solid crimson by this time, and her pale complexion had become almost transparent. Her eyes glowed up at him like hot coals dropped in snow. Longarm heard Ballenger groan. He turned away from Marge and regarded the wounded man carefully.

"Help me," the man cried. "I'm hit bad."

"You're dead, Ballenger. Gutshot."

"A drink, then! Give me some of that whiskey."

"I'm saving it for Marge."

"Let him have some, Longarm," she said, her voice reedy, thin. "He needs it worse than I do."

Longarm found two bottles already opened, and gave one to Ballenger and the other to Marge. He sat beside Marge as she tipped the bottle up and swallowed. She drank it like water, then looked with wide eyes at Longarm.

"The cabin's tipping up," she said, smiling faintly, "and my head's just sailing around. Oh, I'm so dizzy, Longarm. And the pain's gone!"

He glanced at Ballenger. The man was bent forward over the bottle. He was very still. Longarm left Marge and approached Ballenger. The man was dead. His dirty white claw of a hand clung tenaciously to the bottle, but Longarm peeled the fingers away from it and brought the remaining whiskey to Marge.

146

"Finish this bottle," he told her. "Then I'll go after that bullet."

She took the bottle from him and swigged it happily. Then her arm dropped and the bottle smashed to the floor. She looked blearily up at Longarm. "Go to it, Marshal! Get that bullet out!"

Longarm had long since dragged the body of Chuck Ballenger from the cabin and buried him. Now he was back, watching Marge's still form lying faceup on the small cot. It was close to midnight, and the only light came from a single kerosene lamp. The chimney was broken off at the top, and the wick burned poorly. The strong, unpleasant smell of the smoking kerosene lamp mingled with the stench of decay and death that hung over the mean cot.

The second Longarm's probing knife had entered Marge's wound, the woman had uttered a sharp cry and passed out. Longarm had probed deeply, but he could not retrieve the bullet. To the best of his knowledge, the slug had slammed off a rib and angled up into her lungs. While Marge remained unconscious, he had done his best to cauterize the wound and pack it to stem the bleeding, after which he had wrapped her tightly in bandages fashioned from what few clean sheets he could find.

He moved stiffly on the wooden chair. Its back was missing, giving him no support. Once or twice in the past hour, Marge had stirred slightly, and he had leaned forward eagerly in hopes that she was coming out of it. But each time she had lapsed back into a deeper, coma-like sleep. He did not like the look of her. Her face seemed to have shrunk into the pillow and her complexion was a glassy white. Whenever he touched her forehead, his hand came away as if scorched. She was being consumed from within.

With surprising suddenness she opened her eyes

147

and turned her face to look at him. "The room is so dark, but that *is* you, isn't it, Longarm?"

"It's me, all right. How do you feel?"

"Hot. I'm burning up. And you didn't get that bullet, did you?"

"No."

"I can feel it inside me, burrowing. Every time I breathe. So I guess I won't be all right, after all. I'm going to die. Like Ballenger."

"Don't talk like that."

"Are you scolding me again?"

"No, of course not." Longarm ran his hand through his hair. "Jesus, Marge!"

"Why, Longarm! You really feel bad about me. That I am dying, I mean!"

Longarm took a deep breath, not trusting himself to speak. She saw his pain and reached out her hand to him. He took it. "Of course I do, Marge."

"Take me back to the Red Dog, Longarm," she told him then, her voice clear but barely above a whisper. "Mary Sweeney will see to my burial. You don't know her, but she's my barmaid on busy nights. You'll like her. She's as big as a house, with a heart to match."

Longarm just nodded. Her hand seemed to be on fire, and her pale cheeks had a fierce, hectic glow. In the dim light, her eyes appeared to be burning through the gloom into his.

"You'll have to get back to that Englishman, Longarm," she told him. "That was Sim Drucker here with Chuck. He wanted Chuck to join him. He's attacking that Englishman's dig. A professor from Denver is paying Sim good money for the job. Sim's a mean one. He'll give that professor his money's worth—and then some."

Abruptly, she began coughing. He left the chair and bent over her. A thin trickle of blood streamed from a corner of her mouth.

148

"Don't say any more, Marge. Save your strength."

"What for?" she asked weakly, smiling up at him. "Kiss me, Longarm. Nice-like."

He leaned down and kissed her lightly on the lips; then, as she closed her eyes, he kissed both her eyelids. He sat back on the chair then, and waited for her to open her eyes again.

He was still waiting moments later when he slowly pulled the sheet up over her head.

Chapter 11

Mary Sweeney was indeed as big as a house. Dressed all in black and dabbing at her eyes constantly with a pink lace handkerchief, she tried to express to Longarm how badly she felt about Marge's death.

They were in the Red Dog, and it was just after the funeral. A full stein of beer was in Mary Sweeney's dimpled hand, and there was a slight trace of the beer's suds on her upper lip. Her face was vast and unwrinkled, heavily rouged, and a study in comic, almost clownish, grief. But just as Marge had said, Mary Sweeney had a heart as big as her girth.

"She was like my own daughter," Mary told Longarm, lifting the stein up to her face again and drinking noisily. She almost wiped her mouth off with the back of her pudgy hand, but thought better of it as she felt Longarm's eyes on her.

"That was a fine funeral," Longarm said. "You really did Marge proud. Those flowers, especially. They were beautiful."

As Longarm had hoped she would, Mary swelled with pleasure at Longarm's compliment. Then she leaned close to Longarm, dropping her heavy hand over his. "I didn't care what it cost, Marshal. It ain't often one us girls gets a chance to go in style." She looked fiercely at Longarm for a moment, her tear-filled eyes bright with sudden indignation. "You know the send-off most of us . . . working girls get. In some back alley they find us, near a stinking outhouse more than likely, a whiskey bottle in our hand—our insides all eaten up by them diseases. And then potter's field in a cheap pine box! Well," she finished triumphantly, leaning back suddenly and finishing the stein, "that ain't the way Marge went!"

"No," agreed Longarm. "That ain't the way Marge went."

"And besides, she was with *you*—and she did a fine thing. You said so yourself."

"Yes, I did," admitted Longarm. "And every word of it was true."

At that moment the batwings were pushed aside and a familiar figure entered. The townspeople had sense enough to keep out of the Red Dog this morning, at least—to give Marge's part-time barmaid and full-time silent partner a chance to mourn in private; but this fellow was not a native of Dog Wells.

It was William Edward Pope, and behind him crowded four unwashed gunslicks. Longarm could almost smell the four from where he was sitting, well back in the saloon's cool interior.

"Saloon's closed!" Mary called out indignantly to the five men. "Death in the family!"

Pope turned quickly, conferred a moment with his companions, then watched them leave the saloon, while Pope himself stayed inside, turned, and waved to Longarm.

"That you, Marshal?" he called.

"It's me. Didn't you hear the lady?"

Ignoring Longarm's question, Pope walked toward them. "You have no idea," he said, "how anxious I am to rid myself of those four ruffians. I pay them well, but they really don't seem to know their place." He smiled. "They are, after all, hirelings."

151

Longarm looked at Mary Sweeney. The big woman heaved her enormous bosom in resignation, then pushed herself erect. "I'll have to get out of these clothes anyway, Marshal. I'll be open for business by one." She sighed resignedly. "And you can guess just how long it will take *me* to change."

Longarm watched the immense woman move off to a flight of stairs in the back, then turned to greet Pope. The tall, thin man shook Longarm's extended hand heartily as he sat down at the table.

"How about one of those cheroots you favor, Marshal?" Pope asked. "I think I could do with one right now. I lost my pipe a few days ago at Dragon Bluff."

Longarm handed the man one of his cheroots, selected one for himself, and bit off the tip. Pope lit a sulfur match and held the flame to Longarm's cheroot, then got his own going. He leaned back, contented, a cloud of smoke enveloping his head.

He hadn't changed or learned much, Longarm concluded as he watched Pope puff away. He was still dressed in his flashy, fringed buckskin suit, topped by the broad-brimmed sombrero. His face, however, was no longer as florid; the sun had bronzed it and the hazel eyes looked almost green. His beard needed clipping.

"You've been to Dragon's Bluff, have you?" Longarm inquired. "I hope that means you and Stewart have given up on that fool vendetta of yours."

"Not a bit of it, Marshal. Dragon Bluff is no longer yielding anything of worth. Both of us have decided to abandon our dig there." His eyes lit and he leaned closer. "It's that Sir Thomas who has sneaked in right under our noses and made the greatest discovery! Have you heard? He's located a rock wall *filled* with articulated skeletons! *Allosaurus*, *Diplodocus*!"

"You know that for a fact, do you?"

"I have informants, Marshal," he replied. "Unfortunately, so does Stewart!"

"So you're going to have to share this discovery with the Englishman."

Pope shrugged unhappily. "I am afraid it looks that way, Marshal."

"Why the change of heart?"

"I'll be honest with you," the man replied, somewhat reluctantly. "There have been, shall I say, unfortunate occurrences. Some of the men I hired seem to have . . . to put it bluntly . . . gone too far in a few instances."

"That so?"

"Yes, Marshal. I am afraid that *is* so."

"You mean a few innocent men have been killed, property destroyed, that sort of thing."

"Well . . . yes, as a matter of fact."

Longarm looked harshly at Pope and leaned a bit closer to him. "This may come as a big shock to you, Pope, but I know all about what your boys have been up to, and I am holding not only those hirelings of yours, but also yourself, responsible. Is that clear?"

Pope swallowed and sat back, troubled. "Why, yes, Marshal. You have made yourself *quite* clear."

"Those four gunslicks that started in here with you. Is *that* your army? Are *those* the boys that have been shooting up camps, attacking teamsters, and the like?"

"No longer, Marshal. I assure you. I have just paid them off, given them even more than I had promised. They are quite content. But they are to harass no more wagons or trouble any more men working at any of the digs in the area." Pope's face became grave suddenly. "However, I must admit, they did seem somewhat reluctant to give up their new employment. Perhaps I paid them *too* well."

"Why do you say that?"

"They know all about that find the Englishman made. And they had the most extraordinary plan for . . . dealing with it."

"But you called them off."

"Most assuredly, though they did seem disappointed. I never saw men so anxious to impress me, so *inventive* when it came to such things."

"You say you paid them well?"

"Almost more than I could comfortably afford, I am afraid."

"Well, that's your answer. They must sure as hell hate to lose an employer as generous as you are. You've hired devils, Pope, and then paid them well to act like the murderous hellions they are."

Pope blew his cheeks out and shook his head. He looked thoroughly chastened. "I see what you mean, Marshal."

"At any rate, I'm glad your men are being called off. Now, what about Stewart? He's got a gang out here too, you know."

"Yes, I know."

"I met a few of his boys not long ago. One of them killed that woman we buried this morning."

"Heavens!" cried Pope, in genuine horror.

"You got any pressing business in Denver, Pope?"

"Of course. You will be surprised to know, I am sure, that I now have a display alongside Stewart's in the exhibition hall. An *Iguanodon*. The skeleton is not as spectacular as Stewart's *Hadrosaurus*, perhaps, but a worthy companion, all the same. We do not speak much, of course, and I must admit, Stewart is not as complete a fraud as I had thought. But his arrogance is still insufferable."

Longarm looked at Pope. He almost smiled at the

man's still-unreasonable animosity when it came to his rival. Almost. He didn't smile because what had come from this petulant, childish rivalry was not at all funny. "Good," Longarm snapped. "When you get back to Denver, I want you to tell him to get out here and call off his men. If he doesn't, I mean to hold him responsible for what they do. I happen to know they are planning trouble for Sir Thomas and his expedition. You tell him that, Pope."

The man smiled nervously. "I will, most certainly."

Longarm got up from his chair then, and stood for a moment looking down at the scientist. "When were you figuring on leaving Dog Wells, Pope?"

Pope looked up uncertainly at Longarm. "I . . . hadn't given that much thought. Perhaps in a few days, after I have inspected this last load of fossils my diggers have taken from Dragon Bluff. I'd like to supervise their loading. Some of these freight handlers are not at all as careful as they should be." He smiled patronizingly. "I am afraid they do not realize how valuable these fossil bones are—for science and for the world."

"There's a train out tonight, Pope," said Longarm, tugging his hat down securely. "Be on it."

He turned and strode from the saloon.

Longarm rode into New Bethlehem a little past noon the next day. The Reverend Thomas Dorr Wilson did not throw down on Longarm this time. He stood in front of his church by the side of the narrow, rutted main street of his utopia, his black-garbed followers lined up neatly behind him, their round-topped black hats forming a solid roof extending back almost as far as the church entrance. A lookout—a somewhat hysterical field hand, judging from the way he lit out across the hayfield—had long since warned the townsfolk of Longarm's coming.

155

Longarm pulled up in front of Reverend Wilson. Resting his hands on his saddle horn, he said, "Must be you don't get many visitors, Reverend, the way you fuss about me. You tell your people they can go back to work now. They don't have to stand like that in the hot sun just on my account. I won't take offense."

"You laugh at our piety, do you?" Reverend Wilson's tone was filled with suppressed outrage at Longarm's banter.

"Piety, hell! You're all a pack of mealymouthed malcontents looking for a place where you can practice your own form of bigotry without the law hauling you in. Like wife-beating. Called any decent woman a whore lately, Reverend?"

"I assume you are referring to Carrie Newton."

"I am."

"That was most unfortunate," Wilson said. "But there is nothing we can do about that poor, damned soul now, I am afraid. Calvin Newton is in God's hands. And the Lord have mercy on them that turned him into what he has now become."

This strange indictment of Newton caused Longarm to lean forward intently. He had come through New Bethlehem hoping for some trace of Newton. The man was severely wounded the last time Longarm had seen him riding off, but he could have made it back to New Bethlehem. Longarm planned to take the man back with him, if he found him. Attempted murder would be one charge. Resisting arrest might be another. There was one thing Longarm felt was certain: as long as Calvin Newton was a free man, he was a threat to Carrie.

Or to anyone else who might befriend her.

"You've seen Newton?" Longarm asked the reverend. "He's been back here, has he?"

"Yes. He returned. He was fearfully wounded. You broke his jaw, Marshal, so you know that much.

But now he's missing an eye. Worse than that, he's gone mad. There was no way any of us could reason with the man."

"You mean he talked back some?"

"He stole from us. Two horses, he took. He raided the settlement's arsenal. He took rifles, many rounds of ammunition. When we tried to stop him, he shot and killed one of our brethren."

"He's gone from here, then."

"Yes. And good riddance. The devil is with him now, so I know he does not go with God." He looked severely up at Longarm. "He was a good worker before your arrival, Marshal. An unyielding man in some respects, but he pulled his weight. And Carrie was a dutiful wife. Do you wonder why we have settled here? Why we have tried to protect ourselves from the devilish influence of that world you represent?"

Longarm was not a theologian, and he did not intend to become one. Nor did he think much of the reverend and his settlement. But he could see how the man might think the way he did. After all, what had happened to Carrie and Calvin Newton could only be seen in his eyes as the direct result of Longarm and his party's arrival in their midst.

"Those horses he took. What can you tell me about them?"

"One was a roan, the other a gray."

"Which way'd he go?"

"South. The same direction from which he had come."

Longarm really did not have to ask the next question, but he felt he should ask it to be on the safe side. "Who's he after?"

"His wife—and you, Marshal. He said you nearly blinded him."

"I did that. He tried to kill me."

Reverend Wilson stepped back. "Go after him,

157

then," he said. "But all of us will pray most ferverently that neither you nor that fallen creature ever return again to this settlement."

"You're not going to wish me luck, is that it?"

"What luck can a godless man such as you possibly have?"

Reverend Wilson turned his back on Longarm then, and with a single wave of his hand sent his ranks of obedient brethren on their way. As his severely garbed followers broke ranks and moved off, Longarm noted that not since he had ridden into the settlement had he seen the face of a single woman or child. New Bethlehem, he decided, gave him the shudders.

As Reverend Wilson turned to look back up at Longarm, Longarm touched the brim of his hat in parting, and urged his mount on past him down the road. He would be glad to put this utopia behind him.

He was still an hour's ride at least from the canyon down which Sir Thomas's dig was located, and was moving up a gentle rise past a thick stand of alders, when the Arapaho band materialized on the crest of the ridge just ahead of him. Astride their ponies, some with lances, others with rifles, they regarded him solemnly and made no outcry. Chief Yellow Horn was the closest. As before, he was in full regalia, wearing his handsome chief's bonnet.

Longarm reined in and held up his palm in the universal Indian sign for peace. He was glad to be running into the Arapaho in a less belligerent fashion this time. The impassive faces of the braves behind Yellow Horn gave Longarm little comfort, however; and he had no difficulty recognizing the glowering visage of Black Horse. The brave sat to the right of Yellow Horn, his eyes boring into Longarm's like gun barrels.

158

"Hello, Chief," called Longarm. "Nice to see you again."

The chief turned his head slightly and said something to those braves closest behind him. Then he kneed his pony toward Longarm. When he was abreast of Longarm, he nodded in greeting and pulled up.

"I do not know if my heart is glad to see the white lawman again," Yellow Horn said. "When will you take me to see the giants of the earth standing up again? Such medicine would be good. Chief Yellow Horn needs such medicine now."

"What's the problem, Chief?"

Yellow Horn waited a moment, to see if he understood Longarm's blunt question. Then he decided he did. "Twisted Foot questions what you tell me. He says you lie. He says the serpents of our ancestors will rise up and kill us all if we make the giants of the earth walk again."

"This here Twisted Foot," Longarm said. "He's your medicine man?"

"He has powerful medicine, yes. He dreams many dreams."

"That so?"

Yellow Horn's eyes betrayed a momentary glint of humor. "Yes. That is so. Twisted Foot has dreamed many things. In his dreams he sees the whites falling into holes and dying. He has seen the dead Indians returning to enjoy the earth and all things left by the whites. He has seen the buffalo returning. But best of all," Yellow Horn said sadly, "he has seen the end of the white man. The whites are no more. They are wiped from the earth, and the land is clean again."

"You believe that, do you?"

"No. It would be good, but I cannot see it. Still, this matters not. I may be wrong. Twisted Foot may

159

see the future, as he says. And so it is my medicine against his."

Longarm saw at once the chief's dilemma. But he knew of no way to resolve Yellow Horn's difficulty. Denver—and that exhibition hall containing what were now apparently two dinosaur skeletons—was a long way off. Again Longarm mentally kicked himself for his impulsive offer to the chief. Now, it seemed, he was about to pay the penalty for promising this chief such a marvel. The one glimmer of hope that Longarm saw was the inescapable fact that both he and Yellow Horn had much to gain by stalling.

Longarm shrugged. "What can I do, Chief?"

"Take me to see the standing giants so that my medicine will be powerful enough to withstand that of Twisted Foot. If you do not do this thing you promised before, he will lead my band against those who now tear at the bones in the cliff. Of all the burial places of the serpents, this place of giants is our most sacred."

He should have been expecting that, Longarm realized wearily. "I cannot take you to see the standing giants, Chief. I am sorry. It is many miles from here, in the great city of Denver. I have much to do here before I can return to that city with you. You must wait."

Yellow Horn shook his head slowly, gravely. "No. Twisted Foot will not wait. You promise to show me this wonder, and now you say you cannot do this. How do I know the standing giants are in this city of Denver, as you say? It is a funny place for standing giants to go, is it not? They belong in the ground, where they sleep long and deep." He looked shrewdly at Longarm. "I think maybe Twisted Foot is right."

"Now, just hold on a mite, Chief. Why not take

160

me to see this medicine man of yours? Let me explain it to him."

"Twisted Foot will not listen. Like his brother Black Horse, he hates all white men."

Longarm sighed. "Let me try, Chief Yellow Horn. Then we will smoke together and be friends."

"You have good tobacco?"

"Yes. But first let me speak to this jasper, Twisted Foot."

Yellow Horn turned his head and spoke sharply to the band. At once, each brave turned his pony. Black Horse moved with as much alacrity as the others, but he did not miss the opportunity to fix Longarm with a murderous glance a moment before he spun his mount. Yellow Horn looked back at Longarm.

"We go now to our camp. We will see how well your tongue can match the dreams of Twisted Foot."

Yellow Horn turned his pony effortlessly and led the way into the alders, with Longarm following. He didn't see that he had much choice in the matter.

Two older Indians, obviously not as feisty as the young bucks, guarded the Indian encampment with trade muskets. One of them broke ahead of the riders and disappeared around a bend in the canyon. A moment later, Longarm and the rest of the party rode into a lush park. A cluster of tipis had been set up in the grassy bend of a mountain stream. Birch and alder stands flanked the stream. The air was clear and sweet. Longarm could understand what it was that made Twisted Foot and other Indians like him wish to return to such an Eden. And also why they hated the white man so much for taking all this from them.

Longarm had no difficulty spotting Twisted Foot. His deformity was obviously congenital, and he stood crookedly in front of his tipi with his bronzed

161

arms folded over his powerful chest. The tipi was set up on a slight knoll, a judicious distance from the rest of the encampment. Before Longarm could dismount, Black Horse had galloped up the knoll to his brother's side and flung himself from his horse to tell him why Longarm had accompanied them to their encampment.

Longarm caught the flash of defiance that transfigured the medicine man's darkly handsome face. Twisted Foot thrust out his chin and rocked back on his imperfect leg, obviously more than ready to challenge whatever Longarm might have to say.

Yellow Horn stood waiting as Longarm dismounted. "My friend," he said, "I hope you have much luck with Twisted Foot. I do not think Black Horse would like to see you ride from this camp alive. I think he still sings in his tipi of that white woman. There is something wrong with his heart, I think, that he likes the white woman too much." The chief shook his head at the thought as he started with Longarm across the fragrant grass toward Twisted Foot's tipi.

Glancing back, Longarm saw that the entire camp was following after them, the males in front, the squaws bringing up the rear. It was to be the white lawman against their medicine man, and Longarm had little doubt as to who their favorite was.

His arms still folded across his chest, Twisted Foot glared imperiously at Longarm as the tall lawman came to a halt before him. "Black Horse says you come here to speak with me of the giants in the earth."

"That's right, Twisted Foot. Chief Yellow Horn says you plan to attack the Englishmen who dig now at the cliff."

"They are tearing out the bones, the sacred bones of the ancient serpents. Only evil can come of this. We shall stop them. When we do that, the powerful medicine of the ancient bones will give us victory over all the white men." There was a loud murmur of appreciation and excitement from the braves listening to this fateful pronouncement. Aware of the effect he had created, Twisted Foot looked past Longarm and pronounced gravely, "I have seen it in my dreams! The white man's bones will become like stone and will be buried in the ground forever. And the serpents will arise and slay our enemies. Their medicine will bring back the buffalo!"

This was powerful talk, and Longarm recognized it as such. No white man could out-promise a medicine man of this audacity. He nodded solemnly instead and spoke judiciously.

"Twisted Foot has seen great things in his dream. They may well be true. I have seen the bones of these ancient lizards set upright, and I too have felt their terrible power. But your band is small. If you attack the Englishman and his workers, some of your people will die. The horse soldiers will come and chase you from this fine park. Let me tell the Englishman of your dream, so that he may decide if he wants to set loose the powerful medicine by releasing these bones from the cliffs."

Twisted Foot looked quickly, proudly around him at his tribesmen. Longarm's ploy of accepting at face value what Twisted Foot had just told him had given the medicine man great prestige among his fellows. That a white man would treat his pronouncements with such respect was almost unheard of for these people. So pleased was Twisted Foot that he found himself speaking with condescending magnanimity to Longarm.

"Go, then! Tell these Pale Eyes that they do evil to our spirits. They must leave the bones of these ancient serpents in the mountainside. Tell them to go, and we will not kill so many of them."

Longarm nodded gravely, as if he had been granted a great boon. "I will tell them, Twisted Foot. But you must promise not to unleash your powerful medicine until I return to tell you of the Englishman's decision."

"I will see to that," said Yellow Horn.

Longarm turned to face the chief. "I accept your promise, Yellow Horn. Now I will walk back to my horse. I have many hours to ride before I reach the cliff where the Englishman digs."

"I will go with you," said Yellow Horn.

Longarm and Yellow Horn walked some distance before either of them spoke. It was Yellow Horn who broke the silence.

"I have many dreams, like all who sleep," Yellow Horn remarked. "But my dreams do not tell of such wonderful events. And when I wake, I soon forget the shadows that visit me while I sleep. You are like me; you do not believe in Twisted Foot's dreams. I am wondering why my friend treats with such respect the dreams of Twisted Foot."

Longarm took out two cheroots and handed the chief one. The chief dug a clay pipe out of a pouch hanging at his side, broke up the cheroot, and stuffed it into the clay pipe. Longarm thumbed alight a sulfur match, lit his own cheroot, and handed the match to the chief. When the chief had his pipe going, he inhaled deeply and smiled contentedly.

"You are right, Yellow Horn," Longarm said, halting finally beside his buckskin. "But I needed time and now I have it. You can use this time also, to regain your leadership from this medicine man who dreams such dangerous dreams. There would have been no time if I had challenged Twisted Foot openly. How can you argue with a man's dreams?"

"That is true, friend," said Yellow Horn, puffing and nodding sagely. "This Indian has tried."

"Now I will speak to the Englishman, as I have promised. You must use this time to speak in the tribal council. Remind your people of what will happen if you do attack the Englishman's expedition. The blue coats would soon be hunting you. And afterward, your tribe would not be happy on agency land. This park is almost like it was in the Shining Times."

"That is so. You speak painful wisdom, friend."

"Call me Longarm," the lawman said as he stepped into his saddle. "If your counsel prevails, Chief, I will keep my old promise to you. Yellow Horn will see the giants standing. I will take you to the great city of Denver. When you return and relate what you have seen, you will become famous among your people."

Impressed, the chief stood back and looked somberly up at Longarm. "There is yet one more thing, friend Longarm," he said.

"What is that?"

The man's dark eyes glinted puckishly. "Does Longarm have any more of those fine sticks of tobacco?"

Longarm laughed, handed down to the chief another cheroot, waved, and rode back across the meadowland. It was getting late in the day, and he hoped he could make it to Sir Thomas's camp before nightfall.

He also hoped he did not meet any more unfriendlies. He was thinking, in particular, of Calvin Newton. And he was worried, very worried, about Carrie and Alf Riley. But first things first: he had to warn Sir Thomas—not only about the Indians, but about a man Charles Ogden Stewart might have unwittingly loosed on him, a gunslick named Sim Drucker.

Chapter 12

It was well past sundown when Longarm was halted by a voice barking coldly at him out of the darkness ahead of him.

"Hold up there, mister! Or I'll let both barrels go at you!" The voice belonged to Bill Reed, and it carried considerable authority.

Pulling up smartly, Longarm peered through the gloom at the dim figure crouching on a ledge above the trail, and caught the glint of moonlight on twin barrels.

"That you, Bill?" Longarm called. "This is Longarm. I see you got here all right."

"Sure enough. Didn't expect you. Ride on by. The camp's up the canyon less'n half a mile. Don't come on too fast, though, or one of them trigger-happy Englishmen will most likely blow your head off."

Longarm waved to Bill and urged his horse on past him, careful to keep at a nice, even, steady pace. He was challenged twice more before he reached the camp, the last time by a surprisingly menacing Denise Ashley. When at last he dismounted beside the still-roaring campfire, Sir Thomas and Isadora welcomed him heartily—but with what Longarm realized was considerable relief. They were like people under siege.

"What's been going on?" Longarm asked as

Sir Thomas's manservant took his horse. "This is a very nervous camp."

"Despite all our precautions, Longarm," Sir Thomas replied, "someone broke into our stores last night and stole considerable quantities of explosives."

"Explosives?"

"Dynamite, it is called," Sir Thomas explained, assuming wrongly that Longarm was not yet familiar with this new form of explosive. "We were using it to clear portions of overhanging rock that were impeding our progress."

"How did it happen?"

"The fellow who was guarding the tent where we've been keeping it was found dead inside the tent this morning, and almost all of our stores of dynamite were gone. His name was Ben O'Brien. A good worker. A teamster I hired in Dog Wells. His throat was cut. We buried him this afternoon."

"It was terrible," broke in Isadora. "Just terrible."

"I suppose it was my fault," said Sir Thomas. "After we demonstrated to you how effective and impregnable our defenses were, I am afraid I allowed the men to relax somewhat. We are in hostile country, Longarm, and I should never have allowed myself to forget that."

Young Tim Dinsdale, his arm still in a sling, brought out a camp chair for Longarm, and then the four of them sat down beside the fire while the cook brought Longarm coffee. Sipping the scalding coffee, Longarm questioned Sir Thomas further in an effort to find out what more the man could tell him. But Sir Thomas could give Longarm little help. No one had seen or heard a thing the night before, nor had anyone been seen at any other time skulking around the camp.

Leaning back in his chair finally, Longarm fin-

167

ished his coffee, then took out his cheroots and offered them around. Only Isadora took one. Longarm lit her cheroot and then his own. After a moment of silent puffing, he cleared his throat and told Sir Thomas what he had learned in the past few days.

He told the man about Pope's gang and Stewart's gunslicks, explaining without too much conviction that he was reasonably certain that Pope had been able to call off his boys, so that only Stewart's men remained on the loose and still anxious to do what they could to hinder Sir Thomas's work.

Isadora was outraged, especially when Longarm told them of his experiences personally with Sim Drucker and his three henchmen. Longarm had delicately decided to mention nothing about his use of the outhouse behind Chuck Ballenger's cabin, but the shooting death of Marge Tucker he related without holding back a thing. When he had finished, the three were awed, and fully aware then of the reckless and thoroughly criminal nature of these men that Stewart had sent after them. Longarm sat silently for a moment to let what he had told them sink in.

Then he told them about the Arapahos.

"My word!" Tim Dinsdale said softly.

"These aborigines, Longarm," Sir Thomas said. "Are you sure they cannot be bought off?"

"Bought off?"

"Trinkets. Blankets. I have heard that they are most taken by shiny objects. Beads and mirrors especially."

"Not this bunch, Sir Thomas."

Isadora looked at her brother. "Do you have enough fossils, Tom?" she asked.

Sir Thomas frowned as he tried to answer that question to his own and his sister's satisfaction. There was no doubt the man would like very much to continue digging the bones out of that cliff; but by

168

this time it was getting pretty obvious that he might just have to convince himself that he had found enough, that his work at this site was over.

Sir Thomas looked at his sister and winked. "I guess maybe I have at that, Isadora. Besides, if I don't get you out of this country soon, you'll become addicted to this man's cigars."

She laughed, relieved. "I am afraid I already am."

Sir Thomas looked at Longarm and explained, "I believe I have just made a very important discovery, Longarm."

"That so?"

"Yes. It is somewhat technical, I am afraid, but suffice it to say that I may have settled a long-standing debate among my fellow paleontologists with this find. Isadora is quite right in suggesting that I have found enough fossils—at least for this expedition. However, I would like to continue at the dig for at least another couple of days. Surely the Arapahos would not begrudge me that much more time."

Longarm took a deep breath. "Maybe. I'll go see the chief first thing tomorrow. I'll tell him you're getting ready to leave, but it will take a while for you to get all your gear together. Maybe I can get you a couple of days. Then again, it may not be necessary. There's a chance Yellow Horn can outwit that fool medicine man of his and take back control of his braves. You may not have to leave if that happens."

"Do you have any faith that Yellow Horn can do this, Longarm?" asked Isadora.

"He's a wily old cuss. And Indians don't get old unless they're pretty smart. Besides, I've given him a powerful incentive. He would give most of that war bonnet of his to see one of these here dinosaurs standing upright—even if it didn't have any skin left

169

on its hide. It would bring him great fame with his tribe."

"Well, then," said Sir Thomas, "I would appreciate it if you would go see this Indian as soon as possible, Longarm."

"Like I said, I'll go see him first thing in the morning. If I can find him. But I don't like this business of the dynamite. Whoever took it is planning some dangerous mischief, I'm thinking. So keep your camp guarded just as tight as before. Maybe it would be a good idea to ship out as many of them fossils as you can, just as soon as you can."

"Good idea," agreed Sir Thomas. "We'll finish wrapping them in the plaster and start loading by tomorrow evening."

Longarm got to his feet. "That means an early start for all of us tomorrow morning. I reckon I'll find myself a spot up in the pines."

"Of course, Longarm," said Sir Thomas, getting up also. "But are you sure you don't want to sleep in a tent tonight? There's room in mine for another cot."

"Thanks, Sir Thomas," Longarm said. Then he looked around at the towering walls of the canyon, the steep slopes of pine. "I guess I don't like this particular setup, that's all. You're all crowded together down here. You make a nice target, and we've got some wild ones out there, watching us maybe right now. I'd feel safer—and a lot more able to help—if I picked my own camp up on those slopes somewhere."

Sir Thomas shrugged and started for his tent. "As you wish, Longarm."

Tim Dinsdale bid Longarm goodnight and started for his tent also. Isadora stayed in her chair. She had almost finished her cheroot. She smiled at him in the darkness. He caught the flash of her teeth and the glow of her green eyes.

170

She dropped the remains of her cheroot in the campfire, stood up, and moved close to Longarm. "Are you trying to make it impossible for me, Longarm? Or just difficult?"

He laughed gently. "Neither, Isadora. I don't like tents, that's all. And I do like my privacy."

"You're a solitary man, aren't you, Longarm," she said. It was an assertion, not a question.

"I guess in my line of work, you have to be. You can't get much done if you're part of a gang."

"I sent Carrie up to your camp one night, and look what happened to her."

"Maybe you should get your sleep, then."

"I'll be the judge of that. You mustn't take me seriously. I was just teasing, that's all. And I don't have an irate husband who's liable to come after me."

"What about your brother?"

She leaned close to Longarm suddenly, and kissed him lightly on the cheek. As she did so, her left hand caressed his other cheek. Longarm was astonished at the electric effect this had on him; he was instantly willing to cut this game short. He turned to face her. She moved closer. Both of his arms were around her in an instant. He crushed her swiftly, hungrily against him and returned her kiss—on the lips. When he had finished with her, he stepped gently back and smiled down into her face.

"I reckon maybe we should forget about your brother," he told her.

She nodded and stepped closer to him, resting her head against his chest. "Yes," she whispered, trembling. "You go up. Find a spot on the highest slope, nearest the stars. Light a small fire. I'll find you."

"Isadora!" It was Sir Thomas.

She pushed quickly away from Longarm. Her

voice sounded strained as she called, "Yes, Tom? What is it?"

"I want you to sleep in my tent tonight. I've already had Jeffrey bring in the spare cot. I think it'll be safer for you."

"But, Tom! That's silly."

"I won't let you talk me out of it, Isadora! A man was murdered in this camp last night. You'll sleep in here with me, and I'll have a loaded shotgun at my side, with Jeffrey outside the tent on guard."

Sir Thomas had left his tent and was walking toward Isadora while he argued with her. When he saw Longarm still by the fire, he nodded to the lawman, pleased. "Still here, Longarm? Good. Perhaps you will add your voice to mine. You know how stubborn Isadora can be. Don't you think I'm right? Wouldn't she be safer in my tent tonight?"

Longarm looked at Isadora and smiled broadly. "Yes, Sir Thomas," he said. "I do believe she would."

"Oh, Longarm!" Isadora said, seeing the humor in it, as had Longarm. She laughed aloud.

"Goodnight, you two," Longarm said, touching his hatbrim to them both.

He stood for a moment, still smiling, as he watched Sir Thomas and Isadora head for the Englishman's tent. A few moments later, his bedroll on his shoulder, he trudged up through the pines, looking for a spot on the highest slope, nearest to the stars. But he would not light a fire because there would be no one looking for him this night—no one, that is, whom Longarm wanted to find him.

Longarm was mounted up and ready to ride out the next morning, when Isadora stopped him, her hand taking hold of the horse's reins. Looking up at him, she said, "I didn't sleep well."

"Why's that, do you think?"

"I was so well protected."

Longarm laughed.

"Anyway," she said, "I'm glad we're getting out of this canyon soon."

"Why?"

"It's awfully dry down here. And that stream, Longarm. It's our only source of fresh water and it's almost completely dry."

Longarm glanced momentarily up at the snow-clad peaks beyond the canyon and wondered at what Isadora had just told him; but he did not question her statement.

"Well, cheer up," he told her. "Maybe Yellow Horn will see his way clear to letting you and Sir Thomas stay a few weeks longer."

"Tom *would* appreciate that, I know."

"But you wouldn't."

"I know I shouldn't complain, Longarm. This dig means everything to Tom. But without water it is so hard to keep clean, and almost impossible for Cookie to prepare meals."

"Maybe we'll get some rain. Tell Sir Thomas I ought to be back sometime after noon."

She stepped back away from the horse and shaded her eyes as she looked up at him. "Be careful, Longarm."

He saluted her, touched his heels to the buck-skin's flanks, and rode off, squinting through the bright morning sunshine. As he left the camp, he passed Bill Reed and Denise loading a freight wagon.

Denny called out to him. She was standing in the wagon on top of a pile of fossils, the chunks of stone in which they were embedded wrapped in burlap soaked in plaster of paris. Already Denny was covered with the plaster dust, her face and hands especially. Longarm pulled up as Denny grinned

173

down at him, her arms akimbo, a broad smudge of plaster on her right cheek.

"Thought you might want to know, Longarm."

"Know what?"

"About Bill and me. We're getting hitched, soon as we finish this job."

Bill Reed was pushing a wheelbarrow full of fossils toward the freight wagon. Longarm glanced over at him. "Just heard the good news, Bill."

The man stopped pushing the barrow and straightened. Mopping the sweat off his forehead with his big red bandanna, he grinned sheepishly. "I went and asked her and she said yes. Never thought I'd let myself in for it, but I did. Guess there's a first time for everything."

Longarm looked back up at Denny. "Congratulations, Denny."

"You ain't jealous?"

Longarm smiled at her warmly, a twinkle in his eyes. "Well, maybe a little."

She grinned then, and slapped her thigh. "I was hopin' you would be. Thanks, Longarm. You're a real gentleman."

Longarm had no difficulty in finding his way back to the park where Yellow Horn's Arapahos had made their camp. But when he got there, he found that the Indians had moved on without a trace. He didn't like that. He had left Twisted Foot with the understanding that after he talked to Sir Thomas, Longarm was to return to the medicine man and tell him whether or not the paleontologist would leave the canyon. From the looks of it, Twisted Foot and his brother Black Horse had had no intention of waiting for his return—or Sir Thomas's reply.

They had already made up their minds to attack. Yellow Horn had lost all effective control of his young bucks, and the medicine man was in charge, along with his brother Black Horse. If the pattern continued, Black Horse would be the new chief. Longarm remembered then what the chief had told him during their first encounter: Black Horse was a young brave and must show courage, must count coup—or no woman of his tribe would have him. If it was true of Black Horse, it was true of every buck in the tribe.

Count coup.

Longarm decided he had better get back to the dig. Sir Thomas and the rest of his workers—and that included Bill Reed and that perky fiancee of his, Denise Ashley—had better move out while they still had a chance.

He turned his horse about and loped across the lush meadowland, intent on getting back to the dig within a few hours, before noon if he did not spare his horse. And he had no intention of sparing it.

It was while Longarm was approaching the side canyon down which he had trailed Calvin Newton and Carrie that he heard the first detonation. The pounding of the buckskin's hooves on the hard, dry ground caused him to doubt his ears at first. But as the second blast thundered down the side canyon, there was no doubt in Longarm's mind as to what he was hearing. A quick glance up at the cloudless blue sky convinced him it could not have been a peal of thunder.

Hauling in the buckskin, Longarm sat the horse silently, his head lifted, every sense alert as he waited for any further explosions. When the third one came, he turned his horse up the side canyon. There was no longer any doubt about it. Someone up that canyon was tossing dynamite. Probably the same dynamite that had just been stolen from Sir Thomas.

By the time Longarm had ridden half a mile into

175

the canyon, he had a pretty good idea who was using the dynamite and what his purpose was: Calvin Newton had returned to punish Carrie. And he'd stolen some thunder with which to do it.

Longarm left his horse a quarter-mile from Alf Riley's cabin, hauled his Winchester out of its boot, then scrabbled his way up the canyon wall to the rim. It was not long before he was within sight of Riley's place—what was left of it, rather.

The roof was gone and only two sides were still standing, their window frames blown out. A black pillar of smoke was still pumping skyward from the blasted-out interior. If Carrie and Alf Riley had been in that shack when the dynamite had been thrown into it, they could not possibly have survived.

Longarm noticed a smoking crater near the mine entrance. Looking more closely at the shaft itself, he thought he detected pieces of supporting timber that had been blown out, and yes, there was a thin pall of smoke coming from the mine. He looked back at the cabin. The smoke coming from it was still dense. Gleaming tongues of flame were visible inside the shack, and occasionally a leaping flame would flash within the bowels of the smoke.

The dynamiting of Riley's cabin had been done after Newton had sent his sputtering sticks into the mine. That seemed to point to a very disturbing possibility: that the bombing of the mine came first, after Calvin had trapped his wife and Alf inside it. The destruction of the cabin was simply a final, obliterating act of spitefulness.

Which meant, more than likely, that Carrie and Alf were dead—while their murderer remained on the loose—and nearby yet, from the looks of that still-burning cabin.

Longarm felt cold beads of perspiration standing out on his forehead. He wanted Calvin Newton. He wanted him bad. Though Longarm had damaged the man considerably, still he managed to rise up again and again to wreak his havoc on Carrie, on Longarm, and now on Alf Riley. As Longarm's eyes peered carefully down at the canyon floor, he noted to himself that even Reverend Wilson and his black-clad followers would welcome the death of this ruined maniac.

Longarm finished his painstaking scrutiny of the canyon. Nothing. Not a movement, not a sound. The canyon floor and the ledge just above it were as still as death. Longarm took a deep breath and moved cautiously out from behind the clump of juniper he had used for cover, and started to angle down the steep slope.

Halfway down, he reached a level, grassy sward and threw himself down on the cool grass to rest up and perhaps have another look around. Hunkered down in the grass, he was just lifting off his hat to wipe the sweat from his forehead when the sharp crack of a revolver came from above him. He had moved his head slightly forward as he reached up for the hatbrim, and that small movement saved his life.

The round whispered past his left ear, slammed into a patch of exposed bedrock, and whined off into the canyon. Longarm flung himself toward a huge boulder and flattened against it. He was out of sight of his attacker, but that gave him little comfort. He knew it was Calvin because the man had used a six-gun, not a rifle; his broken jaw still made firing a rifle too painful. And the shot had come from just above him. Calvin had missed with his sixgun, but he could still have a few more sticks of that dynamite.

Longarm wasted no time thinking about it. Moving around the boulder, he found himself facing a smooth wall of rock that offered him precious little purchase, except for a single high crack and a tough little jack pine clinging to a narrow shelf just above it. Longarm ran at the wall, managing to reach the crack and then stretch to his full height as he grabbed one of the jack pine's roots. For a moment he thought the root was going to pull out under his weight, and he almost dropped his rifle in order to grasp a second root with his right hand.

But the root held, and Longarm was able to pull himself up onto the shelf. Easing himself along the treacherous path, he came to a fairly large cleft in the rock and ducked swiftly into it, crouching, his rifle held out in front of him. Beyond the cleft he caught the bright, sunlit gleam of a trail leading steeply upward.

It was at that instant that the world just behind him disintegrated in a deafening, shuddering blast that flung him almost to the end of the cleft. Dazed, he turned his head to look back. A swirling cloud of dust and debris was pumping up from a spot just below the cleft in the rock. Longarm was right. Calvin Newton was up there, and he had plenty of dynamite.

Longarm turned his head and peered out at the trail. It remained empty, and still seemed to offer a quick way up to his attacker. He hesitated only an instant to lever a fresh cartridge into his Winchester's firing chamber, then darted from the cleft and raced up the steep trail. It twisted diabolically as it followed around boulders and the tall, grotesque fingers of rock sculpted out of the sandstone. His low-heeled, army-issue boots made little noise on the steep trail, but they were not silent. He kept climbing steadily for some time before he broke suddenly into a grassy pocket. Two horses were grazing on a shaded portion of the flat. They lifted their heads from the grass to gaze at him, their ears flicking nervously.

Longarm halted, moved against a wall of limestone outcropping that rose sheerly almost straight

178

up, and looked quickly around. The horses turned and went back to cropping the grass. Longarm listened. He was certain that these two horses were the same mounts Calvin had stolen from New Bethlehem. Finding no trace of Longarm, Calvin would eventually have to return to the horses. Since Longarm reasoned that he was now above Calvin, he decided to stay right where he was and wait for the man to make his appearance.

He was still waiting when he saw Calvin's shadow on the grass near the horses. The sun was directly behind Calvin and showed him high above Longarm, standing slowly, carefully erect. Longarm saw his danger at once and darted out onto the grass and spun about, his rifle already at his shoulder. Calvin was in plain sight, standing on the limestone ledge, an already lit stick of dynamite sputtering in his upraised hand. Longarm's sudden move had startled him. He hesitated.

Longarm fired—not at Calvin, but at the stick of dynamite in his hand. It was something he would not have attempted had he given it any thought. But everything was happening too fast for deliberation, and he squeezed off the round almost the instant he saw Calvin above him.

It was a fine shot: the dynamite exploded above Calvin's head, taking his hand and most of his arm, and flinging what was left of the man off the rock. He struck once on his way down, tumbled over, and disappeared from Longarm's sight. The detonation was still resounding powerfully among the rocks when Longarm reached the lip of the canyon and looked down. Less than ten yards below him, Calvin Newton was flat on his back. The man had landed on a narrow red tongue of sandstone that jutted out high over the canyon floor.

Peering down at Newton, Longarm was appalled at what he saw. He was not sure at first that the man was still alive. It had been a considerable plunge, and that dynamite charge had gone off no more than a few feet from his head. Peering closer, Longarm caught sight of the man's chest. It was rising and falling, faintly but regularly. Longarm should have been surprised, but he was not. Something demonic possessed this man.

His chin was still wrapped in that bandage Longarm had wound around his head. It had swollen grotesquely as his beard continued to grow under it. Another bandage, this one not quite as filthy, was wrapped around the side of his head, covering the eye Longarm had blasted. A good deal of the hair was gone from one side of his head, and the flesh where the hair had been now looked like raw meat. Newton's remaining three limbs were twisted unnaturally, and here and there the jagged ends of broken bones protruded bloodily through his clothing. Yet he still breathed.

Longarm saw the man's painful efforts to move. The one remaining eye flickered open. Longarm could not be sure, but he thought Newton could see him looking down at him. The sight of Longarm appeared to galvanize Newton. His chest heaved convulsively, and for a brief moment he managed to lift the bloodied stump that had been his right arm. He almost appeared to be shaking it at Longarm. Then it crashed to the ledge, still feebly pumping blood.

Longarm glanced up at the clear sky. A buzzard was drifting high, like a cinder caught in an updraft. Soon, Longarm knew, it would catch sight of Calvin Newton and begin to drop. Others would join it. The humane thing would be to kill Calvin with a clean shot through the head; otherwise, with Calvin unable to move, the buzzards would squat on his chest and begin tearing with their voracious beaks at his still-living flesh.

180

Leaning carefully over the rim, Longarm brought his rifle up and caught Calvin's ravaged face in his sight. Calvin's remaining eye was distended in fury as it stared unblinkingly up at him. Longarm lowered the rifle, thought a moment, then stepped back away from the canyon's rim. He would let the vultures handle the *coup de grace*. They would not be as merciful as a bullet, maybe, but they would get the job done.

A moment later, as Longarm followed the steep trail back to the floor of the canyon, the shadows of three swooping buzzards flickered across his path.

Chapter 13

The strong smell of cordite still hung in the mine's entrance. Longarm worked his way into the shaft cautiously, trying not to dislodge those beams that were still standing. He had to pick his way over tangled and blasted debris, and it got no better as he progressed further into the shaft.

At last, where the stench of the blasting powder was the strongest, he came to a slight depression in the floor. He eased himself into it and picked his way through the gloom across the crater until he was brought up short by a solid wall of rock and rubble, with a few posts and beams sticking out through it. The dynamite had brought the roof of the shaft down at this point.

Longarm scrambled up the sloping wall, pulling himself along by grabbing hold of the beams poking through. He was within a foot of the roof when he heard the faint sound of a pick striking steadily at stone. Poking his head still closer to the cave-in, he thought he caught the sound of voices coming from the other side of the cave-in. He withdrew his Colt and rapped its barrel smartly against a boulder wedged under a crossbeam. Almost immediately there was an answering rap from the other side.

"Can you hear me?" Longarm cried.

At once Alf's voice came, faint but audible. He was telling Longarm that he could hear him. Then came Carrie's higher, clearer voice calling his name.

"I'm going for help!" Longarm yelled back. "I won't be long!"

Holstering his Colt, Longarm scrambled back down the slope of debris and hurried from the mineshaft. He had told them he wouldn't be long, and he hoped that wasn't a lie. But he was worried. How much air remained in that mineshaft?

The last thing he heard as he grabbed his buckskin's reins and swung into his saddle was the faint, eerie *tink* of Alf Riley's pickaxe. Strange that he hadn't heard it before when he first entered the mine; yet now it seemed as clear and as tangible as a bird's song in the morning.

Longarm could smell the fire a mile down the canyon. His horse caught the bite of it on the wind about the same time he did. Clapping his heels to the animal's flanks, he covered the remaining mile swiftly.

Bursting around a bend in the canyon, he was stunned by what he saw. The pine-clad slopes on both sides of the canyon were afire, and a hot wind was sweeping the flames down the slopes toward the camp. As Longarm rode his skittish mount into the camp, he saw Sir Thomas frantically trying to direct the evacuation. To Longarm's astonishment, the man seemed only recently to have begun to break camp.

Dismounting, he strode swiftly to the Englishman's side. "What's keeping you, Sir Thomas? You'll be trapped in this canyon if you don't haul out of here now!"

The man frowned in dismay. "You're right, Longarm. We wasted valuable time trying to extinguish the blaze on that north slope. Only when we had almost succeeded in creating a firebreak did we become aware of the fire on the other side. My God, Longarm! These fires were deliberately set!"

183

Longarm glanced up grimly at both slopes. Yes, that figured. It was the kind of action a man like Sim Drucker would favor. He looked back at Sir Thomas.

"You'll just have to ride out of here without all this gear, then. Take only what you can haul on your back!"

"But all this expensive equipment, Longarm! And the freight wagons. They are loaded with fossils. I can't abandon them!"

"Well, drive them out of this canyon now—before you get cut off!"

The man nodded quickly. "Yes," he said, slapping Longarm on the shoulder. "That's good advice."

Sir Thomas started down the slope toward the wagons, calling out to the teamsters. Longarm looked around for Isadora and saw her grimly packing a huge trunk just inside the entrance to her tent. When she saw him approaching, her face brightened.

"Oh, Longarm! Isn't this terrible! But I'm so glad you're here. Tom is beside himself. He almost stopped the fire, but another one started!" She glanced down at her clothing piled on her cot. "I don't know *what* to pack first!"

"Don't pack anything. Leave everything here and ride out of this canyon. You'll all be cut off in less than an hour, from the looks of this."

"Leave all my things, Longarm!" She was distraught.

"You heard me."

Longarm turned then, and looked back up at the closest slope. The fire was crackling along sharply now, its flames leaping from tree to tree, sending rocketlike cinders skyward. The roar of the onrushing flames was getting louder by the minute, and a sharp, acrid pall of smoke had already fallen over the canyon floor, giving everything a pale blue cast

184

and digging at Longarm's eyes, which were beginning to smart. Turning his head, he saw that the pines on the far side of the stream actually seemed to be burning more fiercely. He then glanced down at the neck of the canyon.

Another, fresh blaze had been set there!

"Look!" Longarm cried, pointing.

"Oh, my God, Longarm!" Isadora cried. "How are we going to get out of here?"

"Whoever set that last fire is still down there. Tell Sir Thomas to move what you can into the stream bed. Shallow as it is now, it's all the protection you're going to have before long."

As Longarm spoke, he started swiftly from the camp, heading in the direction of this new fire.

"Longarm!" Isadora cried. "Where are you going?"

"Never mind! Do as I told you. Hurry!"

As Longarm ducked into the pines just beyond the camp, he began to run, his Colt out. There was a patch of untouched timber between the burning slope and that new section of burning pine at the canyon's entrance. He expected to find his quarry in the unscathed timber, or near it, perhaps close to the canyon wall. For those who had set that last blaze, this was the only direction they could take if they wanted to escape the blazing canyon.

Crouching low, he scrambled past a crackling wing of flaming pine that was sweeping rapidly toward the canyon floor. It almost trapped him; and as Longarm outdistanced the fire, he had to use his hat to slap his way through a section of flaming underbrush. At last he was beyond the burning timber, scrambling up a slope toward the still-untouched stand of pine.

He was almost out of it, and could see beyond the trees to the white walls of the canyon, when he heard the thunder of pounding hooves. He turned toward the sound and thrashed through the underbrush, his elbow held up in front of his face to ward off the branches as he plunged along. He broke into the clear just as four horsemen, one of them with his arm in a sling, appeared directly ahead of him, galloping up the slope in single file along a shale-littered trail that followed the base of the canyon.

They saw him the moment he broke out of the timber, and grabbed for their sidearms. But Longarm had his Colt already in his hand. He pulled up and fired carefully at the lead rider, the fellow with the shoulder wound—the one who had shot Marge Tucker.

The man was hit. He slumped forward over his horse's neck, pulling his mount sharply to the right and off the trail. The horse stumbled, then righted itself and plunged down the slope, heading toward a section of blazing timber.

But Longarm was unable to follow the man's course for more than an instant, as he found himself returning fire from the remaining horsemen. A bullet slammed into a tree behind him. He tracked the closest rider and squeezed off a shot. The fellow peeled backward off his horse. The last rider had his rifle out by this time. Longarm flung himself to the ground, steadied his gunhand with his left, and fired. The rider dropped his rifle and fell loosely off his horse.

The fourth rider, Sim Drucker, disappeared up the trail.

Longarm heard a man screaming from below. He got to his feet, turned, and saw dimly the figure of the first one he had shot. The man was staggering about in the midst of a flaming patch of timber. His horse, wide-eyed and frenzied, was plunging wildly in ever-widening circles, as first one flaming barrier and then another crashed down in front of it. Longarm caught one last glimpse of the gunslick who had killed Marge. He was spinning blindly under a crashing pine, its entire length a seething ribbon of fire. The man disappeared in the flames. His ragged screams did not cease suddenly.

Turning back to the two downed riders, Longarm approached the nearest body carefully, his .44 at the ready.

The fellow was dead, a bullet through his temple. It had gone in neat as a nail, but had come out the other side like a fist. Longarm looked away from him and headed toward the next one, the fellow with the rifle. As Longarm neared him, the man groaned and pushed himself to a sitting position. When he saw Longarm approaching, he grabbed for his Winchester, but it was out of reach.

Longarm smiled and leveled his Colt .44 at the fellow's head, sighting coolly along the barrel. "Give me an excuse, you son of a bitch," Longarm told him coldly.

At once the man's hands shot up. He did not appear to be seriously wounded.

"Get up!" Longarm barked.

Slowly, painfully, the gunslick got to his feet. It was then that Longarm recognized him. He was Charlie, the first cardplayer Longarm had dunked in the outhouse. At almost the same moment the fellow appeared to recognize Longarm.

His lean face went beet-red with fury, his sad, mournful eyes blazing with sudden indignation. Longarm laughed softly, meanly. "I see you got cleaned up some, Charlie. Not much, but some."

"I ought—"

"There's plenty of things you *ought* to do. One of them is burn. And I think I'm going to see to that right now. Hellfire may have seemed like a long way off when you got up this morning, but you and your buddies have given me all I need to roast you right now."

187

"I'm hurt!" the man bleated, his lean figure quivering with fear. "You already done shot me!"

"Where?"

The man moistened his lips desperately. "Here! Right in my side!"

Longarm approached the fellow warily, instructed him to turn around, took his sidearm, then checked his side. His belt was cut through and the skin was broken. A heavy shield of coagulating blood ran from his waist to his thigh. But the bleeding had already stopped. The belt had saved him.

"You ain't hurt bad enough to bother with," Longarm told him.

With the barrel of his Colt, Longarm prodded the man back down the slope until they reached a grassy ledge that led over a raging piece of burning timber. The smoke was so thick that Longarm found it difficult to see the man ahead of him clearly.

"All right," Longarm told the man. "Hold up. This is close enough."

They were standing on bedrock, the thick smoke coiling up from the slope below. Longarm was breathing through a handkerchief he held up to his mouth. He moved around the wounded gunslick until the fellow was facing him with his back to the drop. Longarm took a step forward and waggled his gun menacingly to force the outlaw closer to the edge. Glancing back at the inferno below him, Charlie turned back to Longarm, terrified.

"For the love of Jesus, mister! Don't do it! I don't want to fry!"

"Why not? You set this damn fire, now you burn in it!"

"There's a way out, I tell you! You can stop this fire before it gets to them down there! I tell you, there's a way!"

Longarm stepped close to the fellow and grabbed him by the collar of his filthy shirt. He had wanted to see this man fry the way the other one had. And then he was going after his boss. Yet this man sounded too frightened to be lying.

"Out with it, you son of a bitch," Longarm snarled. "What the hell do you mean? How can this hell you planted down there be stopped? How?"

"The dam!"

"What dam?"

"The one Pope's gang built, up the canyon. They been trying to cut off the water to the camp, so that Englishman and his party'd pull out. But they couldn't dam all the water, not enough to drive them out. So Drucker, he talked to Tracy, and they decided to give you fellows a hotfoot. We didn't mean to hurt nobody, just scare you all out of here!"

It sounded just crazy enough to convince Longarm. People didn't have to be very smart to wear guns and get drunk and set fires.

Longarm flung the sad-eyed gunslick to the ground away from the ledge, aimed carefully, then pulled the trigger. A hunk of real estate near the man's right hand exploded, showering him with the dirt. "Where's the dam?"

The man pointed frantically up the canyon. "It's a couple of miles north! Pete Tracy and Dawson found a narrow bend in the canyon. They used dynamite to cause a rockfall, and it blocked the canyon. Then they just added more rocks as the water piled up behind it."

Longarm stepped closer, his handkerchief still held up to his mouth. "You want to live, mister?"

The man nodded eagerly.

"There's two horses back there. Ride with me down to the camp, then show me the way to that dam!"

"You mean ride through . . . through *that*, down there? Then up the canyon?"

"You heard me."

"The man's mournful eyes went tragic. "I don't have no choice, do I?"

"You got a choice. You can stay here or go with me."

"You mean burn or go with you. Hell, I'm liable to burn either way."

"If you go with me, you might have more of a chance to stay alive—for a while longer, anyway."

"That's the deal?"

"That's it, mister."

The man shrugged resignedly. "My name's Charlie. Charlie Terhune."

"Let's go get them horses, Charlie. We got us some riding to do."

Despite the stream's shallow flow, Sir Thomas had done a pretty good job of wetting everything down, wagons and anything else he could haul or carry into the stream. Longarm quickly gave them the reason for the stream's lack of depth. And then he told Sir Thomas and Isadora what he planned to do.

"Blow up the dam, Longarm?" Isadora cried.

"In less than an hour, those fires will be reaching the shore of this stream. By that time the smoke and heat will exhaust most of the oxygen in this canyon. I've seen what canyon fires can do. The heat will blister you and drive the animals mad. But maybe I can drown this fire. Soon as you give me the dynamite, tie these wagons down, and let them float, with all of you inside. And then let the animals loose so they can swim free."

"But that means dumping all my fossils!" said Sir Thomas.

"Which do you want to save, Sir Thomas? Bones, or you and the rest of your party?"

"The answer to that is obvious, Longarm."

"Then fetch the dynamite."

"I'll get it, Longarm!" called Bill Reed. He and Denny, along with the rest of Sir Thomas's crew, had been listening intently. "It's over here in our wagon. We been trying to keep what's left of it from blowing up.".

"Is it dry?"

"It's dry enough," the man replied, mopping his streaming face.

"It better be," Longarm muttered, as he looked around him and saw the growing wall of fire that was marching through the pines toward them.

Protected by their slickers, over which they had thrown thoroughly soaked blankets, Longarm and Charlie Terhune rode up the almost dry stream bed. The dynamite they carried under the slickers, in pouches slung over their shoulders.

They had all they could do to keep their horses from bolting as the flames crackled closer. At one treacherous spot, they had to dismount and lead their horses through a veritable wall of flame. They kept their soaked blankets on themselves and over the heads of their mounts and managed to keep going until at last they were through the worst of it, beyond the pine slopes.

They mounted up and rode on through the winding, sheer-sided walls of the upper canyon. Pretty soon they found they could discard their blankets and slickers, and Longarm was able to blink away the tears in his stinging eyes. He began to watch carefully the rims of the canyon towering high above them.

"Over there," Charlie said finally, pointing to a narrow game trail that wound up the flank of one wall. "That'll bring us up behind the dam."

A shot rang out from the opposite rim of the canyon. As the round ricocheted off the wall beside

191

Charlie, he cried, "Jesus!" and spurred his horse toward the trail.

Longarm followed close behind as two more rifle shots cracked from the rim. After about fifty yards, shouldering fingers of rock shielded both riders from the canyon's rims. The firing ceased.

Turning back to face Longarm, his face drawn with fear, Charlie cried, "They seen us! They know we're comin'! We better give this up, Longarm! If a bullet hits these pouches, we'll blow clear to the moon!"

Longarm drew his Colt and smiled at Charlie. "Shut up and keep going, or *I'll* blow you clear to the moon!"

The man turned back around in his saddle and rowelled his horse savagely up the narrow trail.

They were almost clear of the trail, approaching the canyon's rim, when a fusillade of shots rang out from the rocks just ahead. The rounds whistled past them so close that Longarm could almost believe he might have seen them, had he been looking sharply enough.

"Off your horse, Charlie!" he cried, snaking his Winchester from its boot. He flung himself off the buckskin and into a narrow cleft in the rocks beside the trail.

Charlie did not wait for Longarm to tell him a second time. Squeezed down beside Longarm in the cramped area, he turned his wide, frightened eyes to the lawman. "What smart idea you got now, Marshal? All we're goin' to do is get ourselves blown into smithereens. We ain't nowhere near that dam!"

"You call out to them buzzards with the rifles, Charlie. You tell them it's you. And tell them you got a friend with you."

"A friend?"

"Yeah. Tell them Bill Reed wants to throw in

with them. If they ask why, say he had a beef with Sir Thomas."

"It won't work," the man bleated. "They all know you. Drucker seen you at Ballenger's cabin, and Pete Tracy and Dawson, they seen you in Dog Wells."

"You just do as I tell you, Charlie. Now hurry it up! We don't have all that much time!"

As another couple of rounds ricocheted off the rock in front of them, Charlie raised his quavering voice and shouted out to the men who he was. It took a while for them to hear him. The shooting stopped then, as one of the outlaws questioned Charlie, asking him who he had with him.

"Bill Reed!" Charlie called back. "He wants to join up with us!"

"You mean he wants to keep his hide from getting blistered! All right, come ahead, Charlie."

Longarm grabbed Charlie's arm. "Tell them you just been hit, you and Bill. Swear at them for shooting first and asking questions after. Tell them you need their help and make it sound desperate, *real* desperate."

Swallowing, Charlie nodded, turned back around, and did what Longarm had instructed. Longarm was impressed at the whining misery Charlie was able to get into his voice as he complained bitterly of his treatment by his own trigger-happy saddlemates. As Charlie bleated out his unhappiness, Longarm climbed to a cleft about ten feet above the trail, and found he had an unobstructed view of the trail and the rim beyond.

"They're comin'!" Charlie called up to Longarm. "What are you goin' to do?"

"What the hell do you think I'm going to do?"

"Jesus! Don't miss or they'll blow me up!"

Longarm grinned down at the trembling outlaw.

193

"Don't worry, Charlie. You're fighting on the side of the law now."

And then Longarm caught sight of the two outlaws scrambling down the trail toward them. He had already levered a cartridge into his Winchester's chamber. Now he sighted on the closest outlaw, one of the men he had seen entering the Red Dog with William Edward Pope. He did not recognize the outlaw behind him. Longarm waited until both men stopped cautiously and peered into the cleft where Charlie was crouched.

"That you in there, Charlie?" the first one called nervously. "You don't look so good."

Longarm caught the fellow's chest in his sights and squeezed off a shot. As the man went crashing back, a neat black hole in his dirty shirt, the other one swung up his own rifle. But Longarm had already levered. His second shot caught this outlaw in the throat. The man's head rolled crookedly back, he lost his hat, and as the steaming blood gouted from his neck, he sank into his own gore, a dead man. For a moment Longarm tracked the first one. But when he saw no movement from him either, he climbed swiftly down, inspected both dead outlaws, and waved Charlie out of the cleft.

"Let's go," Longarm said impatiently.

The man had been frightened earlier. He was petrified now as he looked with wide, staring eyes at Longarm.

"I said let's go!" Longarm commanded harshly.

On weak knees, the fellow scrambled out of the cleft. Longarm grabbed him by the shoulder and shoved him roughly ahead of him, past the two dead men.

"Lead the way, Charlie. I want to see that dam! We're wasting time!"

A few moments later they were peering over the

canyon's rim. Longarm was astonished. A clear lake of sparkling water extended as far back as he could see from the crude but effective dam.

"Whose idea did you say this was?" Longarm asked Charlie.

"Pete Tracy and Dawson. They figured when Pope found out how neatly they had scared off that Englishman from this new dig of his, Pope would have to come across with more money."

"But it wasn't Pope's idea?"

Charlie shook his head. "No. The pipsqueak's been tryin' to pull out of his deal with Tracy. But Tracy wouldn't have none of it."

"So I see," muttered Longarm, glancing back down at the dam. "Where'd you get that dynamite you say Tracy used to blow that rock into the canyon?"

"Dawson stole it from the Englishman."

"Alone?"

"There was a crazy guy with him. His face was a mess and most of it was hidden in bandages. He was with us awhile, and when Tracy started talking about the dam, he was the one suggested we use the dynamite and told us where we could get it."

"You killed a man to get that dynamite."

"It wasn't Dawson. It was the other one—and he lit out with half a case of the stuff before he got back here. Dawson said he was glad to see the son of a bitch go. He was a real looney."

"Yeah," Longarm said, looking back down at the dam. "He was that."

"How we goin' to get down there?" Charlie asked, the trace of a whine creeping back into his voice.

"We'll climb down. Now!"

"We can't!"

"Why not?"

Charlie pointed. "Behind that big rock, you can

195

see down onto a ledge. Down there's where Tracy and the rest of his boys is camped. It's level with the dam and gives them a clear view of it. Soon as we reach it, they'll have us in their sights."

"We can see them from the other side of that boulder, you say?"

Charlie nodded.

"Let's go," Longarm said.

"Where?"

"Follow me."

Peering carefully around the boulder, Longarm saw that Charlie had been telling the truth. Well below them, there was a broad ledge with a narrow trail leading from it, back into the rocks. Saddles and other gear were dumped around the remains of a campfire. The place was littered with the detritus of sloppy men, sloppy men who were bored. Watching a dam had not proved to be all that exciting.

Three men were visible. One of them was Sim Drucker. The other two Longarm recognized as members of the gang that had crowded into the Red Dog Saloon with Pope. "Which one is Tracy?" Longarm asked Charlie.

"The big man, the fellow with the red hatband and the fancy boots. The one beside him is Dawson. He's a mean one, he is."

Longarm studied the three men. Only one of them, Dawson, was watching the dam. Tracy and Drucker were passing a bottle back and forth while they searched the rim above them anxiously, with shaded eyes. If Longarm tried to pick them off from this distance—the range was almost two hundred yards—he could not possibly get them all. There was enough cover around that ledge to make it possible for anyone that Longarm did not pick off to hole up and keep Longarm from that dam long enough

196

to let every living thing fry in that seething canyon below them.

Even as he thought this, he glanced southward and saw the dark pall of smoke pumping up from the blazing canyon. The smoke was growing in intensity with each passing moment.

Drucker suddenly yelled up at the rim of the canyon. "Hey, Pound! Withers! You get them two? What's going on?"

Longarm took out a cheroot, lit it, and glared sideways at Charlie. "If you let out a sound, I'll toss you down there onto that ledge. You won't bounce, you'll blow up."

"Listen! Like you said, Longarm. I'm on the side of the law now!"

"Remember that."

Longarm reached into his pouch and pulled out three sticks of dynamite. The fuse protruding from each one was short enough—perhaps too short. He had a roll of safety fuse in the pouch, but he decided to go with the length he had. As he placed the three sticks of dynamite down carefully in front of him, Charlie shrank back.

Longarm looked back down at the ledge, measuring the distance once more. Then, reaching down, he plucked up a stick of dynamite and held the lighted end of his cheroot to the fuse. He flung the dynamite at the one watching the dam. Before the first stick blew, Longarm had touched the cheroot to another fuse and flung the second stick of dynamite at the two remaining men. The first blast swept the man watching the dam off the ledge. The second stick landed behind the other two. The blast sent them flying. One of them was flung along the ledge, his head smashed into the base of a rock slab. The other one, Drucker, was already on his feet, scrambling crookedly toward the path leading into the rocks. Longarm lit the next stick of dynamite and threw it after him. The dynamite detonated in the rocks above the trail, but Drucker had already disappeared from sight.

"Those rocks down there," Longarm said to Charlie. "What's the fastest way down to them?"

"This way," Charlie said, setting out along a narrow game trail that led down into a stand of jack pine.

A moment later, the click of iron on stone caused Longarm to reach out and pull Charlie back, then slam him against a wall of rock. He was just in time as Sim Drucker's riderless horse bolted past them both, nostrils flaring, eyes wild. With a finger to his lip, Longarm cautioned Charlie to remain silent, then continued along the narrow trail, his rifle held ready in front of him.

The chink of spurs warned him of Drucker's approach.

Longarm crouched and waited. Drucker appeared on the trail ahead of him less than ten feet away, his eyes starting from his head, a sixgun in his hand. Obviously intent on overtaking his horse, he could probably still hear that blast ringing in his head.

"Hold it right there, Drucker. I'm a deputy U.S. marshal!"

The man pulled up and straightened. He was incredulous. "You!" he cried. "A federal marshal! Chuck said you was just a drifter after his woman!"

"Drop the gun, Drucker."

"No! Don't drop it!" cried Charlie from behind Longarm. "I got the marshal covered, Sim! We got him between us! He didn't know I had this gun!"

Drucker's eyes lit as he saw Charlie with the gun. Longarm didn't bother to turn around; cursing himself for letting Charlie get behind him, Longarm flung himself to the right behind some rocks. Charlie's first shot ricocheted off the rock wall inches

198

above his head; but it was a clean miss, and that was all Longarm could hope for at this juncture. Spinning about and levering rapidly, Longarm sighted over a low rock just as Charlie fired a second time. The slug tore Longarm's hat off his head, but the lawman returned Charlie's fire coolly. Out of the corner of his eye, he saw Drucker streaking past them both.

Longarm's round caught Charlie square in the chest. As it slammed the sad-faced gunman back against a tree, the fleeing Drucker didn't even look back. Longarm started up from behind the rocks to take after Drucker, but—incredibly—Charlie Terhune was still game. Bringing up the small Smith & Wesson .38 he had hidden somewhere on his person, he squeezed off another shot at Longarm.

Seeing Charlie's movement out of the corner of his eye, Longarm ducked back down behind the rock. The bullet clipped a piece off it and went whining up into the blue. Longarm peered carefully around the side of the rock. Charlie was sitting down now, with his back to the tree, his eyes glazed, but the revolver was still in his hand and still pointing in Longarm's general direction.

Longarm shook his head grimly. He didn't have forever. Levering a fresh cartridge into his firing chamber, he crabbed swiftly out from behind the rock and fired point-blank at Charlie. The round tore into Charlie's thin, mournful face, demolishing it.

Longarm stood up slowly, a wary eye on the dying man. As he walked closer to inspect Charlie, Longarm heard Drucker's horse. The animal was galloping away, undoubtedly with Sim Drucker aboard.

Longarm peered unhappily down into the wreckage of Charlie Terhune's face, wondering what in the hell it was that made men always do such damn fool things. *Old son,* Longarm told himself, *when*

*are you going to learn? There's just no way you can
see a man's intent in his face—or in his manner.
You damn well better keep that in mind, or the next
time will be the last time.*

Longarm bent, snaked the pouch of dynamite
carefully off Charlie's shoulder, and hurried on
down the trail. He had a dam to blow.

Longarm was not expert at setting charges or at
blowing up dams. But he did the best he could under
the circumstances, setting the charges below the level
of the water backed up behind the dam, doing his
best to set them in strategic places that were also dry.
The dam was a makeshift, and there were many
leaks, which explained why so much water did manage to follow the stream's course. He linked all the
fuses with a main fuse, then nudged the fuse with the
lit end of his cheroot and scrambled up the dam to
the ledge.

He kept going until he was in the rocks behind
the ledge. Ducking down, he waited, saying a silent
prayer that his charges had been set and lit properly.
Directly in his line of vision, he saw the sprawled,
stiff body of the outlaw Tracy, the man Pope had
hired to harass his rivals, Stewart and Sir Thomas.
If anything happened to Sir Thomas or any member
of his expedition, Longarm promised himself that he
was going to haul Pope *and* Stewart in for conspiracy
to commit murder and make the charge stick.

The first charge went off. Longarm had expected
a bigger blast. He waited for other, more powerful
detonations. But nothing happened. Dismayed, he
stood up and started back onto the ledge. That was
when the entire dam blew sky-high. Longarm had
no time to duck his head as the awesome blast swept
past him. Then the shockwave hit him and he was
flung painfully against a boulder. He found he could
not breathe. Gasping, he crumpled to the surface of

the ledge. And then, gradually, as a light rain of wet debris and mud fell upon him, he found he could breathe again.

Turning, he ran to the far end of the ledge. The dam was gone. All that was left of it was a boiling mass of boulders, mud and debris, swirling in a great brown froth down the canyon. As Longarm stood there watching that awesome fist of water punching its way through the narrow canyon's walls, he had no doubt that it would extinguish the burning timber in the canyon below.

But was the cure worse than the disease?

He turned and ran from the ledge, anxious to find his horse and get back to Sir Thomas and the others. But as he hurried back up the trail, he remembered a sound he had last heard coming from within Alf Riley's mine. The faint, chinking sound of a pick axe striking at stone.

If Carrie and Riley were still in that mineshaft, were they still alive?

Chapter 14

As Longarm rode back into the lower canyon, he could see where the boiling wall of water had swept through, reaching halfway up the slopes in some cases. It was like a giant bathtub with its ring of dirty water along the sides. Only no amount of soap and water could wipe from this land the black stain left by the ravaging fire. In fact, flames were still tearing at the few stands of timber remaining high on the slopes along the base of the canyon's walls.

The wagons became visible as soon as Longarm rounded a bend in the canyon. The ropes had held, preventing the wagons from being capsized and swept away. Two of the largest wagons were still floating on the now muddy but full-throated stream. Surprisingly, quite a few horses and mules were still on their feet nearby. They could not have lost many, Longarm realized. A mud-spattered but happy crowd of survivors was racing along the bank of the stream toward him. Longarm dismounted when they caught up to him and found his hand being pumped gratefully by Sir Thomas, while Isadora impulsively flung both arms around his neck and kissed him.

"Anybody hurt?" Longarm asked, pleased and somewhat abashed by all this show of appreciation. "I see you were able to save most of the wagons and animals."

"Yes, we were," Sir Thomas said, beaming. "And not a one of us was hurt."

"But it *was* very close, Marshal," said Tim Dinsdale. "We're all pretty well scorched, I'd say."

"Another ten minutes, Longarm," said Isadora, "and I am afraid . . ." She shuddered at the thought.

"Never felt such terrible heat," admitted Sir Thomas. "No matter how low we crouched in the wagons. Their sides were smoking in some instances, and the flames seemed to fill the sky."

"We were like pigs roasting in an oven, Longarm!" said Bill Reed, as he pushed close and took Longarm's hand. He shook it powerfully. "Never thought I'd be glad to see an avalanche of water coming at me, but I was."

Denny was at Bill's side. She went up on tiptoe and kissed Longarm fondly on the cheek. "I'd rather drown than fry," she told him. "But I'm glad I didn't have to do either one. I want to get married and have children before I die."

"You will, Denny," Bill Reed said fondly. "I'll see to that."

"The thing now is to get on our way," Longarm told them. "And the sooner the better. Now would be a good time for them Arapahos to show us how welcome we are."

Sir Thomas nodded, turned to those crowded around, and began issuing instructions. They did not have very much gear left to pack, it seemed, and there was now plenty of room for them all in the wagons, and enough livestock to pull them. As the men hurried off, Longarm and Sir Thomas, with Isadora at his side, walked back to what remained of their encampment.

"How many of them fossil bones were you able to save, Sir Thomas?" Longarm asked.

Sir Thomas laughed ironically. "How many, Longarm? Very few, I am afraid. All we have succeeded in doing is redistributing those fossils throughout the canyon. When future paleontologists dig them up centuries hence, they are going to wonder at the burlap and plaster of paris wrapped around them. Strange creatures these, the scientists will muse, capable of wrapping their own bones for posterity."

Longarm laughed. He was glad the Englishman was taking it so well. "Do you think that burlap and plaster will last that long?"

"No, Longarm, I don't. It was just a humorous thought that occurred to me."

"I'm glad you're taking it so well."

The man sighed. "This kind of work, Longarm, develops patience before anything else. You have no idea how many blind alleys must be explored, how diligent one must become." Then he brightened. "However, as I told you earlier, I *have* made quite an exciting discovery, and *that* bone I have preserved intact!"

"You should have seen him," Isadora cried gleefully. "He had both arms wrapped around it when that wall of water swept over us!"

"My dear, you exaggerate," Sir Thomas protested, embarrassed. "I had my arm around you as well."

Isadora laughed, delighted at her brother's discomfiture. "Yes, you did, Tom. But I knew that if push came to shove, you would have chosen the bone, not me."

Sir Thomas smiled down at her, his eyes alive with affection. "Why, now that I think of it, Isadora, I do believe you are right."

"That discovery," Longarm said. "Can you tell me about it?"

"Of course. Simply put, I think I have found incontrovertible evidence that these ancient dinosaurs

204

—or dragons, as the Indians call them—were not all vegetarians, after all. Some of them were meat-eaters and preyed on the herbivorous variety."

"That's just what you were looking for, Sir Thomas, wasn't it? I remember you explained all that to me before. The herbivores and the carnivores."

"Yes, precisely, Longarm. And so I have found what I hoped to find."

"So you see, Longarm," Isadora said happily, "it hasn't been a complete failure, after all."

"I'm glad of that," Longarm said. "But what is there about that bone to prove this?"

Sir Thomas beamed. "Tooth marks! Unmistakable evidence. Those marks were made by the enormously powerful teeth of a carnivorous predator."

"You can tell all that by a few marks—on a single bone?"

"Of course, Longarm," said Isadora. "It's a science."

Longarm nodded. "I reckon it is, at that. It's like tracking a man. Only you people are tracking animals."

"Precisely," said Sir Thomas eagerly, obviously pleased with Longarm's example. "Only we are tracking these animals through *time!*"

"Well, I sure hope you get that bone safely out of here, then. I'm still worried about them Arapahos. That medicine man, especially."

"Please, Longarm," Isadora said, almost pleadingly, "the worst *must* be over by now. Surely those savages will let us be, now that we're on our way out of here."

"I hope so, Isadora," Longarm said. "But where Indians are concerned, I don't trust their kind intentions if I can help it. We'd better move out, and move out fast." Then Longarm looked gravely down at Isadora, his concern alerting her. "Do you remember Carrie Newton?"

"Why, of course, Longarm."

"Well, the sooner we get out of here, the sooner I can use your men to dig her and Alf Riley out of a mineshaft. They've been trapped in there since early today. But I've been too damn busy to get back to them. They may be able to dig out for themselves, but I'd sure rather give them a hand if I could."

"My God, Longarm!" Isadora cried. "Trapped in a mine! How awful!"

"How did it happen?" Sir Thomas asked, as concerned as his sister.

"It's a long story. I'll explain later. But right now, I'm real anxious to haul out of here and get back to that mineshaft."

"All right, Longarm," said Sir Thomas. "I am as eager as you are to be quit of this place. I promise you, we'll be on our way well before nightfall."

"I'd sure appreciate that, Sir Thomas."

Sir Thomas was as good as his word. By late that same afternoon, a weary and bedraggled party had left the canyon. Bill Reed and Denny were driving the lead wagon, which contained most of the gear Sir Thomas had been able to salvage. There were a few fossil bones in the remaining six wagons, but there were far fewer than what Sir Thomas and his men had prepared for shipping earlier, before the fire and what had followed.

Sir Thomas had employed—in addition to himself, his manservant, Isadora, and Tim Dinsdale—sixteen men to dig and catalogue and prepare for shipping the fossils they dug from the cliffside. Now these sixteen men and the nine teamsters, including Denny, were armed with rifles as well as handguns. A few brandished shotguns. It was a formidable force, its weakest link perhaps the cook in his ancient

206

chuckwagon, and Longarm hoped it would be enough to intimidate the Arapaho.

And if the Indians were not intimidated, Longarm had a surprise for them.

The wagons had almost reached Riley's canyon when the Indians decided not to be intimidated. An Arapaho arrow, like silent lightning, plunged out of the sky and impaled a bearded oldtimer standing beside Longarm in the rear of the second wagon. So suddenly did the arrow strike the man that he uttered scarcely a murmur as he sank to his knees, his rifle clattering among the bones. For a moment the fellow's round, startled eyes were fixed on Longarm. But only for that moment, as the man collapsed facedown, the green-striped shaft solid in his back, pointing straight up.

All this happened in an instant. In addition to more arrows, a thin volley of rifle fire commenced as Longarm cried out, "Leave the wagons! Get in under the cliffs!"

He leaped from the wagon and headed for a sloping field of boulders under a dark, overhanging shelf of rock. Glancing back, he saw Sir Thomas and Isadora following him—and behind them, Bill Reed and Denny.

Crouching down behind a rock as the rest poured past him, Longarm caught sight of two more men, one a teamster, stumbling around with Arapaho arrows in their backs. And then, as everyone found cover, the firing from above them ceased.

Sir Thomas and Bill Reed were crouched beside Longarm.

"Son of a bitch," Bill Reed whispered, his voice hoarse with fear. "They got Sam, Mike, and poor Jimmy Dickson."

"The worst of it," Longarm said, "is that one or two of them may not be dead. Arrows kill slow.

If we stay here long, we'll be hearing them calling for water."

Sir Thomas shook his head. "Ghastly," he said.

The silence that fell over the canyon was uncanny. There was neither a birdsong nor a human voice to break the awesome, waiting silence. The Indians were apparently grouping their forces—for a charge down the canyon, more than likely, Longarm realized. Now Black Horse and his fellow braves were going to be able to count coup.

He turned to Bill. "Find everyone you can. Tell them to expect an attack before dark. They might even charge us on horses. If they do, tell the men to aim for the horses and don't waste any ammunition."

Bill nodded and, keeping in close to the cliff wall, slipped away.

Longarm looked back out at the abandoned wagons. The mules and horses were standing almost contentedly in their harnesses, waiting, while a cloud of flies buzzed thickly around the chuckwagon. The only reason the Indians hadn't shot down the animals was that they evidently planned on making use of them later. The lead wagon, the one Bill Reed and Denny were driving, was being hauled by four fine horses, two blacks and two roans. They stood alertly, patiently, their tails whisking away the flies, their massive flanks quivering.

Longarm's eyes narrowed as he studied them a moment longer. Then he came to a decision. He patted his inside pocket to make sure he had at least one cheroot left. Then he checked for matches, after which he opened the pouch slung over his shoulder and inspected each of his four remaining sticks of dynamite—that surprise he had in store for Black Horse.

"Cover me," Longarm told Sir Thomas. "It

won't do much good, probably, but do it just the same."

"What are you going to do?"

"I'm going to try to make it back out there to Bill Reed's wagon. When those fool Indians make their charge, I'll have something for them."

"Oh, Longarm!" Isadora cried. "Do be careful!"

Longarm turned and looked back at her. She was crouched in the shadows alongside Denny. "I mean to be *very* careful," he told her.

Longarm left the shadows of the rock overhang and darted out onto the canyon floor. The nearest wagon was the third one behind the lead wagon. Longarm took cover under it and waited. He had not drawn any fire from the Arapaho. If they were still up there, they were being very careless.

If they were still up there.

Longarm crept forward under the wagons until he reached the first one. Clambering swiftly over the high side, he dropped into the bed and burrowed under the gear that had been packed in it. None of the wagons had canvas tops on them, since most were ore wagons, used primarily to haul raw chunks of ore from the mine to the railroad sidings.

Noticing that he had drawn no fire from the Arapaho, either while he clambered into the wagon or while he lay quietly in among the gear, he peered out at the driver's bench and was pleased to see that, despite the urgency of the terror that had caused Bill Reed to flee his wagon, the man had still had enough presence of mind to wrap the reins around the brake handle.

Longarm ducked back into the wagon, crouched low, took out a cheroot, and stuck it into his mouth. He did not light it. That would have to wait.

● ● ●

The sun had slashed a bright orange band across the top of the canyon wall when Longarm first caught the thunder of approaching horsemen. Black Horse and the rest of his crazy band were really going to do it, after all.

Their day was gone, the buffalo now only found in small, scattered bands, the white man aboard his Iron Horse pouring into their lands—but still these crazy Arapaho were going to make one last charge. Lances tugging in the wind, coup sticks brandished wildly, they would swoop down on the hated enemy and count coup one more time before the sun set forever on this tiny band of renegade Arapaho.

Longarm wondered if old Yellow Horn would be a part of this madness. He hoped not. He realized that he wanted to show the old chief those ancient giants standing upright again.

The Arapahos' sharp war cries came clearly now, echoing between the canyon walls. Abruptly, they swept into view in full gallop aboard their splendid little war ponies. They were all in full war regalia, and as Longarm had expected, they were brandishing not only their bows, but rifles of all descriptions, as well as lances and coup sticks. Bare from the waist up, their faces banded with green warpaint and their long, braided hair flying out behind them, they were a fearsome and magnificent sight.

With a heavy heart, Longarm saw chief Yellow Horn in the front ranks, his war bonnet flying out behind him, a bright new Winchester held high. He had made his peace with the young bucks, it seemed, and was helping to lead the charge.

As Longarm had instructed, Sir Thomas's men held their fire. Not until the Indians swept still closer did they open up. Perhaps the men were too unnerved by the sight of these warriors coming at them in full cry. Whatever it was, the Indians' casualties were light. Only a few riders went down.

210

Swiftly, Longarm reached over and untied the reins from the brake handle. Then he pulled the reins back with him into the wagon. He had already taken out his cheroot. Now he struck a sulfur match on his thumbnail and protected its flame for a moment, aware every second of the increased volume of the Arapahos' war cries. He held the match to the tip of his cheroot, sucked in quickly, and got the cheroot lit. Then he reached up past the seat, released the brake lever, and with a sharp yell and a slap of the reins, urged the four horses into a fast gallop—straight toward the charging Indians.

The horses responded. The wagon rolled forward, gaining speed slowly but steadily. Longarm kept down behind the seat and out of sight. Again he cried out to the horses and slapped the reins. It was difficult driving the wagon while crouched down out of sight in the wagon's bed. But Longarm was hoping that the onrushing Indians would not see him at all, but would think the horses had simply bolted.

The rifle fire from Sir Thomas's men was heavy now. A few rounds were punching into the high sides of his wagon, while others sang by just above his head. Longarm dropped the reins, slumped down still further with his back to the seat, and fished a stick of dynamite from his pouch.

He held the lighted tip of his cheroot inches from the fuse and waited. The horses kept plunging bravely forward. The Indians' war cries almost drowned out the rumble of the big wagon's wheels —and then Longarm was plunging through the Arapahos' front ranks. He crouched down still lower, facing backward as the charging braves, their backs to him, swept into his line of vision.

He touched the cheroot to the fuse and heaved out the stick. He was fishing for a second stick of dynamite when the first one blew up in the midst of the first rank of Indians. The carnage was fearsome.

211

Longarm thought he saw Black Horse go down. He concentrated, lit the second piece of dynamite, and hurled it at the second rank of Indians now swerving frantically away from the wagon. Longarm's horses, maddened by the explosions behind them, needed no more urging to gallop on through the Indians. As Longarm swept past the suddenly demoralized warriors, he tossed his third stick of dynamite into their midst. The damage was awesome, the sight one that made Longarm flinch away.

He heard the sound of someone scrambling onto the wagon's seat behind him. He dropped his cheroot, drew his Colt in one fluid motion, and spun about. A maddened brave was leaning over him, his lance held high. Longarm shot the brave twice, in rapid succession. The force of Longarm's two slugs punched the Indian back off the wagon seat. Another sound behind Longarm warned him; he turned just as a warrior finished scrambling from his pony into the rear of the wagon. This one held his rifle like a revolver and would have killed Longarm if the horses, out of control now, had not swerved wildly just as the brave fired. The shot went wild, and Longarm pumped two quick slugs into the Indian's bare chest.

As the Indian tumbled backward over the side, Longarm holstered his Colt, picked up his cheroot, and stuck it into his mouth. Then he jumped from the wildly careening wagon. The pouch flying from his shoulder, he landed heavily on the rocky canyon floor, careful to keep the pouch's one remaining stick of dynamite from coming down hard. Scrambling to his feet, he ran for cover among the rocks.

A party of four Indians spotted him running and galloped after him. Crouched among the rocks, Longarm waited unhappily. He still had his lighted cheroot and the stick of dynamite. The cries of the charging warriors reverberated in the narrow canyon. They began firing at him with their rifles as they rode closer, their slugs ricocheting among the surrounding rocks with a fearsome, whining clamor. He was soon able to make out each Indian's face, and to his surprise, he saw that one of the braves was Twisted Foot. The medicine man sat his pony awkwardly, but handled the animal well, and he was the one leading the others, his face twisted into a mask of exhilarated hatred.

Longarm grabbed the stick of dynamite, looked away from the onrushing war party, and touched the end of his cheroot to the fuse. It sputtered, hissing like a cornered wildcat. Braving the hail of bullets, Longarm stood up and heaved the sputtering stick of death carefully. It exploded under the lead pony—the one Twisted Foot was riding. The blast lifted his pony and flung the paint beside it to the ground. Both Twisted Foot and the warrior on the paint were flung to the ground like punctured dolls—only it wasn't sawdust leaking from their bodies as they crawled slowly away; it was blood.

The remaining two Indians also lost their mounts, but managed to keep their feet under them as they left their stunned ponies behind. Longarm pulled out his Colt again and fired at the nearest Indian. The bullet caught the Arapaho high in the neck, blowing a hole in his windpipe. Choking on his blood, he stumbled to his knees and, with one last remaining burst of fury, flung his lance at Longarm.

Longarm ducked aside. The lance clattered harmlessly past him. He had one more Indian, and his Colt was empty. Longarm waited upright. The last Indian pulled up, flung his rifle away and drew his hunting knife. Then, with a shattering cry, he charged the remaining distance. Longarm palmed the small derringer from his vest pocket, waited until the last moment, then fired both barrels into the crazed warrior.

The Indian, though wounded mortally, lurched toward Longarm, who ducked to one side and backed up. The Indian stumbled drunkenly after Longarm, the two small holes in his chest bleeding neatly down his front. Again he reached out his knife hand, and again Longarm backed away. The Indian cried out something and lifted the knife over his head.

Longarm could take no more. He turned his back on the dying warrior and walked away, leaving the protection of the rocks. He did not look back when he heard the dead Indian fall heavily to the ground.

Sir Thomas's men had finished mopping up by the time Longarm rejoined them. What few Indian survivors there were had galloped off. The combined firepower of Sir Thomas's riflemen and Longarm's dynamite had decimated the war party.

"Do you think they'll be back, Longarm?" Isadora asked as she stood huddled beside her brother. Her voice was hushed, her face pale and drawn from having witnessed so much slaughter.

"I doubt it," said Longarm. "I hope not."

"Longarm!" It was Bill Reed.

"What is it?" Longarm asked as Bill hurried toward him.

"There's an old Indian over here. He's hurt pretty bad, but he says he won't die until he speaks again with his friend Longarm."

Longarm winced. Chief Yellow Horn. He had hoped the old chief might have escaped the slaughter somehow. "Where is he?"

"Over here. Near the wall," Bill said, hurrying back the way he had come. "Denny's with him."

When Longarm came upon Yellow Horn, he was dismayed to see that the chief had been wounded fearfully in the shoulder and chest, and the wounds were still bleeding, despite Denny's efforts to bind them tightly with strips torn from a man's shirt.

Yellow Horn brightened at Longarm's approach. He raised a faltering hand in greeting and glanced skyward. It was past sunset, but the sky was still light; dusk was filling the canyon rapidly.

"The day is dying, Longarm. And I am dying with it. It is a good day to die, but I cannot say I want to go now. It would have been good medicine to see those standing giants in the great city of Denver."

"You may yet see them, Yellow Horn."

"You are foolish, Longarm. You hurled the thunder at us and the rifles spoke from the shadows of the cliff. Many bullets has my body swallowed, and through the holes they left, my spirit steals away. It is all done now. The dreaming. The singing. And the buffalo will not return." He looked piercingly up at Longarm. "How is it with Twisted Foot?"

"He is dead, I think."

Yellow Horn nodded. "He will dream his dreams no more. But his was not a bad dream to dream. We do not count many coup this day, but there are many brave Arapaho who will not eat agency beef or sleep under rotting army blankets. And that is a fine thing."

"Yes," Longarm agreed. "That is a fine thing."

Yellow Horn glanced up at Longarm, his dark eyes glinting with a familiar mischievousness. "Does Longarm have one of his sticks of tobacco?"

Longarm took his last cheroot from his inside pocket. "It's the last one I have. It's yours, Chief."

"No. Cut it in half. I do not think I will smoke long this night."

As Longarm took out his pocket knife, Yellow Horn dug his stone pipe from his pouch. But it was in pieces. He looked at it sadly. Longarm glanced over at Bill Reed.

"Bill, do you have a pipe handy?"

"No, I don't, Longarm."

"I'll go get one from Sir Thomas," Denny said, eager to help.

"Never mind," said Longarm. He could see by now that Yellow Horn would not be able to last more than a few minutes longer. "There's no need."

Longarm went down on one knee beside the chief and cut the cheroot in half. Then he trimmed the ends carefully and handed the chief his half-sized cheroot.

"Smoke it as I do," said Longarm. "We will share the tobacco together. You will not need your pipe."

Longarm snapped a match to life and lit the chief's cheroot and then his own. Yellow Horn's eyes lit as he inhaled the strong tobacco. He leaned back and closed his eyes, drawing deeply on the cheroot. Longarm made himself comfortable beside Yellow Horn.

After a moment, he glanced up and saw Denny standing with Bill Reed's arm around her. She was crying softly. Chief Yellow Horn opened his eyes and looked up at Denny. He seemed to be peering at her from a long distance.

"You are the woman that Black Horse wanted," he said to her. "I think he is a crazy Indian to want a white woman. But you are a good person. Maybe Black Horse can see better than his old chief." Yellow Horn looked at Longarm. "She makes me think of Black Horse. What of him, Longarm?"

Longarm shook his head slowly. "He's gone with Twisted Foot, I'm pretty sure."

The old man sighed. His face seemed to collapse inward and his eyes grew vague. He held what was left of the cheroot with a palsied hand. But he was still smoking it, still inhaling deeply. He leaned his head back and closed his eyes. This time Denny's weeping could not open them again. After a while,

216

Longarm gently took what remained of the cheroot from the old chief's dead lips and stood up.

He flicked the butt into the darkness, finished his own smoke, and with Bill Reed and Denny, he walked back to the wagons through the sudden darkness.

Chapter 15

Later that same night, as Sir Thomas prepared to move his wagons out and leave behind the stench of death that hung over the corpse-littered canyon, a posse of riders from New Bethlehem rode toward them out of the night.

As Reverend Wilson explained it, the pall of smoke earlier in the day had alerted them, and the sound of gunfire that followed at dusk had brought them now to investigate. Sir Thomas invited the reverend to join him in tea by the campfire. After a cold but formal and most correct conversation with Sir Thomas—he was, after all, a scientist who endorsed Darwin's new theory of evolution, a devil's inspiration if ever there was one—the leader of the settlement sought out Longarm.

"What can you tell me of Brother Newton, Marshal?"

"He's dead, Reverend."

"Do you have any details?"

"Guess it won't hurt to tell you that before he died, he tried to kill his wife—and right now she and the fellow taking care of her are trapped in a mine because of Brother Newton."

"Trapped, you say?"

"That's right. If you could spare a few of your men, we could ride up there now and help dig her out."

"Carrie Newton is with a man?"

"That's right."

"Alone?"

Longarm nodded.

"And he's not her husband."

"Not that I know of."

Reverend Wilson drew himself up to his full height. "I was going to search out Carrie Newton and allow her to return to New Bethlehem. I listened to the voice of God within me—and had decided to forgive her. But I see now, it was the devil that spoke to me! Carrie Newton is damned! I wash my hands of her!"

"You can't spare the men?"

"I *will* not spare them! I told you. I wash my hands of her."

"She was alive, last I knew. I told her I would get right back to her. That was this morning. I'm riding up there now with Bill Reed and a few others. If you don't send anyone, Reverend, I am going to have to conclude that you are not a man of God."

Reverend Wilson's face darkened in outrage. "That is your opinion, sir."

"Here's another opinion. If you don't get on your horse and hightail it out of here with the rest of your brethren, and do it *now*, I'm liable to disremember that I carry a badge in my wallet and do serious injury to a blasphemous fake who is trying to pass himself off as a man of the cloth. Tell me, Reverend Wilson, do you have a record? Bunco, maybe? Real estate? Phony stock?"

With a startled gasp, Reverend Wilson turned and rushed off through the night. Less than a minute later, as Longarm trudged through the darkness to find Bill Reed, he heard the rapid hoofbeats of galloping horses as Reverend Wilson and the New Bethlehem posse rode swiftly off.

Longarm smiled slyly. His shot in the dark had found a target, it seemed.

• • •

The blazing campfire on the bench above the canyon floor told Longarm all he needed to know. He glanced over at Bill, riding beside him in the darkness. Two others, Jim Ford and Frank Barnham, had volunteered to go with Longarm and were strung out along the trail behind them.

"It looks like Riley was able to dig himself and Carrie out," Longarm remarked to Bill.

"Looks that way, all right," Bill responded. He remembered Carrie from that time in New Bethlehem when she had risked so much to tend the wounded Dooley, and he was obviously as relieved as Longarm to see that bright, beckoning campfire.

Bill turned in his saddle. "No need to sweat it, men!" he called. "Looks like they're out of the mine. But there'll be hot coffee for us when we ride in."

When they rode up onto the bench, Longarm saw that the fire had been built just in front of the mine entrance. Standing beside it, peering into the darknsss, were the figures of Alf Riley and Carrie Newton. Longarm called out at once to reassure them, and at the sound of Longarm's voice, Carrie uttered a small cry of pleasure and started to run across the bench toward them, Alf at her side.

Longarm dismounted as soon as he got close enough, and in a moment Carrie had flung herself into his arms. Riley, coming up after her, grinned and stuck out his hand. Longarm shook it.

"What kept you?" the man asked, smiling. "You said you'd be right back."

Longarm smiled back at the man. "That is a very long story, Alf."

"And he ain't just beatin' his gums, neither," said Bill Reed, stepping forward and shaking Alf's hand warmly. "Glad to see you both got out of that

220

all right." Then he looked at Carrie and smiled almost shyly. "Glad to see you again, Carrie."

Carrie, pleased at the greeting, brushed an errant lock of her thick hair back off her pale forehead and smiled back at Bill Reed. Then she moved back close to Alf Riley as the other two rode up, dismounted, and were introduced around. Sir Thomas had given all four riders provisions to take to Carrie and Alf. Once Longarm had explained to the Englishman about the condition of Alf's cabin after Carrie's husband got through with it, Sir Thomas had insisted. As soon as Longarm had started up the canyon for Riley's mine, Sir Thomas had set out for Dog Wells.

Carrie was delighted to get the provisions. Longarm and the others unloaded them and Carrie showed Ford and Barnham where in the mine entrance they could leave them. As Carrie moved off with the two men, Alf led Longarm and Bill Reed over to the fire and gave them fresh tin cups of lavahot coffee.

"There wasn't much left of that cabin," Alf explained. "But I managed to find some coffee in a cannister. You should have seen the cannister." He peered up at Longarm. "You got any idea where that crazy son of a bitch of a husband of hers is holin' up, Longarm? I'd like to kill the bastard."

"You won't have to," said Longarm. He glanced up at the dark walls towering into the bright, moonlit sky. "He's up there somewhere, on a ledge, providing nourishment for your local buzzard population."

"That so? Up there, you say? Near the rim?"

"Yes."

"We were dug out by noon, Longarm. It wasn't no sweat, really. I know how to use a pick. That's all I been doing these past ten years. And now that I think of it, this afternoon I did notice some feastin'

221

vultures. They was crowded onto a narrow sandstone ledge way the hell up there. The last of them waddled off, dropped into the canyon, then managed to struggle back up over the rim and fly off a little before sunset." He smiled happily at the thought. "You mean that was the last of Calvin Newton I watched disappear over that canyon rim today?"

"Looks like it, Alf."

"Damn!" the man said, shaking his head. "Ain't that a shame, now." He grinned up at Longarm. "You know that son of a bitch did me a favor?"

"You mean . . . Carrie?"

"Sure. Carrie. But something else too. Something real crazy."

Bill Reed, standing beside Longarm, moved closer to Riley, as interested as the tall lawman. Riley turned to watch as Carrie, returning from the mine with the two men, passed close by the fire on the way to get the rest of the provisions. When she was out of earshot, the grizzled miner turned back to Longarm.

"It's the damnedest thing. I been working this here mine for close on to four years. I been getting my share of gold dust, but nothing really grand, you understand, just enough to keep me coming back for more. And then this critter Newton finds Carrie and me inside the mine and tosses a stick of dynamite in after us." He paused, chuckled, and shook his head again.

"What the hell's so funny about that, Alf?" Bill Reed asked.

Riley leaned still closer, his eyes bright in the dancing light from the campfire "Well, the thing is, I had this feeling all along that there was a vein somewhere in that mineshaft if only I could find it. But I never was able to come onto it. Then that fool blew out a shelf and nearly buried me and Carrie alive. So what should I find while I'm digging myself out?"

"You gonna tell us, you old coot?" growled Bill Reed good-naturedly.

"He don't have to tell us," said Longarm, laughing. "That blast of Newton's shook loose that vein of gold Alf was looking for. Right, Alf?"

His eyes dancing with the wonder of it, Riley cried, "Longarm, it's a mother lode! I ain't told Carrie yet, but I'm as sure of it as I am that you two are standing here!"

"Congratulations," said Longarm. "I'm glad—for both of you."

Riley calmed down a bit after that, and told them how Newton had caught Carrie bringing water to him while he worked in the mine. Unable to goad the two of them into coming out, the man blew up the cabin, then flung a stick of dynamite into the mine. Though the blast rocked the two of them something fearful and brought down the roof of the shaft, they were both so far back that neither one was hurt. When they emerged later that day, and Carrie saw what her husband had done to the cabin she had already begun to fix up, she had broken down and wept.

"But I'll build her a new one," Riley said. "A grander one, for sure."

"Yes," said Longarm, smiling. "I guess you will, at that."

Carrie and the two men joined them a few moments later, and after a short visit, the six of them bedded wearily down around the fire.

Early the next morning, after a hearty breakfast that Carrie cooked for them over the open fire, Longarm and his party saddled up. Alf was poking around in the demolished cabin when Carrie stole up beside Longarm just as he finished cinching up his saddle.

"You going to be all right now, Carrie?" he asked her.

"Oh, yes."

"You mean you won't miss the good life you left behind in New Bethlehem?"

Carrie shuddered at the thought, and shook her head vigorously. "You have no idea, Longarm, how happy I have been here with Alf. He has nothing, poor fellow, but this hole in the mountain that he digs in hopefully day after day, but he is a kind and gentle man. He has riches in his heart, Longarm —and that's enough for me."

"It's nice you feel that way, Carrie."

"I am very thankful, Longarm—to both of you."

Longarm mounted up. The others had already stepped into their saddles and were waiting for him. At that moment, Riley hurried across the bench toward them.

"Hold on there, Longarm!" he cried. "I got something here for Sir Thomas!"

A moment later, standing with one arm about Carrie's shoulder, Alf tossed up a charred but still serviceable pouch of gold dust to Longarm. The lawman hefted it, then smiled down at Riley.

"I'm sure this is more than enough, but Sir Thomas will appreciate it. I'll thank you for him, Alf."

Longarm touched the brim of his hat to Carrie, turned his horse, and rode off the bench alongside Bill, the others trailing behind. After they had gained the canyon floor, Longarm glanced back to the bench and saw the two of them waving goodbye. All four waved back.

Bill Reed said, "Carrie's in for a surprise, ain't she?"

Longarm nodded.

"Think it'll change things between them?"

"Might. But I doubt it. Them two are already

224

fixed in their ways and they know they got something there that money can't buy."

Bill Reed said nothing more, and Longarm took one last glance back up the canyon, his eyes searching for that ledge where he had left Calvin Newton. When he found it, he saw one lone, scraggly buzzard picking over the remains. As Longarm watched, the buzzard opened his wings and pumped slowly up into the pale blue morning sky.

Six days later, on a Monday morning, Longarm cautiously pushed open the side entrance to the Rocky Mountain States Exhibition Hall just across the avenue from the Windsor Hotel and stepped inside. He was in a small, familiar anteroom; a frosted door faced him. Longarm pushed through the door and found himself once again confronting that towering skeleton that Charles Ogden Stewart was presenting to the city of Denver.

Pope had called it *Hadrosaurus* and had mentioned a dinosaur of his own he was erecting also. Longarm walked around a corner and saw an even more fearsome dragon, facing the other way. This was obviously the one Pope was constructing. It was not yet finished. Portions of the enormous tail were scattered on the floor behind it, great lengths of wire stretched loose under the tail. This was Pope's *Iguanodon*, his attempt to outshine Stewart. It was not as tall a creature, but it was surely just as terrifying and sure as hell just as awesome. As Longarm stood gawking up at it, he found himself wishing that Chief Yellow Horn was standing beside him, gazing up in wonder at the standing giant, one of Longarm's cheroots crushed in his stone pipe.

But this was not why Longarm had come to the exhibition hall this morning. He had only recently returned from a fruitless effort to track Sim Drucker, the leader of the henchmen that Stewart had hired.

Billy Vail's repeated telegrams ordering Longarm to give up on the search had finally brought him back. According to Vail's thinking, since Sir Thomas was safe in Denver, Longarm's mission had been completed successfully.

Well, maybe so. But Longarm had fed a lot of buzzards to protect that British peer of the realm, and Sim Drucker—as well as the man who hired him—had been responsible for most of that sad slaughter.

Longarm remembered where the working quarters of the paleontologist and his assistants were located. He skirted around a massive foot, ducked under an extended, intricately articulated neck, and headed for a large door on the other side of the hall. He had almost reached it when he heard an angry shout from the laboratory beyond, and then the sound of something crashing to the floor. Almost immediately afterward came the bark of a sixgun.

Longarm burst into the workroom and saw, cowering in front of a massive pile of crates, the two paleontologists—with Sim Drucker in front of them, his sixgun out and still smoking. Stewart, it appeared, had just been shot. A growing red stain was showing on the shoulder of his white smock.

Longarm was so pleased to have found his quarry that he froze for a second, contemplating his man. That was all the time the desperate Drucker needed. He swung his sixgun and fired. The bullet struck Longarm's cross-draw rig where the holster was attached to the belt. Longarm felt as if he had been punched. The impact of the bullet spun him around. As he hit the waxed, dust-littered floor, he skidded into another towering pile of empty crates, most of which promptly tumbled down upon him.

In the confusion that followed, Longarm was able to draw his Colt. Crouching down under the avalanche of crates, he swiftly ascertained that his .44

226

was undamaged and charged out after Drucker. But the outlaw was already through the door, running across the exhibition hall. Longarm flung a shot after him, but it went wild. A piece of bone high on the backbone of Stewart's reconstructed dinosaur disintegrated. Longarm heard a cry of dismay from both Stewart and Pope, crowding into the doorway behind him.

Drucker turned and fired back. The slug gouged out a piece of the door. The outlaw ducked behind the leg of Stewart's *Hadrosaurus* and threw another wild shot in Longarm's direction. Longarm could see that the man was not thinking or shooting very well. He darted from the doorway, keeping the long tail of the *Hadrosaurus* between him and the crouching Drucker, who could see Longarm coming, but could not get a clear shot. He darted for Pope's incomplete skeleton and tried to duck under the *Iguanodon's* tail. Abruptly, he went down, cursing wildly.

Holding his fire, Longarm ran over cautiously and was in time to see Drucker, a piece of wire caught securely around one boot heel, frantically attempting to free himself. In a frenzy, he leaped to his feet and yanked at the wire with all his strength.

There was a high-pitched groaning sound; the entire backbone of the giant lizard shifted horizontally. The great skull nodded assent and turned slightly, as if it sniffed something dangerous coming up behind it. The groaning became a squeal, and then a loud series of cracking sounds, like an old man's joints going, and instantly the entire, massive structure collapsed. A huge cloud of plaster dust filled the spot, behind which the ancient pile of bones crunched to the floor.

And under all that squirmed a frantic, panic-stricken Sim Drucker.

Longarm waved away the clouds of plaster dust and ignored the shrill cries of dismay coming from

227

Pope, who was still right behind him. He caught a glimpse of Drucker on his feet now, but still entangled in the wire.

"Hold it right there, Drucker!" Longarm barked.

The outlaw did nothing of the kind. He whirled and fired twice at Longarm, the slugs coming uncomfortably close. Longarm returned the man's fire carefully, deliberately, aiming for the torso. Drucker was slammed violently backward; but his foot, still ensnared, was yanked out from under him; he was flung heavily down on his back.

Skirting the enormous pile of shattered bones, wire, and plaster, Longarm approached Drucker, his sixgun still extended. The fellow was flat on his back, unconscious. His face and clothes were a ghastly white from the plaster, and so thick was the dust on him that the blood oozing from his wounds appeared black. Longarm bent closer.

"Drucker?" he called softly.

The man did not respond, and there was little, if any, chest movement. Longarm went to replace his Colt in his holster and discovered that it was hanging crookedly from a nearly severed gunbelt. So he just stuck the revolver in his belt.

The sound of anguish behind him he could no longer ignore. He whirled impatiently. Pope was standing with tears in his eyes as he gazed in shocked disbelief at what was left of the skeleton he had been laboring to reconstruct.

"Marshal!" the man cried. "It's ruined! Ruined! The bones have been cracked and splintered in so many places, they are useless! Some have been reduced to little more than powder!"

Longarm wanted to tell the man to shut up, that it didn't matter all that much. Less than ten feet from this blubbering schoolboy with a passion for bones, a man lay dying. He was an outlaw, yes, and not a

228

very fine human being—but he was a man and he was dying.

Stewart, his face showing clearly the agony he was suffering from his shoulder wound, had been standing behind Pope, watching with undisguised joy his rival scientist's despair. Now he could hold himself back no longer.

"What are you blubbering about, you fool!" he cried, wincing from the pain his outburst caused him. "That specimen was nothing! A shadow of what I have over here! Your efforts at reconstruction were laughable." He clutched at his shoulder; the entire right side of his smock was heavy with his blood. Steady droplets of bright scarlet dripped from the hem of the coat to the floor. But this did not stop Stewart's tirade. "You had nothing! Nothing to compare with my masterwork! You see! It stands upright still, unscathed! It is a judgment on you and all the lies, the calumny you have heaped on my head for these many years!"

"Stop that, Stewart!" Longarm cried. "This is no time for that!"

The scientist whirled on Longarm. "And who are *you* to tell me what to do! This is *my* laboratory. Here I labor for the good of all mankind. I serve science, not you or your petty laws." He flung his head back proudly. "As long as my construction stands, it will remain a monument to my skill and to my devotion to science and the truth! Look at it, Marshal! It stands triumphant, while this toady's fraudulent exercise in futility is reduced to dust!"

Stewart, Longarm realized, was close to the breaking point by this time; it was a result of having to work for so long in this hall beside a man he despised, as well as Drucker's searing slug that was still burrowing into his flesh. But Longarm didn't care what the man's reasons were.

Longarm withdrew the Colt from his belt, took

fresh cartridges from his coat pocket, and inserted them into the firing chamber. When he had a fully loaded his revolver, he raised the gun and aimed carefully at the wire snaking up from the backbone into the skull of Stewart's towering *Hadrosaurus*. He fired. The round burned through most of the wire, the sound of its ricochet high and frightening. The wire stretched a bit, and the entire skeleton sagged.

With a shriek, Stewart lunged at Longarm; but he was too far gone. He stumbled weakly and fell to the floor, his face ashen, his eyes wild. Ignoring him, Longarm fired a second time at the same spot. This time the wire snapped. The entire structure settled dangerously, but held. The neck and head sagged forward a little; the tiny, ineffectual forelimbs high up under the gaping jaw trembled.

Longarm caught sight of another wire, this one heavier and obviously supporting the powerful hind quarters of the dinosaur. Two quick shots severed the wire. The erect *Hadrosaurus* seemed to scrunch itself closer together, as if a sudden cold wind had passed through its gaping bones.

Longarm had two more rounds left. He aimed for the dinosaur's great frontal ridges, just under the gaping eye sockets. He fired. The round knocked the head to one side. He did not need to fire again. As Stewart screamed hysterically, the great reptilian head hung for an instant, the entire structure hanging with it. Then, with the same suddenness that took the other one down, the great, towering skeleton disintegrated. The crack of fracturing bones and the *ping* of snapping wire filled the air as another great cloud of plaster dust billowed up around the crumbling dinosaur. It was over in an instant.

Longarm turned to Stewart. The man was still on the floor, his head hanging. Deep, painful sobs came from him. Longarm stuck the Colt back into his belt and walked over to the scientist. The man did not

230

look up at him. Longarm looked over at a pale, shaken Pope.

"Get out of here and find a copper. Hurry it up. There's two men here hurt bad, and maybe one's already dead! Get a move on!"

Pope ran from the exhibition hall.

Longarm looked back down at Stewart. "You ever hear that about them that sows a wind, Stewart?"

Stewart looked slowly up at Longarm. Tears were running down his haggard, shockingly white face. He nodded dully. He had difficulty focusing his eyes.

"They reap a whirlwind, Stewart—and that's just what you got."

"You had no right!" Stewart gasped. "No right at all!"

"Stewart, there's too many people dead right now because you thought *you* had the right. I guess I won't have much luck trying to haul you and Pope in for what you did. But maybe you two will remember what happened here today."

"But it was for science," the man gasped. "I did it for science!"

"That what you call it?"

"You must believe that!"

"You may serve science, whatever the hell that means, but I serve the law! And the next time you go hunting for bones in these parts, I suggest you remember that."

The man moistened his dry lips. He was breathing with difficulty. Unable to speak, he just nodded dully.

Longarm left the scientist and walked back to Sim Drucker. He shook his head wearily when he looked down at the outlaw's slack face. The man was already dead.

The Windsor Hotel was just across the street from the exhibition hall, but it was almost three hours

231

before he got there. As he strode wearily into the hotel's bar, a familiar voice hailed him.

Longarm looked over and saw Sir Thomas sitting at the end of the bar. The man was alone, and he looked as if he were dressed for travel. The Englishman waved Longarm over. The two shook hands amiably. Longarm could tell that the man was genuinely glad to see him; and for his part, Longarm liked the Englishman—but at the moment, any reminder of these past weeks brought the lawman little pleasure.

"I heard the news," Sir Thomas said somberly. "I mean about what transpired over there earlier—in the hall. One of Pope's assistants was just in here at the bar, getting very drunk."

"Because he was unhappy?"

"He was celebrating. Seems both Pope and Stewart are heartily disliked by their underlings."

Longarm nodded and ordered a shot of Maryland rye.

"I understand Stewart was visited by one of those thugs he had hired to attack us," Sir Thomas said. "Is that correct?"

"That's about it, all right. The outlaw's name was Drucker. Pope told us what happened. Bronson was scared some because he knew I was on his trail. So he tracked Stewart down, looking for money to get him out of the country."

Sir Thomas laughed softly. "He was under the impression these scientists were wealthy?"

"Hell, the way they were throwing money around, I don't wonder them outlaws were fooled. Anyway, the poor son of a bitch showed up this morning, made Stewart get rid of his assistants, then told him what his price was."

Sir Thomas smiled slightly. "What was his price?"

232

Longarm shook his head, bemused. "Twenty-five thousand dollars, that's all. And that was a comedown from fifty thousand."

"My word!"

"Stewart just laughed at the man—so Drucker shot him."

"How badly is he hurt?"

"He'll live, more'n likely. But the doc on the wagon said he's going to have a game right arm from now on."

"Tragic."

"Maybe."

"I want to thank you, Longarm, for what you did for us."

"Yeah. I did a whole hell of a lot of good. I let you take back one bone." Longarm smiled warmly at the man. "You still got it, complete with all them teethmarks?"

Sir Thomas nodded happily. "It's in my steamer trunk—well packed, I assure you—and right now it is on its way to the train station."

"You're leaving Denver?"

"I am, yes. I am very anxious to return to the British Museum—and strut around with this very significant find. I am very pleased with it, Longarm. I only wish it hadn't cost so much—in human lives, I mean."

"I know how you feel," Longarm said, lifting the shotglass of rye to his mouth and downing its contents. "I reckon I feel the same way."

"I don't think I'll ever forget that last night in the canyon, the sight of those aborigine women and the old men, coming to claim their dead. And the sad procession afterward as they took them away. It was such a foolish, gallant charge. It reminded me of . . ." Sir Thomas paused.

"Of the Light Brigade?"

Sir Thomas nodded quickly. "Precisely."

"Maybe," said Longarm. "It *was* a mistake, them Arapaho coming at us like that. But we were ripping out the bones of ancient serpents, remains that held a wonder for them, made their land special, sacred."

"I suppose so."

"And then, like Chief Yellow Horn put it, not a single one of them dead Arapaho warriors will ever have to eat agency beef or sleep under rotting army blankets."

Sir Thomas pondered Longarm's reply for a moment, before shrugging and consulting a gold pocket watch. "Time to go, Longarm. My train leaves within the hour."

"Next time you're through here, look me up."

"If I am on another expedition, I most assuredly will do that. Incidentally, Isadora has not yet had her fill of Denver."

Longarm smiled. "I was just fixing to ask about her."

"She has decided to stay on for a few more weeks."

"That so?"

"She's upstairs, Longarm. In room 312. It would be nice if you could find the time to show her around the Mile-High City. I am sure she would appreciate that. I know she thinks very highly of you."

Longarm walked with the tall Englishman to the carriage stand and bade him goodbye. As Sir Thomas climbed into a hack and set out for the train. Longarm watched him go for a moment, then turned, a smile lighting his face, and walked back into the hotel.

Room number 312, it was.

"Who is it?"

"Longarm!"

Almost at once the door was flung open. Longarm held out the bottle of champagne. Isadora took it with a cry of delight.

As she closed the door behind him, she said, "But you don't need this to make yourself welcome, Longarm."

"It's the hotel's best. I think I needed it. This day hasn't started off too well." He smiled suddenly. "But it sure is looking up some now."

"My brother saw you?"

"I met him downstairs in the bar."

"I was hoping you two would meet."

"And let me know you were still in Denver?"

She looked at him for a long moment, savoring his sudden and most welcome appearance. "Yes," she said. "To let you know I was still here."

She looked spectacular, almost as if she had been expecting him. Her flashing green eyes were matched by the long, green corduroy dress she was wearing. The thick, luxuriant curls of her dark hair, unpinned, fell almost to her waist. She had looked good in jodhpurs, but she looked a whole hell of a lot better in this green dress.

"A headache kept me from going to the station with Tom," she said, walking slowly toward him. "But the headache left the moment you walked in. We started much that we didn't finish back there, Longarm. Do you remember?"

"I remember," he said, as she stepped into his arms. "This time there'll be no interruptions."

"Just the champagne and us."

They kissed. It was a long kiss, and Longarm found himself lifting her in one swift, easy motion and carrying her into the bedroom. She had left the champagne behind, he realized, but he didn't let that bother him as he let her down gently beneath

235

him and lost himself in the scented wonder of her abundant hair, and then the sweet warmth of her breasts.

They could have the champagne after . . .

Chapter 1

There was no snow in Denver that morning, but the air had a definite bite to it. Longarm snapped awake at dawn, as usual, and told his stomach to quit growling until breakfast time. When his innards kept reminding him that he'd had a scanty supper the night before, he rolled out of bed. A bottle of Maryland rye with just a heel left in it stood on the bureau. Longarm swallowed the whiskey and started dressing. The air in his unheated room was too nippy even for a whore's bath, and in any case, he'd just drunk the whiskey he would have used to sponge himself down.

Dressed, with his Colt in its cross-draw holster belted on at the precise angle that suited him best, Longarm set his flat-crowned Stetson on his crisp hair and, with a final twirl of his sweeping mustache, set out to face the day. Breakfast came first, and he took his time. A second cup of coffee and a cheroot brought the morning around to the hour when George Masters would have his barbershop open for the day.

A half-hour later, shaved and trimmed, his tanned jaws still cool from a good rub-down with bay rum, Longarm was ready to see what his boss had on the docket. It was time, Longarm thought as he entered the Federal Building, that Billy Vail found something better for him to do than to cool his heels in Denver. And, after sweeping past the pink-cheeked young clerk who tried without much success to guard Vail's office door, Longarm passed on his sentiments to the Chief U.S. Marshal himself.

"Funny you feel that way," Billy Vail grunted, pawing through the ever-growing stack of paperwork that littered his desk. "I just got this on the overnight wire from Washington."

Longarm reached for the message, but Vail was already reading it over to himself. The wire was lengthy, and Longarm took out a cheroot and lighted it to pass the time. He'd smoked the thin cigar a third of the way down before Vail looked up and shook his head.

"Well, Billy?" Longarm asked.

"It's a good thing you've got a hankering to take on a job. This one is just about the right size to fit those number-twelve boots you favor."

"You going to tell me about it, Billy? Or am I supposed to read your mind?"

"Oh, it's not any secret. Seems somebody sneaked back into politics after getting himself a bad name in Washington, and he's trying to weasel himself back into a job there. The Attorney General himself's taking a hand in seeing that he won't make it."

"I'm betting you can't call names to me, though."

"You'd win your bet. But it's a name you'd be likely to remember, if I was able to give it to you. Which the boss says not to do, of course."

"You can tell me about the job, I guess?"

"Oh, sure. It's a little bit of a long story, so settle back and knock that ash off your damned cigar before it falls on my new carpet."

Longarm had been around Billy Vail so many years that he could read the signs of an ugly job, and this looked like one of them. Whenever an especially mean assignment came out of Washington, Billy began picking at him. Tossing the partly smoked cheroot into the brass spittoon at the corner of Vail's desk, Longarm settled back in the red morocco chair.

"Go ahead, Billy. Let's have it."

Vail looked at the message, knitting his bushy eyebrows worriedly. He asked, "Do you recall ever running into a Texas Ranger by the name of Maddox? Clayton Maddox?"

"Can't say I do. Which company's he with?"

"*Was* with. At the time we're talking about, it was A Company."

"In Austin, eh?" Longarm shook his head thoughtfully. "I never did spend a lot of time there. Mostly just stopovers between trains. What's our interest in Maddox?"

"Back in '66, he was one of the Ranger renegades that joined the Texas State Police."

Longarm grunted. Every lawman in the West, no matter how late he'd come to wear a badge, knew about that sorry episode in Texas history during the Reconstruction years. When the carpetbaggers out of the East had taken over the white-pillared state house, they'd learned early that the Texas Rangers lived by a code that wouldn't allow them to carry out the kind of orders the Eastern conquerers were issuing to humiliate and subdue the spirits of those who'd supported the Confederacy.

After dissolving the Rangers, the Reconstruction government had replaced them with a motley crew of gunmen, thieves and scalawags that had been called the Texas State Police. This force was not only ready to carry out any kind of instructions the occupying rascals issued; its men were ingenious in evolving humiliations of their own.

Longarm said, "So Maddox turned his back on his own kind. Well, I reckon he wasn't the first one, and

241

I don't suspicion he'll be the last. There's bad apples in every barrel, Billy. Even the Rangers. Hell, we both know that."

Vail nodded, leaned back in his chair, and ran a pink, thick-fingered hand across his shiny scalp. "Sure. Anyhow, Maddox worked around in the little jerkwater towns close to Austin—as city marshal, deputy sheriff, whatever he could find—until a year or so ago. Then he got the itch to go back to the Rangers again."

"And they didn't want him," Longarm guessed. "Well, he'd be a little bit long in the tooth for a Ranger, wouldn't he, Billy? The war's been over quite a while."

"Oh, Maddox wasn't all that old. He was on the light side of twenty when he first joined up. He'd only be a few years older than you are, right now."

"Which ain't all that grizzly, I reckon," Longarm said. "But I still don't see what all this has got to do with us."

"Just hold your horses. I'm getting there." Vail shifted his bulky frame in his chair and studied the message again for a moment. "The last time he tried to rejoin the Rangers was about a year ago. And he wasn't in any mood to take no for an answer. When the captain he was trying to persuade kept turning him down, they got into a slanging match. I suppose they said a few things that they oughtn't. Anyhow, Maddox pulled down on the captain. Killed him."

"That's still not our affair," Longarm objected. "Hell, let the Rangers handle their own cases. Murder's not in our jurisdiction, Washington's told us that enough times."

Vail shook his head. "But Washington's not worried about the killing. It seems Maddox knows where there's two things that Washington wants real bad."

242

Longarm waited patiently. When Vail kept studying the message for the third time, Longarm lighted a fresh cheroot.

Vail finally looked up and said, "First of all, Maddox knows where there's over a hundred thousand dollars in carpetbagger loot hidden away. Graft money, most of it."

Longarm whistled. "That's enough to interest anybody, I guess."

"And along with the gold, there's papers tucked away that point a right dirty finger at two bigwigs who're getting ready to give the President a real bad time when election comes up next year."

"And that's the kernel in the nutshell, I guess?"

"Seems to be. So what we're supposed to do is locate Maddox and find out where the gold and the papers are."

"Well, now. That's a real nice job for somebody," Longarm said, keeping his voice noncommittal, as though he didn't know what was coming next.

"Glad you think so," Vail said amiably. "I don't guess there's any reason for you to put off leaving for Austin any longer than it'll take you to get your gear together."

"Now hold on, Billy!" Longarm objected. "If this Maddox killed a Ranger captain, the Rangers are going to be after him."

"That's right," Vail agreed brightly.

"And they know a lot more about him than I do, where he'd be apt to run to."

Vail nodded, and Longarm went on, "So how am I supposed to find this damn Maddox when the Rangers can't?"

"That's up to you," Vail replied, no sympathy in his voice.

243

"Damn it, Billy, this is a big country. I need a place to start from."

"Try Mexico, Washington says."

"Now come on, Billy! I was down there not too long ago, and there wasn't too many folks sorry to see me leave."

"All the information they've sent is that Maddox was heading for Mexico, the last trail of his the Rangers turned up."

"Hell, Mexico's almost as big as this country," Longarm pointed out. "How'm I supposed to know where to start?"

"That's what you're getting paid for," Vail said patiently, "but the word is he had a niece who lived with him 'round about Austin somewheres, and nobody's said anything about her going with him, so she might still be there. Maybe you can sniff her out. You got a reputation for being able to get all sorts of things out of fair young maids; maybe you can get some information out of this one."

"I'm grateful for what the good Lord sees fit to send my way," Longarm replied, smiling thinly.

"I don't know about the good Lord," Vail said, "but the clerk's got your orders ready about now, and a travel voucher. I don't see much reason for you to be wasting your time hanging around here."

"When you put it that way, Billy, neither do I." Longarm unfolded his six-foot-plus body from the red morocco chair, and stretched. "Seeing as Washington's in such an all-fired hurry, I figure I'd better be, too. Only one thing I need to find out before I go. You got any notions about where this Maddox started from to Mexico? Austin's a pretty big town now, maybe five or six thousand people in it. I'd waste God Almighty's length of time if I didn't have some kind of starting point."

Vail looked at the message again and shook his bald head. "Not a clue in here. Not even the towns where Maddox worked before he did the killing. Just that they were all close to Austin. I guess you'll just have to pick one out yourself."

Longarm nodded. "As good a way as any, I reckon. Better than Austin, anyhow. You didn't mention it, but I got myself a hunch that if I go nosying around asking too many questions in Austin, there's going to be some Rangers run across my trail and come looking for me to find out why I'm interested in their renegade."

"It's your case from here on," Vail said. "Handle it any way you see fit. Just don't spend the Department dry finding Maddox. Don't forget, I'm the one that's got to account for whatever money you waste."

Longarm grinned. He touched the brim of his hat as he turned away. At the door, he looked back and said, "If you don't hear from me for a while, I'll still be on the job. I wouldn't want you worrying, you know."

Vail grinned back. "You worry about yourself. I'm damned sure not going to lose any sleep over you."

Walking down Champa Street on the way to his roominghouse to get his kit, Longarm moved at a faster pace than his usual city saunter. He carried most of the railroad schedules in his head, and if he hurried just a little bit, he could get the morning Fort Worth & Denver City southbound express to Fort Worth.

There, he'd make connections with a Katy local that would put him into Taylor to connect with an I&GN express to Austin. He could be in Austin by midnight. If he didn't shake a leg, though, if he lollygagged around and missed the morning express, it meant the milk train that night and a series of short hops on dusty, slow-moving locals, and he'd make Austin about noon tomorrow. He looked around for a hack, and saw one within whistling distance. As long as Washington was in such a stew, Longarm didn't mind adding a half-dollar in cab fare to his expense sheet.

He made the train with time to spare, checked his saddle through on the baggage car, and settled down in the smoker. There was the usual array of drummers, ranchers, and men whose dress and actions gave no hint as to their occupations or interests. Longarm leaned his Winchester against the wall of the coach between his seat and the window and settled back to relax as the express pulled out of the depot, wound its way slowly through the growing city, and then gained speed as it hit the mainline south. He was leaning back with his eyes closed when the conductor came through collecting tickets.

"Longarm!" the trainman said, pleasure in his voice, when he stopped at Longarm's seat.

"Jim Pearson!" Longarm extended his callused hand to grasp the one the conductor extended. "It's been a while, ain't it!"

"A long while," Pearson agreed. "And I can't think of anybody I'd rather see on board today."

"Something bothering you, Jim?"

"There sure as the devil is. Fellow up in the day coach next to the baggage car. I've seen his face before, but I can't remember where. And I've got a hunch he's trouble."

"You want me to sashay up front and see if I recognize him from somewhere else, or from our wanted flyers?"

I'd sure appreciate it. If he's a bad one, I want to keep an eye on him."

"Be a pleasure to help you. You sure helped me, that time the derailment just about had me whipped down, over in the Indian Nation."

Longarm stood up and started toward the front of

the car. He was still some distance from the door when a man wearing a bandanna over the bottom of his face burst in, the big Navy Colt he was waving preceding him at arm's length.

Longarm didn't go for his own gun. Nobody but a fool would try to draw on a man who already had his weapon out and his finger on the trigger.

"Now, everybody just hold still, and don't do nothing foolish, and we'll get this finished up without you men getting hurt," the intruder said in a voice loud enough to reach the back of the coach. "All I want is your money and jewelry. I'm going on to the back, to give you time to get your wallets and watches out, and to take off your rings and stickpins. When I pass by you, just drop your contributions in my hat, and that's all there'll be to it."

A buzz of voices rose in the smoker. The holdup man quieted them quickly by firing a shot through the coach roof.

"Do what I told you to. Now!" the holdup artist shouted in the silence that followed the shot. He started along the aisle as the passengers began fumbling in their pockets.

Longarm followed the example of the other men, holding his head down so his hatbrim would hide his face from the approaching bandit. If the robber was an old hand, there was a good chance he'd recognize a Deputy U.S. Marshal who managed to get around a good bit.

Turning his head without drawing the bandit's attention, Longarm kept his own face shielded and his eyes on the man's back as he went down the aisle between the coach seats. At the back, he took his hat off and began moving slowly up the aisle again, stopping beside each seat to let the passengers drop their tributes into the hat.

Jim Pearson had stepped up behind Longarm. The holdup man noticed Pearson for the first time when he reached the spot where Longarm stood. He said, "I was wondering where in hell you'd got off to, Conductor. First thing you better do is hand over your gun. And don't try to tell me you ain't got one, because I know better. Just take it out nice and slow and drop it in my hat, along with your money and that expensive railroad watch all you conductors wear."

Pearson complied without speaking. The gunman switched his attention to Longarm. "All right. You next."

To divert the man's attention, Longarm said mildly, "You're going to have to settle for just a watch off of me. I don't carry any money."

"Like hell you don't! Nobody travels on a train busted, mister, not unless he's a hobo, and sure as shit stinks, you ain't dressed like a bum! But I'll take your watch first, then I'll just go through your pockets myself while you hold my hat and see whether or not you're lyin'."

Longarm brought up his right hand slowly and hooked his fingers around the watch chain. As he'd anticipated, the man's eyes followed the movement. The instant Longarm was sure the gunman's attention was focused on his right hand, he brought his left down with a flashing swoop that knocked the stickup artist's gun downward and to one side.

In reflex action, the man triggered the Navy Colt. The bullet smashed into the coach floor. By the time the gunman had recovered his wits and was trying to bring the revolver up again, his wrist was locked in the steel-tight grip of Longarm's hand, and the marshal's derringer was pressing its cold brass muzzle on the man's ear just above his bandanna mask.

"Now, then," Longarm said calmly, "suppose you just open up your hand and let that pistol drop on the floor. Then we'll take a look at your face and see if I don't know you from somewheres."

Though the bandit's eyes flashed hatred, he obeyed. Pearson picked up the fallen weapon and covered the man with it. Longarm returned his derringer to his vest pocket and jerked the mask down from the holdup artist's face.

"Well, if it ain't old Gus Posey!" he said. "You can't have been outa the pen more'n a few weeks, Gus. Wasn't it two years you got for that post office job I sent you up for the last time we locked horns?"

Posey replied sullenly, "Damn it, Marshal, a man gets turned outa the pen with ten dollars and a suit of clothes. He's got to make hisself a grubstake some way."

"You ever think about doing an honest day's work?" Longarm asked. When Posey didn't respond, he shook his head and said to the conductor, "Well, Jim, I guess if I handcuff old Gus, you can shut him up in the baggage car till we get to Trinidad, can't you? That'll be our last stop in Colorado. If you carry him any further, getting him accommodated in a jail's going to be a little more complicated."

"Don't worry, Longarm," Pearson answered. "I'll send a message ahead from our first stop, and there'll be somebody waiting at the depot to take him off your hands."

Longarm nodded. Then, raising his voice, he told the passengers who'd been watching wordlessly, "Come claim your wallets and watches and jewelry, gents. This fellow won't have any use for them, not where he's going."

Austin looked just about as Longarm remembered it from his last visit.

And that was a while ago, he told himself as he walked along Lamar Avenue from the depot toward the Iron Front Saloon. He recalled the saloon very well indeed, and hoped it still had the big free lunch table that had fed him so well the last time he'd had to stop over in Texas' capital city. To his relief, the Iron Front was just the same. As far as Longarm could tell, there were even the same barkeeps handling the spigots that dispensed Pearl beer.

With a foaming stein in one hand, and a plate holding a generous assortment of cold cuts, cheeses, and pumpernickel in the other, Longarm glanced around to find an empty table. Everywhere he looked, all seats were taken, until he spotted a small table for two in a far corner of the barnlike building, with only one of its two chairs occupied. He threaded through the narrow aisles between the tables until he reached his objective.

"Mind if I join you?" he asked the occupant.

"If you've a mind to. Most people don't bother to ask."

As Longwarm was putting his plate down, the stranger frowned. "Your face is familiar. I know I've seen you somewhere."

"Not likely, friend," Longarm said as he arranged thick slices of venison sausage on a slice of pumpernickel. "I don't get to this part of the country much."

"No, I don't think it was in Austin that I saw you before. Or even in Texas. It was—" the stranger snapped his fingers. "Of course! I remember you now! You're a U.S. Marshal. Denver. And your name's—

Longarm had been studying his tablemate. He saw a youngish man with a full, twist-tipped mustache, carefully pomaded hair showing below the brim of a back-tilted derby, a rounded face with a suggestion of a beginning double chin, and dark, mischieviously twinkling eyes. The man was dressed in the standard uniform of city dwellers: starched white shirt with a high collar, a puffy black cravat, and a black broadcloth suit. He had neither the looks nor the attitude of a crook or a con man, so Longarm decided he'd be safe in admitting his identity.

"You've placed me right. But if I ever did see you before, I don't recall your face."

"We were never introduced. I was in Denver covering the trial of Texas Jim O'Conner. He was a local badman, and I thought we ought to give him a little notoriety."

"You're a newspaper fellow, then," Longarm guessed between sips of his beer.

"That's right. Porter's my name. Will Porter. But I sign most of my pieces with my pen name. O. Henry. You might've noticed it in my paper? It's called *The Rolling Stone.*"

Longarm, his mouth full, shook his head.

Porter sounded disappointed as he said, "No. I guess you wouldn't. We only send a few copies up to Colorado. I suppose the only readers the rag's got in Denver are the exchange editors of the *Post* and the *Rocky Mountain News.*"

"Hell, I don't even read the *Post,*" Longarm said.

"Look here, Marshal," Porter went on. "I've been thinking about trying my hand at a few short stories about this part of the country. I'll bet you've had a lot of things happen to you that'd be new to people back East, where I come from."

"Things happen to just about everybody, I reckon," Longarm pointed out noncommittally.

I don't mean just *things*," the young newspaperman explained. "I mean unusual things, funny things, even serious ones, that could only happen out here in the West." He saw that Longarm's stein was empty, and waved to one of the white-aproned waiters. In a few moments, the waiter set freshly filled steins in front of them.

"I'll tell you what," Porter suggested. "I'll buy the

drinks if you'll do the talking. How does that sound?"

Longarm shook his head. "If I was feeling like seeing the elephant and hearing the owl, I might take you up on that, Mr. Porter. But I'm here on business, and I've got a long ride ahead of me tomorrow."

"Looking for a badman?" Porter asked.

"I reckon you might say that." Longarm suddenly had a thought. If young Porter was a newspaper reporter, he just might know something about Clayton Maddox. He said, "But before I get on with my business, I'd like to see an old-time Ranger and swap a few yarns with him. You might've heard about him. His name's Clayton Maddox. I disremember where he was the last time I heard. You wouldn't happen to know anything about him, would you?"

Porter looked at Longarm narrowly. "Clayton Maddox used to be a Ranger. But they're after him now, or didn't you know that? He shot Captain Elzey, right in his own office. Maddox was a town marshal up in Georgetown when that happened. He's on the run now. Nobody knows where he is, but the Rangers sure would like to."

"I'd heard he'd had some trouble," Longarm said. "I guess his niece is gone, too, then."

With a grin and a knowing look, Porter nodded. "You don't have to say anything more, Marshal. If you know Amy, I'd guess you're more interested in finding her than her uncle."

Longarm managed to look sheepish. "Georgetown, now," he said thoughtfully. "To the north a ways, as I recollect?"

"About forty miles. Well, Marshal, my invitation still stands. The night's just a puppy yet. Do me a favor and let's go out on the town together."

"No. I thank you for the invite, but I better not." Longarm stood up. "Fact of the matter is,

I just stopped in here for a quick bite before I look me up a hotel. So I'll bid you goodnight and go find me one."

Longarm stopped at the bar and bought a bottle of Maryland rye to wake up with the next morning, then stepped out on the street.

As he looked around for a hackman who belonged to one of the half-dozen hire carriages that stood outside the Iron Front, he hummed softly to himself a bit of an old song that came into his mind every time he found himself in Texas:

"Come all you Texas Rangers, wherever you
  may be,
I'll tell you of some troubles that happened
  unto me.
My name is nothing extra, so that I will not tell,
But here's to all you Rangers, I'm sure I wish
  you well . . ."